For a moment, they lay still. She wondered if it was getting close to dawn.

She could look outside, she supposed, to see if there was any glimmer of light in the east. Yet, she was reluctant to move. It was warm under the jacket, pressed close to the fire. She was conscious of his warm body. She had never been so close to a man before. There was an intimacy that was both disconcerting but also not disconcerting. She couldn't find the right word—exciting and yet with an underlying contentment. She looked to him. His lips lifted in a smile.

"What is it?" she asked.

"I was only thinking that this felt oddly comfortable."

"Yes," she said.

They lay side by side, staring at the ceiling, and she felt his hand reach out to touch her own. Awareness darted through her, a tingling excitement and a feeling of being more alive, as though every particle of her body, every inch of her skin, was sensitive.

"Everything feels more real with you," he said softly. "Like I have been sleepwalking or living in a gray world turned multicolored overnight."

Author Note

Historical research is always fascinating, and this book encouraged me to explore Cornwall's colorful smuggling past. *Caught in a Cornish Scandal* is set just after the Napoleonic Wars as the smuggling trade began to decline. Two factors contributed to this: growth in coast guard services and the reduction of excise duties on imported goods.

Many smugglers avoided capture, but consequences were dire for the less fortunate. Smuggling was a capital offense. However, the poaching of deer, stealing of rabbits, pickpocketing and numerous other petty offenses could also result in the death penalty.

On a more uplifting note, Sam and Millie decide to open a school at the end of *Caught in a Cornish Scandal*. This is a reflection of my own belief in the importance of education for all, regardless of socioeconomic status, ethnicity or gender.

In writing this, I learned about the inspirational individual John Pounds, a cobbler who began in 1818 teaching poor children reading, writing and arithmetic without charging fees. This resulted in the development of the ragged schools movement. Individuals like Thomas Guthrie and Anthony Ashley Cooper, 7th Earl of Shaftesbury, furthered this concept, resulting in many free schools for poor children.

This is a time when one needs uplifting stories. The idea that one individual, John Pounds, could make such a difference emphasizes the power one person can have to promote positive change. It reminds us that our choices matter and that we can support and encourage each other to ensure equity and opportunity.

ELEANOR WEBSTER

—

Caught in a Cornish Scandal

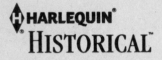

HARLEQUIN®
HISTORICAL™

**Recycling programs
for this product may
not exist in your area.**

ISBN-13: 978-1-335-50615-3

Caught in a Cornish Scandal

Copyright © 2021 by Eleanor Webster

All rights reserved. No part of this book may be used or reproduced in
any manner whatsoever without written permission except in the case of
brief quotations embodied in critical articles and reviews.

This is a work of fiction. Names, characters, places and incidents
are either the product of the author's imagination or are used fictitiously.
Any resemblance to actual persons, living or dead, businesses,
companies, events or locales is entirely coincidental.

This edition published by arrangement with Harlequin Books S.A.

For questions and comments about the quality of this book,
please contact us at CustomerService@Harlequin.com.

Harlequin Enterprises ULC
22 Adelaide St. West, 40th Floor
Toronto, Ontario M5H 4E3, Canada
www.Harlequin.com

Printed in U.S.A.

Eleanor Webster loves high heels and sun, which is ironic as she lives in northern Canada, the land of snow hills and unflattering footwear. Various crafting experiences, including a nasty glue-gun episode, have proven that her creative soul is best expressed through the written word. Eleanor is currently pursuing a doctoral degree in psychology and holds an undergraduate degree in history and creative writing. She loves to use her writing to explore her fascination with the past.

Books by Eleanor Webster

Harlequin Historical

No Conventional Miss
Married for His Convenience
Her Convenient Husband's Return
A Debutante in Disguise
Caught in a Cornish Scandal

Visit the Author Profile page
at Harlequin.com.

Reading was not initially easy for me,
and I dedicate this to my first teachers,
my parents. They taught me both a love of
reading and perseverance. I dedicate this to all
educators. Without their diligence, few of us
would be able to enjoy the many splendors
of the written word. As always, I recognize
the support and constant encouragement
demonstrated by my husband
and daughters.

Chapter One

Cornwall—January 1818

Rain stung Millicent Lansdowne's cheeks. Wind sliced through the coarse seaman's cloth of her borrowed shirt. Tangles of wet hair fell into her eyes, blinding her as she pulled on the oars. The darkness suited the enterprise and yet she longed for the merest sliver of a moon. The only relief from the gloom came from the intermittent flash of the lighthouse lamp shimmering across huge troughs of water and towering, omnipresent rocks.

Millie had lived on the Cornish coast most of her life, but had never smuggled. She'd never even considered it…until now.

The buffeting wind stole her breath so that she gulped at the air, panting with effort. The muscles in her arms cramped. Her hands ached as she clutched the oars, but she dared not pause even to flex her fingers for fear that her small vessel would be dashed against the jagged cliffs. She glanced apprehensively seawards. Somewhere, hidden behind the rough seas and salt spray, *The Rising Dawn* waited with its bounty of brandy.

Yesterday, the decision had felt less foolhardy. Yesterday, the weather had been better and the danger so much less immediate.

But this was necessary. Smuggling had served Cornwall and its people well in times of crisis. And this was a crisis.

Millie had accepted her own duty to marry a dull man twice her age, but she *would not* let her sister marry a man without morals or conscience. She would not. She had failed to keep her brother safe, but she would not, *could not*, fail Lil.

Clenching her teeth, she pulled back on the oars with renewed energy, shifting away from the rocks and towards the open sea. It was the flicker of movement that caught her attention. She paused briefly, peering at what seemed like an improbable hand waving from the sea's belly. She hunkered forward, as though this slight shift would make her better able to see. She shouted, but her voice disappeared, drowned by the wind.

The lighthouse beam swung around. Again, she saw flailing arms, the frantic limbs silhouetted against the light.

She acted instinctively, sprawling across the gunnel as she pushed the oar out over the water. 'Here! Grab on!'

The oar dipped, pulled by a heavy weight. She saw a man's face, mouth open in a silent shout. He caught at her arm, gripping so tightly that she half feared she would be dragged into the sea. The boat sank into the trough, soaring up again on the crest of the next wave.

She clutched at wet cloth, flesh and muscled arms, pulling and tugging until the man floundered aboard. He tumbled to the boat's bottom. For a moment, she could do nothing except pant, staring at the inert figure briefly outlined in the light's glare.

Then the splintering crash of the waves jolted her into

desperate action. With frantic energy, she pulled on the oars, fighting wind and current, inching away from the white-flecked foam of the crashing breakers.

But relief was a transitory, fleeting thing.

Even as she pulled clear of the cliff face, she felt the ship's presence. *The Rising Dawn* was the stuff of legend; the smuggler's ship that could outrun the fastest cutter. The ship's transom towered above her, a black bulk, invisible save for a signal light which swayed with the sea's movement. In the distance, one of the village boats scuttled back to shore, a small shadowy outline, disappearing fast into the wet darkness.

And then she was alone.

Her heart thundered. Her chest felt tight, unable to expand to properly breathe as she looked nervously upwards towards the deck. The torchlight moved, illuminating a single person, his craggy brows, nose and the folds of his face deeply shadowed.

'Who's there?'

Her mouth felt dry. 'Heaven sent!' she shouted.

'You new?'

'Yes.'

'We'll lower—'

Whatever the sailor was going to say died on his lips as the man at the bottom of her boat coughed, retching up the contents of his lungs into the bilge. Not dead, it seemed.

'What the hell's that?' the sailor asked, moving the torch so that its weak light shone down into her vessel.

'He's injured,' Millie shouted.

'Didn't ask about his health. Who is he?'

'One of your men, I presume. He was drowning.' Her tongue felt huge and unwieldly in her dry mouth.

'Not ours.'

The drowned man pulled himself to a seated position, staring blearily, blood trickling across his forehead. She could have wished him dead longer.

'Best come aboard as you've brought company,' the sailor shouted, his mouth a black hole, save for a single tooth.

Fear snaked through her. 'No! That was not the agreement...'

Instructions and warnings had been clear enough. A smuggling ship was no place for a female. Ferrying goods to shore was foolhardy enough, going aboard could spell disaster.

She grabbed at the oars, pulling her vessel away.

A shot rang out, audible even over the wind and waves. Gasping, she looked towards the single flickering light. The sailor stepped forward so that he was illuminated. He did not speak, merely beckoned her on board. She shook her head, gripping the oars more tightly. He shifted the pistol. The metal glinted as his lips stretched in a wide, almost toothless grin.

Sam's head thudded. The pain was so great that sparks flashed before his eyes like the fireworks at Vauxhall. He tasted salt water, blood and bile. He coughed, rolling on to his side, before again slumping to stare upwards into the black heavens.

Where was he? He could make no sense of the voices, the lurching movement, wind or rain. Everything had the surreal, disjointed quality of a bad dream. The effort to think, to push away the blank fuzziness overwhelmed him and he felt himself slip again into the inviting nebulous state which was neither sleep nor consciousness.

Seconds...minutes...hours later, he wakened once more. He was being moved, handled by rough hands and dropped or tumbled to the ground. He lay quite still, orienting himself in a world spinning and lurching.

He forced his eyes open. He could see his own fingers splayed on wet rough planking and, beyond that, a black seaman's boot.

'Captain! 'E's awake,' a man bellowed from somewhere above his head, the words inordinately loud so that they ricocheted about his skull.

Sam pulled himself painfully on to his knees. Briefly, everything blurred as his head thudded. Then the thunder lessened and he found himself looking up into the distorted visage of an old man, his features eerily lit in the swinging torchlight.

For a moment, he distrusted the evidence of his own eyes. It seemed he was on a ship. The man opposite looked to be a pirate, or as good as. The sea was so rough that Sam put his hands back on the deck for balance. Rain fell. His hair was plastered to his forehead. Water ran into his eyes and down his cheeks. He could feel the rain's sting and the cutting cold of the wind.

It made no sense. He'd come to Cornwall to visit his elder sister and her new baby. He'd travelled from London in a private carriage. Why was he on a ship? Had he been attacked on the highway? Except he'd made it to Fowey. He'd seen his sister...

Before his thoughts could clear, he was brought back to the immediate present as another man strode over, the sea boots huge, mere inches from his face.

'Best get rid of them.' The command was cold, without emotion.

Instinctively, Sam reared up, only to be struck by the boot. Helpless, he crumpled to the deck.

'You cannot kill us. I work for you.' The words were calm, unflinching and reasoned.

Sam turned quickly. His head thudded with the movement. A scrap of a lad stood beside him, wet hair and shirt plastered to his skin.

The first man, older and with just a single tooth, did not even acknowledge the lad. Instead he continued to chew his tobacco with a singleness of purpose. With methodical motions, he reloaded the pistol. The 'Captain' was already turning away, as though their execution no longer merited his attention.

Sam pulled himself again to a seated position, fighting down the nausea induced by the movement. He would not have them discuss his murder as though he were a kitten to be drowned. 'Sir,' he said. 'My absence will be noted.'

'Indeed,' the lad said in clear, crisp, surprisingly educated tones. 'Besides, you have no idea of this fellow's identity. He might be some bigwig.'

'Good Lord,' Sam said, before silencing himself. Even in the dim light, the lad's silhouette had a delicacy of feature that was not masculine and the wet shirt definitely showed a femininity of form.

Perhaps this was, indeed, an illusion or nightmare too bizarre for reality. Was he to believe that he and this female had been captured by pirates? Was this some elaborate ruse? A practical joke or crazy wager? A hallucination after too many brandies?

The clear calm reasoned voice spoke again. 'It makes no sense for you to hurt us. You were happy enough to accept my services.'

'That was before you started bringing strange, unknown folk to my ship,' the Captain said, turning back to his captives.

'I did not bring anyone to your ship. I did not want to be on your ship. I wanted to collect the merchandise and return to shore.'

'Leaving him as a witness.'

'He was out cold.'

'He was throwing up his guts in your bilge.'

'Either way, he certainly did not seem capable of witnessing much,' the woman said.

The Captain held up the lantern and Sam could feel his scrutiny. Shrewd eyes glinted, deep set within leathery, pockmarked skin. He lowered the lantern. 'He looks capable enough now. And I cannot see any other solution. Killing 'im seems the best policy.'

'Not unless you want every Bow Street Runner investigating the situation,' Sam said, collecting his thoughts and forcing the words out. Even if this was a bizarre hallucination, he refused to be the snivelling coward in it.

There was a silence interrupted only by the regular squelch of the older sailor's tobacco.

'When I want the opinion of a toffee-nosed Brit on my own ship, I will ask for it,' the Captain said. 'And I wouldn't mind adding an aristocrat to the minnow population.'

He chuckled at his own joke. Sam swallowed. He wished his thoughts would clear. Everything was a blur of disjointed images: his sister, the baby, dinner. How could he argue for his life when he had no idea why he was here or how?

'But that's just it,' the girl said in her clear tones. 'I know him. He *is* a gentleman. From London.'

Sam startled. Good God, she was right. But how did she know him? Had they met? Had she attended dinner with his sister? He had no recollection of her and she certainly was not dressed for it.

'I am Mr Garrett,' he said. It was an effort to say the words, as though their enunciation required conscious thought and labour. He felt less that he was providing information and more that he was clinging on to a fact, as one might a life ring.

'There, you see!' the girl said with some energy. 'As posh as they come. He is quite rich and might well be worth more to you alive than dead.'

The words hung in the air.

Millie held her breath. Despite the storm, the wind had dropped so that even nature seemed to be waiting. A variety of expressions flickered across the Captain's face. He was not smart, but she detected a natural cunning.

'What's your meaning?'

'Likely, he has a family that would pay for his return.' She made her voice calm despite her nervousness. She knew nothing of Mr Garrett's family. Indeed, even her belated recognition felt as though it had come from a force external to her, an image dropped into her mind from a lifetime previous. Later she would be fully conscious of the oddness of this coincidence—finding themselves together on a smugglers' ship off the Cornish coast—and would feel a stunned disbelief.

Right now, she felt nothing.

'It would put me and the company at risk. And I do not like loose ends,' the Captain said.

She swallowed, biting her lip. Sal's husband had warned her. Smuggling was different now. The war with France was over and the coast rife with excise men. Fear and risk had grown exponentially and, with it, a harder, crueller breed of smugglers. They would forgive no mistakes and demonstrate little humanity or mercy.

The Captain nodded to the sailor who again raised the pistol.

She saw the glint of metal. She saw the movement of his finger on the trigger. Instinctively, she held her breath, squeezing her eyes tight shut, ludicrously bracing herself for impact as though taut muscles might deflect steel.

The shot did not come. Instead, peering through her lashes, she saw the Captain's gaze had turned towards the rocks and then seawards. The ship had drifted too close to shore.

'Luck's with you fer now.' He turned away. 'Wind is dropping. Best to git out.'

'What do I do with 'em?' the sailor asked.

'Tie 'em up and git 'em below decks. I'll decide what to do with 'em later.'

Millie exhaled, limbs wobbly like so much blancmange. The Captain strode towards the foredeck, already bellowing orders. The old man stopped chewing tobacco long enough to emit a piercing whistle, producing two younger sailors.

With rough efficiency, they pulled her arms behind her. Coarse rope was twisted tightly around her wrists as they did the same with Garrett before jerking them upright.

'Git!' the old sailor said, spitting out his tobacco.

She walked unsteadily across the wet, slippery planking, stumbling with the ship's continued movement. To either side, she saw figures and heard the rustle as huge sails were hoisted.

Beyond the ship, hidden in the dark, was her home… more remote than the moon, stars or any constellation. She hadn't told her family about the plan. She'd expected to do this quickly, efficiently, under the cover of darkness. She'd be in and out and back for breakfast.

In an evening's work, or a few evenings, she'd ensure that her mother did not have to go to debtors' prison and her sister need not marry a lecherous, middle-aged man.

Instead, her absence would be noted, her reputation ruined so that even Mr Edmunds would not want to marry her. Granted she did not particularly want to marry Mr. Edmunds, but the union would have offered her mother and sister some financial stability.

Risk-taking and misplaced optimism were the hallmarks of the Lansdowne family. Her father had lost his money in investments gone wrong. Her brother had lost his life in gambling gone wrong. And now she—apparently—might well lose *her* life in smuggling gone wrong.

She'd promised she'd keep Lil safe. She'd promised.

But, like her father and brother before her, she had failed to save Lil, instead making her more vulnerable.

'Git!' the sailor holding her said, his rough voice jolting her back to the present as he shoved her into the small doorway leading below deck.

She lurched unsteadily down the steps. The stench struck her first. It was a solid wall, a mix of sweat, stale food and human waste. Instinctively, Millie pulled back, only to feel the pistol at her spine. She continued forward into a corridor that was dimly lit by a single lantern. It swung, casting weird shadows within the narrow confines. The smell worsened.

'Stop 'ere!' The sailor thrust open the door and rough hands pushed her through so that she stumbled over the sill, falling to the floor.

She heard Garrett also stagger.

'Best get 'em tied up.'

The older man's gaze passed over her body so that she was painfully aware of the thin cotton shirt and the damp cloth clinging to her chemise. She pushed herself back, flattening her spine against the wall, as though this slight distance might provide protection. She struck her shoulder as she did so and, wincing, realised a hook stuck out of the wall. With efficient movements, one sailor grabbed the rope, looping it over the peg she had hit and wrenching her arms back with a painful twist.

'That ought to keep you still.' His smile widened. She shivered, although it was not cold in the belly of the ship.

The men turned. The torch flickered with their movement, distorting their silhouettes. They stepped into the corridor, taking the light with them and letting the door slam.

The bolt slid into pace with a final metallic click.

Sam could see nothing. The darkness felt impenetrable, as though made of a substance more solid than air. As for his fellow captive, he could discern no part of her form or face. The only evidence of her presence was the intake of her breath and the shuffling sound as she shifted against the wall.

'How do you know me?' he asked into the fetid air.

'I have an excellent memory for faces.'

'We have met? How? Who are you?'

She made no reply. He heard her swallow.

'I know you are a woman. There is no need to dissemble,' he said.

'It is not in my nature to dissemble.' Her voice was sharp. There was that clipped tone, a clarity of enunciation which did not sound like that of a local villager.

'You are not from the village.'

'I was born just outside Fowey.'

'But you are educated.'

'Being from the village does not preclude education,' she said.

'No, but it makes it less likely. What is your name?' He sensed her reluctance. 'I am hardly in a position to tell anyone and I imagine your absence may soon be noticed.'

'Millicent Lansdowne.'

He startled. He knew the name. They were small land-owners in the area. He had known her brother, Tom. He had eaten at their house when they'd still had a place in London. And drunk with Tom when he'd imagined his heart broken.

Granted, the Lansdownes had lost money, but they were a decent family. Why would Tom's sister be here? In a smuggling vessel? Involved as part of a criminal enterprise? It was a role totally unsafe and unsuitable for any female, never mind one from a decent family.

'Miss Lansdowne?' He looked in her direction as though to discern some clue even in the darkness. 'Why are you here?'

'As I recall, we weren't given much choice and were rather thrown into these confines.'

'No, I mean, out here…at sea? Working for these people.'

'Financial gain.'

He almost admired her composure except her brazenness shocked him. Good Lord, surely she felt something: shame or embarrassment or something.

'But these men are…are pirates. Your family owns land. Your brother would be…distressed,' he said.

'They are smugglers. And my brother rather forfeited the right to such distress when he took a nose dive off his horse. It is hard to emote from the grave.'

Her voice was blunt to the point of coldness. Sam had forgotten about Tom's tragic accident. He'd become quite wild after his father's death, gambling, drinking, duelling and taking crazy risks.

'I'm sorry,' he said. 'I forgot.'

'You may have other things on your mind at present.'

Good God, he did not know if this was dry wit or unpleasant hardness. He did not know if he was shocked, appalled or fascinated.

'My condolences,' he added. 'On both your father and brother's passing, I mean.'

'Mr Garrett, I realise that gentlemen of fashion feel the need to fill in the silence with small talk. However, that is not required here.'

'I was merely expressing my condolences.'

'I am not particularly at ease with small talk or condolences.'

Just then the ship pitched sharply and he applied himself again to the ropes, determined to loosen them. They would have no chance of escape if the ship sank, tethered as they were.

'*The Rising Dawn* is a seaworthy vessel,' she said, as if reading his thoughts. 'It has been crossing between Cornwall and France these many years.'

'I am reassured.'

'And I know someone on board. I hope... I am certain he will help.'

'You *know* someone? A young lady shouldn't know smugglers,' he said.

'Young ladies in Cornwall sometimes do.'

His mind was still reeling. He had vague memories of Tom's mother, Mrs Lansdowne—a typical matron, as he recalled. 'What does your mother say?'

There was a pause. 'She doesn't know, but I am certain she would express disapproval quite volubly.'

He did not know what to say. All young ladies of his acquaintance held their mothers in high esteem or at least pretended to do so, when in public.

'And this friend will help? So far, they have not been exactly hospitable.'

'"Friend" may be an exaggeration. I hardly know Sally's husband. And he would not consider me a friend, more an acquaintance. He strongly disapproved of the idea and was quite cross with me when I made it clear I would be going through with it.'

The man, whatever his other shortcomings, showed some sense. 'But you think he will help?'

'Yes,' she said.

Her certainty of assistance was naive. Sam wanted to disillusion her, but it felt unkind. Besides, right now, she was his only ally so it made little sense to antagonise her.

'I will attempt to loosen the knots in case he does not come,' he said.

'Indeed, it is always wise to have an alternate plan.'

'It might have been wiser for you to stay on shore,' he muttered.

'But fortunate for you I did not. And you're welcome, by the way.'

'Pardon?'

'I saved your life,' she said.

'I— Yes, I suppose you did. Thank you. What happened exactly?'

'You were drowning. I rescued you at some inconvenience to myself.'

'Right.' He vaguely remembered searing pain in his lungs, the choking taste of salt water and then a desperate fight for air. He felt a confused muddle of emotion: shock, gratitude, curiosity, intrigue and even admiration. 'Er...thank you. You are unusual. I mean, you are very composed, given the situation.'

'I suppose that has always been my role. My mother has a predilection for hysterics. Father was absent and tended towards grandiose gestures. Someone had to be sensible.'

He wanted to say that, given their situation, sense did

not seem to be her greatest attribute but this again felt unkind. Besides, the woman had saved his life, no mean feat given the storm and weather.

'Well, thank you for my life, I mean,' he said, conscious that this statement seemed inadequate.

'Truthfully, I am not as "composed" as I might seem. In fact, in retrospect, I rather wish I'd chosen not to do this.' She sounded less airy and he felt an unexpected sympathy.

'Why did you?' he asked. 'I mean, if you do not mind me asking?'

'My father lost a lot of money, as you might know. My brother gambled. We are in some financial difficulties and my sister may have to marry an unpleasant person. I wanted to help. This seemed like the best solution.'

'I'm sorry,' he said. He heard her swallow and the rustle of cloth as though she had shrugged or shifted against the wall.

He felt a certain empathy. She must have been desperate.

'So now you know my story. Why did you end up in—?' she started to ask, but was silenced by the grating grind of rusty metal against rusty metal.

Sam stiffened. He felt his eyes widen as though this would help see in the heavy darkness. He tugged at the ropes, twisting his fingers against the rough hemp until the tips felt raw.

The door swung inwards, banging against the inner wall. Lamplight spilled into the dank confines. A figure of immense size filled the doorway, his uneven features visible within the light.

Chapter Two

'Jem!'

Relief filled the woman's voice.

'Hush, woman. Do not be shouting from the rooftop,' the man said, his words a harsh whisper, which seemed at odds given his size.

He moved forward, his shoulders so broad that he had to angle himself sideways to proceed through the door. Once inside he was unable to straighten, but stood, hunched, his head bowed by the ceiling.

'Fool woman...do not you remember my last words to you? Pick up the merchandise, I said. Pick up the merchandise and chase straight back to shore. And here you are locked up in the brig.'

'I did not choose to board. Your Captain would have shot me if I hadn't complied.'

'He wouldn't have if you hadn't collected strays.'

'I could hardly let this gentleman drown.'

'It would have been wiser.'

'As you may know, wisdom does not run in my family,' she said wryly, but with a bitter undertone.

'Look,' Sam said, 'I hate to break up this reunion, but can you cut through these ropes?'

'And who might you be?'

'The aforementioned stray. Samuel Garrett.'

Breathing heavily, the man squatted beside Sam. He pulled out a knife, hacking through the ropes with a steady rasp of steel on hemp. The ropes sprang loose, falling to the ground.

'Thank you.' Sam flexed his wrists, then pulled himself upright. It hurt to stand. His muscles had cramped and the movement made his head thump so that the Spartan confines spun. For a second, he feared he would fall, but the room steadied, or rather steadied as much as the lurching vessel would permit.

The man, Jem, cut through the remaining ropes at Millie's wrists so that she also stood, stretching gingerly.

'Where are we going? Are we heading down the coast?' she asked.

'Across to France,' Jem said.

'What?'

'France,' Jem repeated as though they were hard of hearing. 'Which reminds me—the Captain wants to see you once we're clear of the coast. Oh, aye, and I have some water and bread outside if you've a thirst.'

The man exited, ducking into the passage, returning with water and bread. He passed the crusts, then poured the water into tin mugs. The water was brackish and the bread hard. Indeed, the ship's movement combined with the putrid stench gave Sam little appetite. Besides, he'd eaten dinner. Dinner... For a moment, the memories felt closer, much as one might see something obliquely, from the corner of the eye.

He tried to focus on the confusing mix of images: candlesticks, crystal, silverware...the smell of rich food and heavy sauces. He remembered his sister, Frances. He had been worried about her. He hadn't seen her for two years. In the afternoon she'd clung to her new baby, but had appeared happy with motherhood. At dinner, she'd seemed different, as if diminished, withdrawing into herself. His brother-in-law was there also, but he couldn't remember him well. Indeed, Sam's memories of dinner remained obscure, as though looking through a thick, blanketing fog.

And then nothing.

His mind was a hole, a blank slate. One moment he was at dinner and the next he was choking and retching at the bottom of a smuggling tender.

It made no sense—a misadventure on a fox hunt, a fall from his horse, even a curricle accident…but drowning off the coast of Cornwall? He did not even like the sea and why would he have walked out in the middle of a ruddy storm?

They drank in silence. The boat was moving less and the wind had decreased, although they could still hear the steady patter of rain mixed with the creak of beams and waves slapping against the sides.

The torch illuminated the small space and Sam studied Miss Lansdowne's features, trying to remember when or where they'd met. He couldn't and her features had an arresting, unusual quality so it seemed strange that he would forget her so entirely. Large eyes dominated a thin, pale face. Her mouth was well shaped but somewhat unsmiling and her brows were dark and straight, giving her countenance a somewhat severe expression. Her forehead was high with wisps of hair escaping from a sailor's cap and her chin jutted forward.

'You said the Captain wants to see us?' the woman asked the giant of the man, breaking the silence.

'Aye.'

'Would you know the Captain's plan as it pertains to us?'

'Not exactly.'

'But you have a notion?'

'I told him as how you was very handy with lace.'

'Lace? I know nothing of lace,' Miss Lansdowne said.

'Yer mum's a fancy lady. You must have picked up summat. Besides I needed to convince the Captain that you had greater use alive than dead. Sal will not forgive me if you ends up dead.'

'Oh.' Her voice quavered. 'I would be somewhat put out, too. He still has a mind to kill us?'

'Aye.'

'And my knowledge of lace will save us?'

'Aye.'

She swallowed. 'I know nothing about lace,' she repeated.

'Well, learn fast. The Captain's been a tad tetchy of late.'

'Tetchy?'

'Not himself. Worried like. Too many excise men about, you know, since the wars ended. Too many wrecks as well, 'e says.'

'Not quite what we are wanting to hear,' she muttered, her lips twisting into a slight smile which softened her expression.

'*The Rising Dawn*'s a good ship. Besides, he'll keep you around. Lace is a growing market, 'e says.'

'Easily hidden, I suppose,' Sam added. 'I heard that the patrols have been stepped up along the coast.'

'Aye. More excise men 'ere than a dog has fleas, begging yer pardon, miss,' Jem said. 'So just make certain we do not get any shoddy cloth, you'll be fine. Might even keep you on for a bit.'

Miss Lansdowne nodded somewhat distractedly. Her fingers rubbed against the rough fabric of her trousers. Sam could feel her anxiety growing. Strange that she could row through a storm, rescue him, conspire with smugglers, but panic over lace.

Perhaps that was a characteristic of fear, like grief. He'd been stoic when his mother died and dry-eyed when sent to school to 'toughen up'. Indeed, even his father's passing had had little impact. Then when Annie Whistler broke their engagement, he'd been a man drowning, shattered. All rational process stopped. One managed for so long and then one did not.

'I… I do not…know if I can pretend…to…to know… about…lace.' Miss Lansdowne's words, punctuated with breathy gasps, brought him back to the present, as her fingers continued to work nervously against the coarse cloth of her trousers.

'Miss Lansdowne. I'd give you a brandy if I had one. Look, if we're going to get out of here alive, you need to be calm.'

She inhaled and nodded, but her eyes still looked too huge in her thin face, as though the panic was there, lingering under the surface.

His years at school had felt like that, a calm surface hiding the panic underneath. He'd survived only by showing a confidence he'd seldom felt. That was always the key to survival: pretence. Indeed, that was Annie's attraction. He'd fallen so totally, absolutely in love, he'd felt himself complete, invincible, whole. Until, of course, she met a duke with double the fortune and double the lands and he'd learned that life was a solitary enterprise.

'Miss Lansdowne.' Sam took her hands. He felt her start of shock, but continued to hold them within his own. 'You are able to do this. Remember you do not need to know more than your mother. Or your sister. You need only know more than the Captain.'

For a moment, she did not react, as though requiring additional time to process the words. Then he saw her exhalation. Her face relaxed with just the tiniest softening of her lips. She looked at him and then away. In the torchlight, her lashes formed a delicate lacey pattern against her cheeks.

'Indeed, he doesn't look the type of gentleman to have a deep appreciation for fine cloth.'

Millie felt the anxiety lessen. The painful bands which had constricted her chest eased. Mr Garret's hands felt warm against her own. She found herself conscious of him as a person. She'd recognised him previously, connecting the features of the half-drowned man with her brother's friend, but that had been an instinctive act of survival. She'd grasped at his identity as she might any tool which could delay execution.

But as his grim expression gentled, she found herself thinking of him not only as a half-drowned body, but as a person, a man. He had a strong jaw, dominant cheekbones and straight nose. His eyebrows were well-shaped and he had a lean strength about him. Even the bloodied, swollen welt on his forehead was not as unpleasant as it should have been. Rather it gave him a warrior appeal.

She frowned. He had undoubtedly received the wound in some drunken scuffle or mad gamble which had led to his near death. He was, as Tom had been, a risk taker. Anyone who ended up half-drowned off the Cornish coast did not seem to be an individual of caution— although, obviously, she had a similar failing.

She should move away from him, but there was a comfort in the warm strength of his grasp. There was an intensity in his gaze and she had the impression that he understood some part of what she was feeling.

This was a fallacy, of course. Mr Samuel Garrett was from a privileged position, a place of power. He could hardly understand the feelings of someone duty bound to marry. Or the sense of inadequacy in knowing that her sister might be doomed to a worse fate, enduring marriage to a worse man.

Millie moved back against the wall, taking her hands from his grasp, turning back to Jem. 'I should have listened to you,' she said. 'You warned me not to try smuggling. I looked for a quick answer. I am more like my brother than I thought.'

'You were desperate, miss, and with reason. No point worrying about that now. You do a good job when we get to France, you might still end up earning a bit. The Captain's a fair man.'

'Won't I look conspicuous?' She glanced down at her seaman's pants and boots.

He frowned as though bemused by her words.

'We'll say yer a cabin boy. You're a drab little thing, not the sort to get attention.'

'That is a cause for gratitude,' Millie said.

Sadly, it was true. Drab and mousy had always been apt descriptions and she felt a familiar longing that she might be more like Lillian. Although, she shouldn't.

Indeed, she should not wish she was like Lil, but that Lil was like her. If Lil had been drab and mousy, she would not have caught Harwood's attention.

Not that 'attention' was an apt word. It was more like 'fixation'. Lord Harwood wanted Lil. He had always wanted Lil. Even when Lil was little more than a child, he'd appear on their estate at odd times, so frequently that Lil seldom went out alone unless he was in London.

Sometimes he'd stop her, smile and say too nice things while his gaze roamed over her body.

In those days, Lord Harwood had been a predator, but a distant one, a shadowy menace but not an imminent threat.

Two days ago that had changed.

Even now, Millie shivered when she remembered Lord Harwood's visit.

He'd smelled of perfume, the scent somehow worse than the stink of vomit and urine which permeated the ship. He wore a dirty wig that was out of fashion and had a sore on his lip. He'd talked to her mother alone and when he'd left, he'd bowed, smiled and strutted, leaving a trail of stale scent in his path.

'Tom owed him money, a promissory note. He showed me,' her mother had said. 'He wants to marry Lil. He said that he would throw me in debtors' prison. And I just couldn't survive.'

'He can't marry Lil. We'll think of something. I'll marry Mr Edmunds, I suppose.'

'Mr Edmunds wouldn't have that sort of money.'

'I'll manage. She can't marry that man.'

Millie had been managing throughout the gruelling six months since Tom's death.

Indeed, her mother had been little help, remaining in her bed for weeks armed with smelling salts and laudanum. Millie had been the one to make sense of the accounts and keep the family out of debtor's prison.

And she had done so. She'd haggled, scrimped and saved. She'd sold livestock, furniture and paintings. She'd even considered marrying the humdrum Mr. Edmunds.

But Harwood would not touch Lil.

And it was this desperate, foolhardy determination

which had led to this moment, sitting on a smuggling vessel with Sally's mountain of a husband discussing lace.

Jem picked up the tin cups as he prepared to stand within the narrow space. 'I'll go back to the Captain. See when he wants to see you.'

'Thank you,' Millie said.

Jem nodded. Taking the lamp, he went to the door, stepping into the corridor. The door clattered shut behind him, blanketing the room in thick darkness.

Millie shivered. She could hear the scrabble of rats across the floorboards, audible now that the storm had lessened. She wondered what time it was. It must be dawn soon, surely. One lost any sense of time within this interminable darkness, deep in the very bowels of the ship. Her family would be worried. Lil would be worried. Sal would be worried. It was Sal who had suggested smuggling. 'We cannot let Miss Lillian marry that man. And your mother is not like to do much,' she'd said.

Millie pressed back against the wall. How long to get to France?

France. France. She'd only been twice to London and now she was going to France. On a smuggling vessel. To look at lace. Would she even recognise shoddy lace?

As a child she'd avoided going to London. Her love had always been for Cornwall and she'd been allowed more freedom than was usual. Her parents had been distracted. Her, lovable jovial father was often inebriated and always busy chasing an improbable scheme. Although, he'd had a larger-than-life presence when he was around, teaching them to row and swim.

Her mother was anxious, too often dosed with laudanum. As the years went by, her mother had withdrawn, shunned by the people she wanted so much to impress, and her father's gambling had worsened, marked by desperation.

'I do not even speak French,' she muttered. She'd shared a governess with the vicarage children, but Miss Collins did not run to French.

'I do,' Mr Garrett said.

'I knew I'd rescued you for a reason.'

For a few moments, they were quiet, surrounded by the dark, the scuttling of rats and the creaking groans of a moving vessel.

'When did we meet, by the way? I have been racking my brains, but I cannot recollect.'

Millie laughed. 'Sorry, that was an exaggeration. It was more a sighting than meeting. It was about a month before Father lost his money and Mother insisted I come to London. I was little more than fourteen. I woke up one night when I heard you and Tom coming in. You were singing and I crept out of my bed and stared through the banisters.'

'You remembered my name? How did you even know it?'

Millie felt a wash of heat through her cheeks. Truthfully, she could still remember how he'd looked that night. Slimmer than now, but tall, well dressed, with broad shoulders and a merry laugh.

'I asked Tom the next day. He called you a "good egg", as I recall.'

Of course, a 'good egg' to Tom meant anyone willing to drink, gamble or otherwise risk life and limb. Tom had been more than two years older than her, but it had never felt that way. She remembered trailing after him, trying to stop him from climbing too high, galloping too fast or swimming too far.

The noise had somewhat abated and the movement of

the ship had lessened so that Millie was no longer bracing her back and legs against the floor and hull.

For this reason, the sudden, lurching movement of the ship was unexpected. Indeed, the vessel shuddered with such violence that they tumbled, sprawling across the bare boards. The sound was louder than a clap of thunder and longer. The grinding continued, rattling through their bodies, the noise mixed with crashing, shouting and running feet.

'What was that?' she gasped.

'We have hit something!' Mr Garrett shouted.

Disoriented, Millie twisted, her body striking a wall. She stretched her fingers across the planking, feeling for the door.

'Here! This way!' he shouted.

She followed his voice, scrambling over the floor.

'Damn—it's locked. Stand back,' he yelled.

She froze in position, crouched low. She heard the impact of his boot and then, at last, the splintering crack of the door. Light and noise assaulted her. Pushing forward, they stumbled into a torrent of water swirling around their feet and ankles. The lamp had broken, igniting the wood and illuminating the corridor's darkness. Flames already twisted and snaked along the beams, the amber light eerily reflected in the flooding corridor.

Millie could feel the fire's heat even as her feet froze. Noise was everywhere, magnified tenfold as water rushed about them, mixed with screams, shouts and the rending of beams and timbers. Men were running in the corridor behind them, pushing and shoving, so that they were moved forward more by sheer momentum than by any rational thought.

The outer deck was equally chaotic. For a moment, Millie stood quite still, as though stricken with a strange paralysis, unable to process the sights and sounds. Men ran by her, scrambling over the deck and into the water. Flames licked up the mast. Sparks showered like angry fire flies.

'Jump!' Sam shouted.

Jolted into action, Millie moved, instinctively searching for escape. Indeed, she never fully remembered how she crossed the deck. She recalled only a mismatch of images; sharp moments set against a blur. She remembered the crazy slide down the steeply angled deck and the shock of the cold, salty water. She remembered the blind panic as she fought for the surface, coughing and choking. She remembered her desperate flailing kicks and the weight of her boots and trousers.

Gulping for air…swallowing water…the blind eyes of a dead sailor…sudden quiet…

And darkness.

Chapter Three

Millie broke the surface.

Gasping, she gulped at the air, feet and arms desperately paddling.

'Swim! No point living on an island if you cannot swim.'

If she'd believed in the supernatural, she'd have said that her father spoke from his grave. Those words pulled her from the briny depths. They cut through her panic, investing her with purpose. Kicking off her boots, she struggled upwards, fighting to stay afloat, even as the waves tossed her about like so much flotsam.

'Mr Garrett!' she shouted.

She stared wildly at the debris, fragments of rigging, casks, men and rope strewn across the ocean, all eerily lit in the fire's ugly amber glow. *The Rising Dawn* had been split down its centre. The bow stuck up, propped on a jutting rock. Masts poked upwards, still burning and starkly outlined against the night sky.

It was a scene more reminiscent of the portals of hell than anything earthly.

The need to survive pulsed through her. She had to

live for her sister and mother. She could not leave them. They needed her. She could not let them down.

Like her father.

Like her brother.

Except she was exactly like them.

Like her father.

Like her brother.

The thoughts flashed through her mind, indelibly etched on her brain. It almost seemed as though she could hear the words in steady, rhythmic incantation.

'Miss Lansdowne!'

The shout grabbed her attention. She jerked around, but could see little. The salt water stung her eyes, the waves obliterating her view. For a moment, she saw him and then, just as quickly, he disappeared. A second later, he resurfaced, gulping at air, arms thrashing.

'Kick off your boots!' she shouted, but her words were taken by the wind.

She swam towards him, conscious of the strong current pushing her back. Mr Garrett clung desperately to a piece of wreckage. She looked towards the shore. The beach was some distance away. Only one or two men seemed to be nearing it. She could see the movement of their arms.

Could she try to push Mr Garrett to the shore? The tide was going out. She could feel its current.

'Won't…make…it… The…tide…' she shouted to Mr Garrett, as she neared him, although she doubted if he could hear or comprehend her words.

Desperately she scanned the scene. The stern had sunk, but the bow was still propped up.

'This way!' she shouted.

Gripping the wood beside him, she started to kick, pushing them towards the remnants of the breached ship.

If they waited there until the tide changed, they'd stand a chance of swimming to shore. Or, conversely, all life would be beaten out of them, smashed against barnacles and jagged rocks.

Somehow, she got them to the wreck. With relief, she felt the rough barnacled rocks under her feet and the slight lessening of the wind as though the wreck was offering them some small protection.

'We'll try to get in to shore when the wind dies,' she said as they hunkered low, hidden behind the wreckage and pressed against the rocks.

The sudden crack was like thunder but sharper, like the snap of a whip. By itself, muffled by wind and sea, it seemed a muted thing. The scream was worse. The scream splintered the night.

Startled, Millie lost her grip on the wood, bobbing under the water. Water shot into her nose. Coughing and retching, she grasped at the wood. A second shot ran out. With increased urgency, she scanned the shore.

'What's happening?' Garrett shouted, his voice hoarse from the water he had swallowed.

Millie stared past the wreckage. She saw a torch flicker. A man was crawling from the water, his silhouette briefly outlined as he moved up the beach on all fours, like a hound. She heard another crack and then, with an awful unnatural movement, the man's arms flung upwards before he fell forward, quite still.

'Dear God. They're…' Her incoherent words petered into silence as she watched at the panicked confusion on shore.

'They're being shot. We have to do something.'

But, as quickly as it had begun, the shooting stopped. The pause lengthened into silence. Instinctively, Millie froze in place, holding her breath and waiting for another scream or pistol crack. She heard nothing save an eerie, deafening quiet, broken by wind and wave, but no human voice or cry.

Millie counted the seconds. Time passed, unmarked save for the lightening sky and the gradual smoothing of the waves.

'We have to go in,' Mr Garrett said. 'We can help.'

'What if they are still here?' she asked through stiff lips, although she had no idea who 'they' were.

'I see a something…a light.'

She peered towards the shore. She could see the dark shape of the land and a light, like a firefly, winding up the shoulder of the cliff. 'I see it.'

They waited, watching the faint light until it disappeared, either hidden by the landscape or the dawn.

'We have to try to get to shore. If we stay here, we will die from the cold. And the tide has turned. It is rising,' he said.

'You cannot swim.'

'I'll kick and hold on to these.' He nodded to the planks clasped in his hands. 'At least we'll have a chance.'

Somehow, they had made it. It was well past dawn and the scene was lit with the dull grey light of a winter morning. The wind had dropped and the tide was coming in, creeping up the rocky shoreline. Finally, her feet were no longer hanging into nothingness. She felt shale, smoother than the barnacles, and slippery tendrils of kelp—or perhaps seaweed—twisted, snake-like, about her feet and ankles.

Crawling on all fours, they inched closer. On either side, she saw the bodies of the drowned men, twisted, half-submerged and moving eerily with the water's ebb and flow. Her gaze scanned the shore as she listened for any sound: the click of the trigger, the rustle of movement or exhalation of breath.

'This is evil.' His expression reflected her own horror.

The carnage continued, men sprawled, their faces contorted into expressions ranging from surprise to anguish. The dull grey light reflected in the puddles of sea water, now blood red.

'You think they have gone?' she asked, although she knew he had no way of knowing.

'They would not have let us get this far if they were still here.'

Millie nodded. They crawled from the water. She held her breath, still half expecting a shot to shatter the quiet. Her trousers clung in cold, damp folds. Her limbs moved awkwardly, numb and stiff, so that she lurched unsteadily, stumbling on the shale. The cold was intense. She wrapped her arms about herself as her body was racked with painful shudders that were almost violent.

Slowly, as if drawn by a force beyond her control, she went to each crumpled figure.

Jem was the third body.

She found him face down and spread eagled. She went to his inert shape. The back of his head was gone, a bloodied mess. Strangely, his face remained untouched.

How was she to tell Sally? The Lansdownes' maid, Flora, was her aunt and Millie had grown up with Sal—they were friends. Bile and vomit pushed into her throat. She swallowed it down.

'He was not a bad person. He just wanted a different life,' she said.

Beside him, she recognised the old man from the night previous, his face contorted into a toothless grimace.

She shivered. The cold inhabited every part of her as

though generated from a frozen core. 'We cannot just… leave them.'

'We'll get the authorities.' He looked over the scene. 'I'm sorry about Jem.'

They stood beside each other in the grey morning, on the grey beach. Sam still wore evening clothes, his tattered cravat fluttering in the wind.

'We have to go,' he said.

In a distant part of her brain, Millie knew he was correct and yet she felt reluctant to move. Her limbs were imbued by that heavy, hopeless lassitude.

'But who? Who did it?' she whispered.

'Wreckers,' he said.

'What?'

'They lure ships. Then grab the cargo.'

'On…on purpose?'

'Yes.'

'And Sally? How will I tell Sal?'

'You will find the words.' He put out his hand to her. She took it. 'You will tell her that he was brave. He saved our lives. If he hadn't untied us, we could not have escaped.'

She nodded. Like it or not, she and this man were each other's best chance of survival. And like it or not, there was nothing she could do for Jem or the others now.

'We will get through it,' she said.

Every bone, sinew and muscle hurt in Sam's body as he pulled himself up the steep embankment. They were bare footed and stones pushed painfully into their soles. Occasionally, one of them would slip, sending a tinkling waterfall of rocks tumbling down.

Neither of them talked. Indeed, Sam was conscious of a numbness, part-shock and part-exhaustion. It felt surreal to realise that he and this woman were the only survivors. Why had a Cornish bay become a slaughter house? And how had he ended up in the sea in the first place? And how the hell were they going to get out of this alive?

The image of those bodies flickered before him. He remembered the rhythmic crack of the pistol. He felt the prickling of goose pimples on his skin.

'Mr Garrett?'

They had reached a slight levelling of the path. Her tone was soft, but something in it made him turn quickly to her.

'Yes?'

'I just realised that there was no cargo,' she said.

'What do you mean?'

'I was told to help unload products from France. I was late coming down, but other boats had made it. Most of the cargo would had been brought in. *The Rising Dawn* was close to empty. And the men would have no personal effects of value. Why would anyone destroy an empty vessel?'

'Rival smugglers, I'd guess.'

'You mean from Cornwall?'

'Most likely. Maybe it was a fight over territory?'

'No.' She shook her head. 'There has always been smuggling, but never this. Seamen wouldn't lure people, other seamen, to their death. They wouldn't—'

'Miss Lansdowne, I do not mean to be unfeeling— those men did not deserve to die like they did on that beach…no one does—but they were criminals.'

She shook her head, saying nothing for a moment as she continued the ascent. 'You're from London. You do not understand.'

'What has London to do with it?' he asked, irritated

as he chased up the path to keep up with her. Did she think there were no criminals in London, no children who had never been taught right from wrong? He knew and that was why he funded schools to support the moral growth of children whose parents were unable to do so.

She made no reply, merely continuing up the trail, moving swiftly, despite her bare feet,

'And what do not I understand? Smuggling is a crime. These are grown men, not children who may not understand right and wrong,' he said.

She paused, glancing back at him, her dark brows pulled together in a way which was almost formidable. 'It is so much easier to understand right from wrong when one is not desperate.'

Thankfully, they were close to the clifftop. Millie scrabbled upwards, eager to distance herself from the man behind. Mr Garrett was judgemental. He did not understand the life of the men in the mines. He did not know what it was like to be forced into a life one did not want. He did not know what it was like to feel one's hope and dreams disintegrate. Or to pore over figures and to know that the best, the only, way to help one's family was marriage.

Marriage to the dull Mr Edmunds. Marriage to a man twice her age. Marriage to a man who had no interest in her other than to acquire the narrow strip of their property which bisected his own.

But that was not the worst of it. The worst of it was knowing that marriage to Mr Edmunds might not be enough to save Lil. Just as her nagging had not been enough to save Tom.

It was never enough.

With a burst of angry energy, she pulled herself over

the cliff's edge, scanning the area to gain a sense of her surroundings. The ground stretched, flat, ugly and utterly desolate, except for a scattering of hawthorn trees, twisted and hobbled by the wind.

She stared. The anger which had thundered through her seemed to solidify, turning cold, as she looked about with growing hopelessness at the harsh, unforgiving landscape.

Tears smarted. What had she expected: a country village and welcoming tea party? She stared at the bleak surrounding with a sense of futility. She'd overcome one hurdle just to be faced with this vast barren landscape, unbroken save for the tors strung along the horizon.

She turned back towards the sea. It shimmered, a dull metallic grey. *In and out and back for breakfast.* That had been the plan. Almost she felt as though a friend had turned on her.

Mr Garrett scrambled over the cliff's edge. It was ironic that this man from Tom's past, who represented everything she did not like about England's aristocracy, should be her sole company. It was an irony that some literary genius would have loved.

With a sigh of exhaustion, he straightened, also staring at their surroundings. The contrast between the first time she'd seen him and now was almost funny. Then, he'd been every inch the fashionable gentleman with his perfectly fitted jacket, high collar and intricate cravat. Now his clothes were close to rags. He'd taken off his coat and held it in one hand, the dark tails hanging torn and wet. His shirt was ripped, several buttons undone, and she could see his chest. His trousers were tattered, his feet bare and the ends of his once-white cravat fluttered in the wind.

'We made it,' he said, surveying the emptiness. 'Where would they have gone and how?'

'Horseback most likely. There looks to be hoofmarks, but it is too dry and hard to see clearly. We will be able to see more clearly in the damper areas.'

'Any clue where we are?'

'I am unsure.'

'At least no one can sneak up on us.'

He smiled. He had one dimple on the side of his cheek that made a slight crease. Millie smiled also. Laughter bubbled inside her. She grinned and then chuckled The emotion grew, swelling up from somewhere deep. It shook her, breaking through the numb paralysis morphing into high-pitched giggles which subsided into a whimper.

He stepped up quickly, reaching out for her, taking her into his arms and holding her tightly to his chest so that she could smell the sweat and salt on his skin. Instinctively, she clung to him. Her fingers tightened on his arms, needing to feel that he was real, solid, alive. His shirt was damp against her cheek. But she could feel the warmth of his skin and hear the thudding, regular beat of his heart.

'Hush,' he said, rocking her as he might a child. 'Hush.'

His words and the gentleness of his tone made things both worse and better. Her sobs lessened. The tight bands about her ribcage loosened and she could breathe more easily. She became aware of the strength of his arms, the way they encircled her, making her feel safe, protected and anchored away from the horror of the beach below.

For several seconds, she was content to cling to this man, this sole survivor, but as the panic lessened, she felt an awareness that was embarrassment mixed with something else.

She had never been so close to a male. Ever.

Her cheek was flush to his skin. His hands encircled her and she could feel her body tight against him. She felt the pressure of his embrace and a consciousness of the exact inches where his palms and fingers touched her back.

She had been clinging to him as though for survival, but the feeling morphed and she became aware of his skin and the movement of his muscles.

She had never touched a man's bare chest or shoulders. She had never felt this sensation of curiosity, awareness.

She jumped back. Her arms dropped quickly to her sides.

'I—I am so sorry,' she said, stammering as heat rushed into her cheeks.

She glanced up. He was standing quite still, his expression unreadable. His hair was still wet and fell forward on to his forehead. She knew a sudden wish to push it back. She pressed her hands tight to her sides.

'I cannot think why I behaved so,' she said, stepping further back, wishing he would say something.

Their gazes met. His eyes were a dark greenish-grey. She looked away. For another moment he said nothing and when he spoke it seemed to require an effort. 'It might have something to do with near drowning and seeing, well…what we saw.'

'I…um…do apologise. It…it certainly won't happen again.'

'I did not mind,' he said.

She supposed he wished to be reassuring, but somehow his tone and his expression made the confusion worsen. Heat fired into her cheeks. Her throat became dry. She rubbed her eyes, which were still damp from the tears.

'Here.' He pulled out a handkerchief and his fingers brushed her hand as he handed it to her. They were warm, yet his touch sent cold shivers coursing through her body.

'You still have a handkerchief?' Her voice sounded strangely husky.

'Every well-dressed gentleman does.'

She took the handkerchief, still damp from the sea. 'Thank you.'

After wiping her eyes, she looked around the surroundings and realised that the landscape was not quite as foreign as she has supposed. 'I feel quite composed now, I suggest we continue to the nearest town,' she said.

'An admirable suggestion. I'll pull out the map.'

'No need to be facetious. Fowey should be that way.' She nodded in a south-west direction.

'Is that a whim or do you know the area?'

'I know it. I walk a lot. I have not been this far, but I recognise the landscape as similar to what I'm used to.' Her words came out quickly, sounding like a hurried babble to her own ears.

He looked doubtful. 'You are a woman of surprises, but I will follow your lead, given I have no better ideas.'

Miss Lansdowne started forward with surprising confidence. The cap had been lost and wind pulled her hair loose in a wild, tousled mop. Although quite short, her stride was brisk and he found himself quickening his pace to keep up with her.

She was an anomaly, different from any woman he had encountered, and oddly appealing. The way she had clung to him, the surprising soft fullness of her body pressed against him, had invoked a gamut of emotion.

Her eyes were huge and blue, not a flat cornflower blue, but a dark, deep blue. He watched her nimble movements and the ease with which she negotiated the rugged path, despite her bare feet. He lived in a world where conformity was paramount. His father had wanted him a certain way, an imitation of all the other sons from centuries past who had gone to Harrow and graduated into White's. He'd hated Harrow and he did not particularly enjoy White's. His father had sent him to school days after his mother's death. He'd learned to survive. But survival had depended on being the person others had wanted, not the person he was.

This girl should be singing and torturing a musical instrument, not running around Cornish bogs in sailor's trousers. He did not know if he envied, admired or disapproved. All three, perhaps?

How did one go from tea parties to smuggling? *Why* would one go from tea parties to smuggling?

'You mentioned being in London some years ago. Have you visited more recently?' he asked, as he followed her brisk steps.

'We are still in mourning,' she said, her tone flat.

'Of course, I am sorry.'

'Yes, people always are.' Again, she sounded almost angry.

Grief did that, the pain mixing with a desolate, impotent wrath so that one did not know where one emotion ended and the other began. He remembered when his mother died and how the pain and shock had shifted into rage.

Miss Lansdowne had suffered two losses: father and brother. Two losses so close to each other would be tough on any family.

'It must have been a difficult time,' he said.

She stopped a few feet ahead of him and turned, her hands set squarely at her waist. Her dark hair blew wildly and there was something about her silhouette, starkly outlined against the moorland's grey sky, which had an untamed wildness that was akin to pagan. He could imagine her as a direct descendant from the druids who had once walked these shores.

'As I mentioned before, I am not comfortable with small talk or condolences. If you must talk, why do you not enlighten me about your aquatic escapades? How did you end up half-drowned off the coast anyway? I still do not even know that.'

'Nor do I,' he said.

'Pardon?'

'I do not know what happened.'

'You do not know?' Her brows pulled into a ferocious frown, as though finding this statement a personal affront.

'No. Everything is blank.'

'I suppose you were drinking.' She spoke flatly, a statement as opposed to a question. It struck him as surprising that such a young female should be knowledgeable about drunkenness.

'My brother's evenings usually started with food and ended in stupor,' she said, answering his unspoken question.

Indeed, Tom had been habitually three sheets to the wind, but Sam felt again taken aback by her bluntness.

'I believe in honesty, perhaps to an unladylike extent.' She looked at him with that disconcerting direct gaze as she again answered an unspoken question.

He paused, caught by her candid blue gaze.

Did she? How would she react if he'd told her that he found her the most fascinating female he'd encountered in years? Or that he wondered what it would be like to kiss her? And that her eyes were a beautiful blue?

He wouldn't say any of this, of course. He would not take advantage of a young woman still emotionally distressed. Nor would he step away from the script deemed appropriate for a gentleman. He paused and wondered which was the greater motivation; character or convention.

She nodded, turning from him and moving forward. 'So what do you remember?'

'The last thing I remember with any clarity is dinner,' he said, stepping after her.

A drunken escapade was a simple explanation. It would make sense; dinner followed by too much port. Except he did not believe it. His memory loss was not merely the blurriness of too much wine. Moreover, he'd been too worried about Frances to drink very much. Even that afternoon she'd seemed oddly quiet, holding her baby as though fearful to put him down. At dinner, it had been worse, as though her body was present, but her mind was not.

'I do not think that my memory loss was caused by too much drinking,' he said.

She glanced back. 'You did hit your head so I suppose it could be that.'

He touched the base of his skull somewhat tenderly. 'Isn't that the stuff of novellas and fanciful stories?'

'There is often a grain of truth in such tales, at least so my sister says.'

'Perhaps. I am not well versed in such fiction.'

'My sister adores them. The more unlikely the better.' Her voice had softened, as though merely thinking about her sister gentled her disposition.

'So might I be a prince in disguise?' he asked, needing to draw out this tenuous connection, this moment of levity, to hear the laughter in her voice and imagine her expression relaxing, her lips curving upwards in that smile which was somehow transformative.

'Her favourite authors would find that entirely possible with all manner of assassins eager for your demise.'

'You say that with too much enthusiasm.'

She glanced back again, her face now serious. 'But is it possible? Could someone wish you harm? Might you have been intentionally attacked?'

He frowned. 'It seems unlikely. My memory of my last twenty-eight years is quite clear and I do not remember any duels, physical skirmishes or enemies to speak of. Although I suppose I might have had a run-in with one of your smuggling friends.'

She shook her head. 'It was a small delivery. I saw the other two boatmen collecting the shipment and they did not seem distressed.'

'Perhaps they are too used to clonking the odd inconvenience on the head to experience any additional concern?'

'No, they are both very pleasant individuals. Mr Jones is the baker and Mr Larose the undertaker. That doesn't sound reassuring, I know, but he is quite the loveliest man. Where were you staying?'

'Manton Hall.'

'What?' She jerked to a stop so suddenly that he almost collided with her. She turned around sharply, her expression again becoming one of hostility. 'Why?'

'My sister lives there.'

'Your sister lives at Manton Hall? Married to Jason Ludlow?'

'Yes, you know him?'

'Not well,' she spoke quickly, all trace of humour gone, almost spitting out the words as though they tasted bitter on the tongue.

'You do not like him?'

She shrugged. 'I do not like him or his friends. However, your situation is easily explained. You and Ludlow made some crazy wager to see who could balance on a cliff, swim across the cove or something equally foolish.'

'Gracious, for someone conspiring with pirates you sound rather judgemental.'

'Smugglers. And I prefer sensible.'

'Which was why you chose to row in a storm?'

She stiffened, swallowing. He saw the movement in her throat and an expression of bleak sadness flicker across her countenance. 'You are correct. I made a poor choice. Poor choices are a family failing.'

'Miss Lansdowne, I did not mean to upset you.'

'I am not upset. Your statement is entirely accurate. My choice may greatly impact my family, who have already experienced so much pain.' There was a raw, pent-up emotion within the flat tones.

'I…look…'

'Might I suggest we focus on working together to ensure our survival as opposed to deciphering the past? Doubtless whatever led to your near drowning will become clear if—when—we get home. Talking is slowing our progress. At this rate we'll never get anywhere before nightfall. Let us continue in silence unless there is something urgent to mention.'

He wanted to argue. He felt angry at her flat dismissal. He also felt peculiarly sad that he'd upset her and irritated that his brother-in-law was condemned while pirating was entirely permissible. Moreover, he was confused that he even cared what this odd woman thought. He was hardly likely to strike up a long acquaintance.

Indeed, it was decidedly more important to determine how he'd ended up drowning and requiring rescue. Despite Miss Lansdowne's strongly stated opinion, he did not like Jason Ludlow sufficiently to drink excessively with him, gamble or take foolish risks.

So why had he have left his sister's house in the middle of a rain storm? Why go to the sea?

And so his thoughts kept circling to no effect. The more he pushed the fuzzier dinner became, as if the very act of thinking thickened the fog.

They continued in silence. He did not like the scenery. It seemed so endless, static, without change. Almost he could think that his mind was playing cruel tricks. He glared at the horizon. Maybe that was it. Maybe the moor turned one odd. Cornwall had not helped Frances. He remembered a woman who loved fashion, the theatre, and all the trappings city life. And now...she seemed hollow, a shell of skin and bone.

And Miss Lansdowne was decidedly...odd. Yet, she did not evoke sympathy. Instead, despite the pain and cold, there was a strength about her as she moved, sure footed, as though she belonged in these wild places.

'Sam! Look!' Millie's sharp tones cut through his abstraction as she again halted abruptly. She pointed towards the horizon. At first, he could see nothing, but then, hunkered against the hillside, he saw the outline of a hut, the grey stones visible against the yellowed grasses. Almost, it seemed like a mirage or illusion.

'Should we go there?' she asked.

'It's out of our way. How far to Fowey? Will we make it by nightfall?'

She looked about the landscape. 'I'm not certain. It is still some distance. And the days are short.'

He glanced towards the sky. They had been walking for hours. Day was sliding into the heavy gloom of late afternoon. The lull between storms was also ending. He could feel the wind picking up, pushing the heavy, black, rain clouds inwards across the moor.

'I wish we could get home tonight,' he said. 'Your family must be so worried for you.'

'And yours.'

'And your reputation...'

'Flora will say that I went out fishing and got caught in the storm. At least, I hope she will.'

'You do that often? Fish?'

'Yes. Though not usually in a storm.'

He stared towards the solitary dwelling. He hated to think of Frances being worried or scared for him. He'd stayed away much too long, only to arrive and then disappear.

'Maybe someone living there could help us get to Fowey quicker. They might have a donkey or cart.' He doubted this, even as he said the words. Even from this distance, the place looked abandoned. He saw no light or smoke from the chimney. 'And, at least, we could find shelter.'

'But what if...?' Millie let the sentence peter into the air. He knew she was visualising the slaughter at the beach.

'It is more likely a peat-cutter's cottage than anything ominous. Besides, if we cannot get to Fowey before nightfall...'

'We'll die of exposure.'

Of course, they could not go as the crow flies. To do so, they would have had to take a short cut through the peat bog with all its inherent dangers.

Instead, she guided them around the high land towards the hill. As always, the moors played its tricks and the hut remained tantalisingly distant. The only thing marking the passage of time was her heavy-limbed exhaustion, the dimming daylight and a growing thirst and hunger.

Millie tried to imagine what her family might be doing. Flora, their only remaining servant, was the most practical. She would take control. Likely she would have urged Millie's mother to lie down, giving her a sleeping draught. Then she would have walked down to the village to talk to Sally. Likely Sal would tell her about the smuggling.

Then a more awful thought struck her; a 'what if' bringing with it an endless series of 'what ifs'. Jem and the others might have been found. If so, Sal and Flora would think she had also died. Mother would likely take to her bed. Lil would be devastated and forced to marry Harwood.

Sweat made Millie's palms clammy. In her imagination, Lil was married before they'd even got back home and spirited away to Harwood's estate. But this was not sensible. The bans had to be read. Not that Millie trusted Harwood to even offer legitimate marriage. He would be the type to get a friend to masquerade as a minister. Really, whether his offer was legitimate or not, it did not matter. He was cruel. She'd heard the tales. She'd seen the maids with bruises, the women bustled back up to London or hidden in some cottage, their bellies growing.

Thankfully, these thoughts were interrupted by the more pleasant sound of the burbling stream twisting through the granite crevasse. It danced over the pebbles, its surface puckered with a scattering of raindrops.

'Thank goodness.' She hurried forward, bending over the clear water and cupping her hands. The relief as she quenched her thirst pushed out less immediate worries.

'A man can manage without food, but water is another matter,' Mr Garrett said.

'The streams running off the tor are usually fresh.'
She drank quickly, relishing the clear chilled liquid with
its earthy taste of minerals. She felt it dribble down her
chin and did not care, splashing her face with the cool,
refreshing droplets.

She sat back, licked her lips. 'Better than the best
wine.'

Glancing up, she caught his gaze and, although he
said nothing, something in his stillness and the intensity of his dark gaze made her oddly self-conscious. She
rubbed off the sweat, salt and grime on her face with a
hurried movement of her sleeve. 'I do not think I will
ever feel clean again.'

'I am not certain if your current efforts have improved
the situation.' He gave that slightly lop-sided grin, the
one dimple flickering.

'You are one to talk.' She flicked water at him. Indeed,
his face was covered by a layer of dirt, which somehow
served to emphasise the grey-green of his eyes and make
the tiny crease on his left cheek more visible.

He laughed as he wiped the droplets from his face
with the remnants of his tattered cravat. Squatting beside
her, he cupped his hands and splashed the water into his
face. They were not physically touching and yet she felt
conscious of his tall, long-limbed body, the tightness of
his trousers against his muscled thighs, the triangle of
chest visible in the 'v' of the torn shirt. She remembered
the warmth of his skin against her cheek, the thud of his
heart and the feeling of his arms about her.

She looked away.

Her focus must be to get home. She must hope that Mr
Edmunds would still marry her. He was her best chance.
And Lil's. Even if he lacked sufficient money to pay off

Tom's debt, she would be in a better position to help Lil as a married woman. Edmunds was decent, if dull.

'Not much further,' she said, standing and looking up the incline. She hated that they had to interrupt their journey, the need to continue pulsing through her. Still it was not practical to collapse from either exposure or fatigue, she thought, stepping ahead with a firm step.

The grey stone cottage was discernible against the yellowed grass. From its exterior, the hut appeared average, of the type often used on the moors.

'Distance is odd here,' Sam said.

'Yes, people say that. The moor is a trickster with mystery and secrets.'

'You speak almost with fondness. You like the moors?' he asked.

'Yes.'

'You do not find it solitary?'

'I find…' She paused, gazing about the desolate landscape. How could she explain that she had always felt a greater comfort outside than within the confines of a salon where she had two left feet and a propensity for tripping?

'Comfortable in her own skin.' She'd coined the phrase after Arabella Raskin's birthday party when she'd turned thirteen. Outside, Millie felt that comfort whereas in the parlour it seemed she had more elbows and knees than the requisite number.

'There is a freedom in the isolation,' she said finally.

He looked again towards the cottage. 'Then its inhabitant must live with considerable abandon.'

'It is likely empty. The peat-cutters leave during the winter months.'

'I suppose we'd best be off before the rain gets really heavy and the light fades further.' He glanced towards the dark clouds rolling in from the sea and hugging the land, the grey mist tangling in the bare branches of the hawthorn trees.

They started forward, stepping beside the silver brook and up towards the cottage. The thick marsh grasses rustled as they bent under their feet. Millie would never underestimate the value of shoes again. The thought of escaping from the wind and rain was alluring. The thought of taking the weight off her feet and letting her body rest even more so.

Yet apprehension slithered down her spine. Goose pimples prickled her skin. She shivered. Her imagination was not being sensible. It seemed to her warped fancy that she felt hostility from the hut's stony walls and malevolence squinting through the one shuttered window.

Crossing her arms, she hugged herself, in part to keep out the chill, but also for comfort. The memory of the drowned men and Jem, his blood puddling in the rock pool, flickered before her mind's eye.

In common accord, they paused in front of the remnants of a stone wall which encircled the property. It was crumbling. Grasses, moss and weeds grew through every space and aperture. There was no sign of occupation, no chickens or cow.

'I'll go in first, in case,' Mr Garrett said.

Millie nodded. 'It is sensible to seek shelter.'

'Who are you trying to convince?' He glanced at her, with that quick fleeting grin. Instinctively, Millie held her breath as Sam stepped forward.

Chapter Four

Aside from the odd cobweb, the cottage was no house of horrors. It consisted of one central room with a hearth on one wall and a small alcove at the back. The air was stuffy, but not unpleasantly so. It had a peaty scent that seemed an integral part of country living. Low beams criss-crossed the ceiling with yellowed straw close to the hearth as though to form a pallet.

The only light came from the open door, but it was sufficient to assure him that the central chamber was empty. Sam turned quickly and entered the alcove. It was also unoccupied.

From behind, he heard the whine of hinges. He jumped, but it was only Miss Lansdowne who had failed to listen, which was not entirely surprising.

'You were supposed to stay outside.'

'I hear well and listen poorly. That's what Flora used to say.' She was kneeling beside the hearth, her fingertips resting on the peat stored beside it. 'It is dry.'

'Good. I will make a fire. You look quite chilled.'

She nodded, leaning forward with sudden concentration. 'There is even a flint.' She picked it up, rubbing her fingers against it with a tiny rasping sound, as though needing this solid proof of its existence.

'And a tin cup. Is it unusual for a peat-cutter to leave such items behind?' he asked.

She met his gaze. 'It is unusual.'

With every moment, daylight was fading into gloom. He shrugged. They had little choice but to stay. 'I'll light a fire. We'll need it tonight for light and warmth.'

She glanced at him with that slight smile, giving her a slightly elfin appearance. 'Mr Garrett, may I enquire if have you ever actually made a peat fire?'

'Well, no,' he conceded. 'But it seemed like the right thing to say. Besides, we need heat so I'll give it a try.'

'I'll do it.'

'You know how?'

'Thankfully, I am no distressed damsel. You get the water while I make the fire.'

'You are unusual,' he said.

'It has been mentioned.'

Her smile grew and something about that slow, transformative smile and the way it suffused her whole face made him feel…odd. It made him wonder again what those soft, gently curving lips would feel like and remember the way she had clung to him, her fingers on his shoulders. It made him want to watch her, to observe her careful, meticulous movements as she bent over the peat. She was not graceful, but she moved with efficiency and with purpose. He felt pleasure in noting her attention as she immersed herself in a task.

She was not self-conscious. She did not pose with more awareness of how she appeared than of the task at hand. Instead, she seemed oblivious of the dark hair falling forward across her face, the gape of her shirt as she pulled out the peat, arranging each strand with deliberation.

Turning hastily, he picked up the cup and hurried outside, letting the door bang behind him. He needed to escape. Likely it was her very peculiarity which fascinated.

Physical desire was a fleeting thing, stimulated by danger. However, he was a civilised individual with emotional control. The woman was vulnerable and he had no need to further complicate his life or waste time thinking about her eyes, or her lips or the pale creaminess of her skin…

He dipped the cup jerkily into the stream.

With Annie, he had welcomed that feeling of being overpowered. It was like losing himself and he had wanted to lose himself then. It was a new chapter. His childhood—with his mother's death, school and then his father's death—had ended. It was the reinvention of self and the finding of meaning in a new identity.

It was also smoke and mirrors. Annie had found her duke and he'd learned that his new identity was no better than the old. When Annie left, she'd taken not only his heart but this sense of renewal, hope and reinvention.

Sam could not let that happen again.

He'd felt broken after Annie. With Frances's help, he'd rebuilt his life. He was now a board member for several charities, he had continued his mother's work, translating ancient Greek, he wrote occasionally for the newspapers, went to the opera and socialised on occasion. He was playing more on the pianoforte and even had a few scribbled original compositions.

He knew a level of contentment.

Sam drank and then refilled the cup, walking back to the cottage. Millie was leaning over a tiny whisper of smoke. The door clattered behind him, but she showed no sign that she had heard his entry. He watched as the peat caught fire, the flame flickering and a whisper of smoke rising.

'There!' she said, her delight obvious. She looked at him as the peat sizzled, the yellow flame providing a flickering light. The fire's heat had warmed her cheeks. Her hair was almost dry and took on coppery highlights.

'You are an individual of many accomplishments,' he said, crossing the floor.

'Building a fire is generally an under-appreciated skill, unless one is a domestic servant or stranded on a moor.' Wry humour laced her tones as she added more peat, blowing on it delicately, with tiny movements of her hand.

'I could almost believe you one of the faerie folk, practising a magical incantation.'

'Merely utilising the physical properties of combustion. Besides, we have pixies here. They are considerably shorter and dance better. I have the stature.'

'But not the dancing?'

'Two left feet.'

'I like dancing,' he said.

'I suppose it is a requisite skill where you come from.' Indeed, this was an understatement. Music and dancing had always been more than just a required skill.

'I come from London. Not some outer constellation within the cosmos,' he said, laughing. 'And I like music.'

'What type do you like?'

'Opera. Although "like" isn't the right word.'

'What is?' she asked, fixing him with that direct gaze, as though she genuinely wanted to know the answer.

He frowned, staring into the flickering flames. His mother had loved the opera. She would go often, and played and sang at home...mostly Mozart and Handel. She'd always been so emotionally restrained except when it came to music. For her, music had allowed communication with others. For him, it was an ability to connect with himself. Sometimes when he listened, he felt an almost physical pain. Its intensity made him want it to go on and yet he also needed it to stop.

'I cannot put it into words. Perhaps that is the key. It is about expressing something that has no other language,' he said.

She looked at him and he had the odd feeling that she understood. It felt that this conversation was more real and intimate than any he had experienced for years.

'Sometimes I feel that way when I listen to the wind and the sea.'

There was a pause, punctuated only by the rain, the wind and the sizzling crackle of the peat. The room was quite dark now, daylight no longer visible through the ill-fitting shutter. The fire's amber glow provided a low flickering light and the air had a smoky earthiness that was not unpleasant. They sat quite close. Glancing sideways, he could see the outline of her silhouette, her face half hidden by the sweep of her hair. He felt an urge to push the brown locks back to better see her expression, her lips, eyes and shadowy lattice of her lashes. He again had that wish to both prolong the moment and the need to break it.

'Water?' he asked, pushing the mug towards her.

'Thank you.' She cupped the mug. Her hands were small but sturdy. She drank, seeming to savour each sip, licking her lips. This was an almost sensual quality about it.

He leaned forward, rubbing his hands to warm them over the fire. 'It's burning well. Who taught you?'

'Flora.'

'Your maid?'

'Maid and friend. She introduced me to Sally—and her family. I also know how to fish and hunt.' She paused,

giving him that slightly impish smile. 'If I had my cata-
pult, I could get us a rabbit to roast over the fire.'

He could see her as an elfin huntress complete with
bow and arrow, a miniature Dianna with a dose of mis-
chief. 'Flora taught you that, too?'

'Yes, and Sally, her niece.'

'Jem's wife?'

'Yes…' She paused, with a tiny sigh. 'Sally and I would
play as children. We became good friends. I learned a lot
of useful skills from her. She told me about Cornish pixies, spriggans and knockers.'

She looked into the flames, smiling, as though privy
to some pleasant secret.

'What in the world is a spriggan?'

'Like a pixie, but nastier.'

'And a knocker?'

'Less malevolent, but tricky. They like to steal tools
or play other tricks, particularly on the miners.'

'You know a lot about Cornwall.'

'It is my home,' she said.

He thought of Annie and all the other women in London. He could not envisage them hunting, weaving tales
of pixies and spriggans or, he reminded himself, cavort-
ing with smugglers.

She was unique, different from anyone he'd encountered.

'Your face is none too clean either,' Miss Lansdowne
said.

'Pardon?'

'You seemed to be scrutinising me.' She eyed him
sternly from under her straight, strong brows, which
were at odds with the delicate heart-shaped features of
her face.

'You are blunt,' he said.

'I warned you.'

'I apologise. I was just thinking that I had never met anyone like you, in London.'

'I doubt I'd survive long in London.' Her nose wrinkled with distaste.

'You do not like it?'

She paused. 'It is not...' she said, after a moment's contemplation. 'It is not that I dislike London. I have only been there twice and it was very foreign to me. I felt as though I was always pretending, trying to impress people about things I did not think important.'

'Like what?'

'The latest fashion. An acquaintance of my mother's once wore a collection of fruit on her bonnet because she thought it fashionable. And everyone complimented her on it.'

'And did the bonnet impress?' he asked.

'Only the flies.' She stretched, smothering a yawn.

He smiled. It was true. Life was about pretending, although he doubted that was limited to London. At school, he'd pretended a love of sports and to have only average intelligence.

His father had married his mother and pretended he did not care that she had a child from a previous marriage, was almost middle-aged, no great beauty, with a vast knowledge of scholarly works and a complete inability to utter a single witticism. None of it mattered because she was rich.

His mother had married his father and pretended to care about the domestic challenges of retaining servants with a mind so brilliant she could read Greek, Latin, astronomy and play several musical instruments.

Even with Annie, there had been pretence. He'd changed to be the person she wanted him to be. It had worked until the duke came along with the title and the lands and then all his pretty play-acting was for nought.

Socrates had said that the greatest way to live with honour is to be what we pretend. What would it be, not to pretend?

Millie gave another yawn and he pushed his thoughts aside, starting to collect some of the straw. 'We should get some rest. I'll stuff some straw under the door jamb. Cut down the draught.'

'My mother calls it a door sausage.'

He glanced at her profile. 'She must be very worried.'

'Yes,' she said in a tone that did not invite further question.

Frances must also be worried. He did not like to think of it. She had seemed so fragile and he hated to think that he was adding to her anxiety. Frances had always been his anchor. Even from a distance, she had helped during those first awful months at school. She'd written long letters with funny anecdotes about cook, nanny, the housekeeper's cat who had somehow landed in the coal scuttle. He remembered her saying that she'd got the maid to post them as his father disapproved, saying that Sam was too much mollycoddled by the women in his life.

Frances had been the strong one, pulling Sam from the brink when he had been set on self-destruct.

'We will get back to them tomorrow,' he said, as though saying it made it the more likely. 'Let's get some rest. I will lie in the small alcove and give you the fire.'

'You will freeze. Stay near the fire.'

He hesitated. 'It hardly seems appropriate for us to be so close.'

She laughed, a wonderful gurgling laugh which lit up the room. 'I doubt being kidnapped by smugglers, escaping a sinking ship and almost drowning was appropriate either.'

He grinned back with sudden lightness of heart. 'You are unusual, brave and with a sense of humour. I cannot think of any other individual who could have endured what you have.'

She gave a breathy gasp. 'Then you really must expand your acquaintances.'

'Here, my jacket is dry at last.' He lay it over her.

'Thank you.' She curled into it and he lay close, making sure that his body blocked the draught which, despite the straw, still whistled under the door jamb.

The wind rattled the shutter while rain drummed on the roof.

'Tell me again…what is it that you like about Cornwall?' he muttered.

'It is beautiful and wild and free and independent.'

'It is that,' he said. 'Goodnight, Miss Lansdowne.'

'Might I suggest, Mr Garrett, that you call me Millie, given the experiences of the day?'

'If you will call me Sam?'

'Sam it is,' she said softly. 'Goodnight, Sam.'

Jason's face was close to his own: so close Sam could see the spittle leave his lips; so close that he could see the pores and broken blood vessels threading his nose; so close that he could see the bloodshot red suffusing his eyes.

Except he couldn't breathe. His throat had constricted. He couldn't see or hear. It was black and cold.

He was drowning, unable to breathe, unable to move. Fear pounded though him.

A scream shattered the night…

'Shh, you're having a nightmare.'

The words came from outside his dream. Sam bolted upright. It was dark. He felt a confused disorientation and raised his fists to ward off an unseen enemy.

'Mr Garrett… Sam…wake up. It's me.'

'Miss Lansdowne.' He lowered his hands. 'I apologise.'

They were at the hut, of course. The memories from the day previous tumbled back.

'You just had a bad dream.'

'Yes… Jason…' Images flickered through his mind but even as he tried to grasp them, they slipped away, ephemeral as mist.

Millie was sitting up with her back to him, prodding the fire into reluctant life. It fizzled and she added more peat, cupping her hands and blowing gently. He shivered, his body cold and clammy with sweat.

'Was it a memory or just a dream?' she asked.

'I do not know. I was with Jason. We were fighting. I was outside.'

'Is that how you ended in the water?'

'I… I do not know.' He shook his head. 'It cannot be. Jason is my sister's husband. I wouldn't fight him. It must be a dream.'

'Maybe someone attacked you both?'

Sam lay back, staring at the plume of tiny sparks twisting towards the ceiling. 'If only I could remember. Sometimes, it is almost there, like when you see something from the corner of your eye but it disappears the moment you look at it.'

She nodded, also lying down. 'So maybe tell me what you do remember? Any detail might help. Just talk about the day. Why you came here.'

He was silent for a moment. It couldn't hurt. He did not feel sleepy and it was still dark. Perhaps it might help him to make sense out of the clogged confusion which was his brain.

'I came to Cornwall to see my sister, Frances. I arrived in the afternoon. I went directly to Manton Hall.' He paused.

'You must have been happy to see her and her baby?'

'Yes.' He spoke, slowly, remembering both Frances's surprise but also her apprehension. It was as though she was coiled too tight, her movements jerky and her gaze unable to linger on any one object. 'But I was worried. I should have come sooner. She had changed.'

'How?'

'She seemed nervous and her maid said that she seldom went out.'

'That much is true, but she was in the family way. Had you been close before she came here?'

'She was four years older than me and I was sent away to Harrow to study. We were as close as circumstances allowed. Frances helped me, during the difficult time after my father died.' He was almost surprised by his words, he seldom mentioned or even allowed himself to think about that time. His father's death, swiftly followed by Annie's decision to marry the duke had led to too many drunken nights.

'I'm sorry,' Millie said. 'About your father.'

'I thought you weren't comfortable with condolences.' He glanced towards her.

'I'm better when they're not directed towards me.'

'It was some time ago.'

'And does time make it better, like they say?' she asked, almost wistfully.

'Yes.' He paused. It felt, suddenly, that whatever was said in this isolated hut and on this isolated moor could not be the usual platitudes. 'There are some days when it still hurts…a lot. When it feels raw, but those days become fewer. With Mother…'

He stopped himself. With his mother it had hurt so much worse because he had not known she was so ill. Logically, he should have known. Even at eight, he should have known. But he hadn't, so the pain had been mixed with shock, anger and a feeling of stupidity. Even now, he wondered if people had sought to keep the truth from him or merely assumed he already knew it.

'What was she like? Your mother?'

He smiled into the darkness. 'Brilliant. Rude. She did not like fools which was unfortunate given her social strata. She could read many languages. Loved music. She was translating *Thesmophoriazusae* from Ancient Greek into English.'

'Thesmo—what? You'll have to enlighten me.'

'Written by Aristophanes. She talked to me a lot about its meaning. I did not listen as much as I should have done. She would also tell me the most wonderful stories and had a Greek or Latin quote for almost every situation.'

'You were close.'

'Yes.' In those last months she'd spent a lot of time with him. Frances was usually with her governess, but he only took lessons in the morning. During the afternoons he would sit with his mother as she told him story after story: myths, legends and make-believe. It was as though she wanted to pack a life time of books and music into a few weeks.

It had been a wonderful time, followed by a pain so harsh it had crippled. His world imploded and he lost not only his mother but his trust. He distrusted happiness. He distrusted people. His distrusted his own intelligence.

'People always want to help, but they never know what to say. They only want you to eat. Just when one wants to eat nothing,' Millie said softly.

'It's true.' He remembered cook making his favourite meal on the day after Mother died. He had eaten little and had felt the guilt of her disappointment. Then his father had shouted at the poor woman and told her not to 'mollycoddle' the boy, which seemed to layer further guilt on him.

'Your sister must have provided some comfort.'

'She wrote often. She cheered me up and helped me to be strong. Maybe that was why I never thought of her as vulnerable. If I had, perhaps I would have come sooner.'

'You came now. That is what is most important.'

Millie glanced at Sam's silhouette, the straight nose and strong jawline, now shadowed with stubble. There was an intimacy in talking like this. She'd read somewhere that it is easier to talk to a stranger. Or perhaps it was the darkness which lessened social restraint or the comfort of being dry and almost warm within this tiny cottage protected from the wind and storm outside.

'I got the feeling you do not like him. What do you know of him?'

'Who?' Millie was momentarily confused because something about his silhouette was distracting. 'Ludlow?'

'Yes.'

Millie thought back to when Ludlow and his mother had first taken the lease on Manton Hall. Indeed, her own mother had been excited. After Father had lost so much money, poor Mother felt banished to Cornwall and hoped the Ludlows would infuse it with sophistication.

In this she was disappointed. Mrs Ludlow, known as an arbiter of fashion and good taste in London, eschewed local society.

Unfortunately, Jason Ludlow was not similarly reclusive. After Father had quietly died of a poor heart, Mother had succumbed further to her nerves while Ludlow became Tom's antidote to the sadness of his home. He accompanied Tom often, going to Manton, London or some country house party. Ludlow had encouraged Tom to take risks but, truthfully, Tom needed little encouragement.

Indeed, Millie was always trying to reason with him and save him from his own demons.

'He was not a good influence on Tom. He emboldened him to seek danger, drink and gamble, but Tom's death was not Ludlow's fault,' she said.

'What happened?'

She stared at the criss-crossing beams and felt the sting of tears. She hadn't wanted him to go. 'Do you believe in premonition?'

'Like having a bad feeling about something?'

'Yes. I asked him not to go. It was a country house party in Devon.'

Truthfully, there was no reason to suspect that it would be any different than any of the other social events Tom attended. Maybe it was no different, he was just less lucky.

'He did not listen?'

'He bet he could jump a hedge. He died instantly,' she said.

The horse had shattered its leg and was shot. Her mother had fallen apart, broken by the loss of husband and son in such quick succession.

'I'm sorry,' Sam said, reaching for her hand.

She accepted his offer. She felt the warmth of his fingers and the comfort of human connection. Loneliness—out of the full gamut of human emotion, loneliness was the sentiment with which she had the greatest familiarity. And duty.

Since her father's financial losses, she'd tried to help her father, her mother, Tom, Lil, even Flora. If willpower could have kept them safe, they'd still be alive. But willpower was not enough. Her parents were too broken, her brother too reckless and her sister too young.

The firelight flickered. Outside, she heard a bird's call and wondered if it was getting close to dawn. They should leave once there was sufficient light. And yet, she was reluctant to move. It was warm under Sam's jacket, pressed close to the fire. She was conscious of his body, the size of him, which was both comforting and something else. She was peculiarly conscious of the present, as though past and future had slid into unimportance.

Indeed, there was an intimacy in this moment with him which was both disconcerting and reassuring.

She looked at his strong features, dimly lit by the firelight. His lips lifted in a smile.

'What is it?' she asked.

'I was only thinking that this felt…nice.'

The touch of his hand changed from comfort to an awareness, a tingling sensitivity and a feeling of being more alive. It felt as though every particle of her body, every inch if her skin had an added vibrancy.

Indeed, everything within the tiny bare cabin felt so completely different from the rest of her life, as if it was a separate moment, stolen in time. It stood out in brilliant, stark relief.

What would it be like, she wondered, to throw duty to the wind? To forget about the 'what ifs'? To forget about Mr Edmunds with his five children and the snuff stains liberally splattered across his too-tight waistcoat? To allow herself to inch closer to this man, to run her fingers across the stubble of his cheek, to feel the muscles in his shoulders?

'You know,' he said thoughtfully, 'I wouldn't have survived the moor without you.'

'You wouldn't have survived the sea without me either.'

He laughed. 'I suppose I should be glad you decided to smuggle.'

'Indeed, you should be grateful for ever.'

'You know, I have never met anyone like you. I feel as though I have been living in a grey world that has turned multi-coloured overnight.'

'I never knew you were a poet.'

'A poet? Now you insult me. Musician, maybe, but never a poet.'

'And what is wrong with a poet?' She raised herself on one elbow. He was quite close, inches away from her. His eyes were intently dark and his lips well shaped and sensitive.

'Aren't they dreadfully foppish? More cravat than person?'

'And musicians aren't?'

'Not nearly as bad. More person and less cravat.'

She giggled. 'I wouldn't know. Cornish sea towns aren't known for poets or musicians.' She touched his cravat, twisting the cloth through her fingers with a rustle of silk.

They were not touching and yet she was very aware

of him and the proximity of his body. 'I'm afraid this won't get you admitted into anything.'

'You mock my cravat? You do realise that an elegant cravat is the pride of every gentleman?'

She met his gaze and felt the rapid-fire thumping of her heart. 'I am sure it was elegant once,' she said, conscious of her uneven breath, as though she had been running.

They were so close she could hear the rustle of his shirt as he lifted his hand, touching her hair and gently tucking a stray strand behind her ear. Very slowly, he traced her jaw. The skimming touch of his thumb made her catch her breath.

He was so close that she could see the tiny crease on the left side of his cheek from that lop-sided dimple and the firm line of his lips slightly lifted in a smile.

Very slowly, he pulled her nearer to him, touching her lips with his own. The kiss was soft and gentle, a fleeting thing, and yet she felt it through every part of her body. It made her heart beat like a wild thing. It made her breath quicken and a feeling that was both shivery, but also searing, flashed through her. She'd never felt this. Or anything like this. Her every sense was filled by him. She heard nothing except his inhalation and the rustle of straw with his movement. She felt nothing except the warmth of his hand, cupping her chin, his lips warm against her own.

'You are very beautiful,' he murmured.

Never before had Millie Lansdowne felt beautiful, but in this moment, and with this man, she felt beautiful.

Sam looked down at Millie's flushed countenance. Her eyes were a dark, intense blue—a mesmerising blue—

her lips were parted, glistening with moisture and her shirt had fallen open, showing a creamy expanse of skin.

The place, the moment, the woman seemed stripped of all pretence, innocent of all lies or subterfuge.

A desperate, raw neediness grew in him. He wanted to pull her close, to feel her, to tangle his hands through her wild hair, drown himself in her eyes and satiate himself with the touch of her skin and lips. This moment had an intensity that made past and future inconsequential.

Her lips parted with a soft gasp as her hands reached up, touching his cheek and the line of his jaw. There was an exploratory innocence about her. He felt the graze of her fingers, as she touched his neck, his shoulders and muscles. This lack of sophistication also excited.

His kiss deepened. He felt her arch towards him. He felt the softness of her breasts pressing against him. He wanted this woman. He wanted this alluring, fascinating female with an almost adolescent urgency.

But he was not an adolescent any longer.

He forced himself to still, rolling away with a muted groan as he stared again at the cabin's criss-crossing beams, now dimly lit by the hint of daylight.

'Sorry,' he mumbled,

His heart thumped like a wild thing. Desire pulsed through him. But he would not seduce a vulnerable girl. Good God, it was not honourable, or sensible, or even safe.

'We must go. Starting to get light out,' he said, abrupt and gruff in his reluctance.

He got up. He looked away as she sat up also, her shirt hanging forward and her hair delightfully mussed.

'I will go outside and get water,' he said, leaving quickly.

It was still dim, but with a hint of dawn brightening the eastern sky. He filled the tin cup, also splashing water on his face. He should take a cold bath, it might bring back some semblance of self-control.

On his return, she was sitting quite composed. He handed her the cup. 'I'm—I mean—I apologise about before. I regret my actions,' he said.

She took the mug. 'Our circumstances are exceptional, likely resulting in our...foolishness. We will leave here and return to civilisation and put this unfortunate experience behind us.'

She spoke crisply, in businesslike tones, with as much emotion as his man of business might display about an unpaid bill. Except for the slight flushing of her cheeks, she seemed quite at ease. Meanwhile, his heart beat like a crazy thing wanting to break free of his ribcage.

'I'd best get more water,' he muttered. 'We should douse the fire.'

Millie glared at his retreating figure. He was positively galloping from the cottage. The door clanged behind him.

Of course, he regretted the kiss. And why wouldn't he? A fashionable gentleman would want someone beautiful, accomplished, witty. She was none of those things. Likely he'd had a moment of weakness brought on by the near-death experience, danger or the cold night.

She pulled her clothes more tightly about her. And what had she been thinking? Her character was not of the sort to forget duty. For the past twelve hours, she'd been damning herself for her foolhardy smuggling escapade and reminding herself that a respectable marriage was her best option, both for herself and Lil.

From now on, she would behave with the utmost propriety. She would search the cabin for anything which might help them on the journey. She would guide them to the nearest habitation. She would return home and hope Flora had concocted some story and her reputation was still intact. She would marry the estimable Mr Edmunds, would somehow save Lil from Harwood and let down neither her sister or mother.

With new determination, Millie stood, looking around the tiny cabin. Wincing, she went to the small cluttered alcove. It contained a broken chair, a plough, cutting tools and straw. Again, she felt a shiver of unease that so many items had been abandoned. She glanced nervously, half expecting to see the cabin's owner had arrived, intent on revenge.

She saw no one and was about to step back into the central part of the cottage when she noted a bin. Perhaps she was fuelled by curiosity or a last-ditch hope to find food. Indeed, potatoes flickered through her mind much like a small child would dream of sugar plums at Christmas.

Kneeling, she touched the rough wood, trying to pull up on the lid. It did not move and she realised that it was padlocked. She twisted the box about. Why would a peat-cutter need a padlocked box?

She scanned the oddments of tools. A blunt knife lay close to the plough and, holding it carefully, she placed the blade under the metal clasp. The knife skidded. She swore as it fell to the dirt floor.

The door clattered behind her as Sam returned. 'What are you doing in there? We need to leave.'

'Give me a moment.'

This time the knife did not skid. Gripping it, she angled the blade sharply, prying off the lock so that it fell to the ground with a heavy clunk.

Millie lifted the lid.

The box did not contain potatoes.

Chapter Five

Millie swallowed. Her hands tightened on the edge of the box while a deep chill seeped into her bones.

She heard the fizzle of the peat fire as Sam doused it with water.

'What is this?' he asked.

She swallowed, glancing back at him in mute appeal. She reached in, touching the cold gold of a woman's locket, as though to affirm its existence and prove it was not a part of a nightmare. Her hand brushed the corner of a child's portrait and the round contours of a man's pocket watch.

'Pearls,' she whispered, pulling up a delicate strand of moon globes. 'A peat-cutter wouldn't have all this.'

'Remnants of the wrecker's hoard. Things he couldn't sell right away.'

She let the pearls drop, the smooth feel of them distasteful. They clinked together, snaking around the child's portrait and the watch. She stared at the collection: signet rings, watches, a locket with tiny blonde hairs trapped beneath the glass.

Relics from the dead.

She remembered Jem's twisted form and sightless

eyes. She remembered the other men, both on the beach and flailing, helpless, in the seas. She stood, stepping back, needing to distance herself.

'We have to leave,' Sam said. 'It is not safe. They may be back.'

Millie nodded. Her throat hurt and she felt the sting of tears. She bent, lifting the lid to close it. The splintered lock dangled.

'You broke the lock? Why?' Sam asked sharply.

'Looking for food.'

'Locked in a box?'

'I thought—'

'You could not have left well enough alone?' he snapped.

'What does it matter? They'd have known we'd been here from the fire.' She dropped the lid. It clattered closed.

'That we'd sought shelter, not that we'd discovered… this.' He gestured to the box with its dangling lock. 'I should never have let us stay.'

'You did not,' Millie said. 'Besides, it would not have been safe to carry on at night.'

He stared at the box, as though its exterior would somehow serve to inform. 'But who did this? Who are they? A smuggling gang, no doubt, but from where? Villagers? Fishermen from further up the coast.'

'Not villagers. Or fishermen. They would not wreck. No decent Cornish man or woman would wreck.'

'Even after discovering this, you're still defending them?'

'Yes,' she said, bristling at the condemnation to his tone.

'Look, I do not know who did this, but odds are they

are smugglers, either from your group or a rival gang. Like it or not, they are criminals.'

She glared at him. His cravat had likely cost more than Jem could make in a year. 'Jem and the other men did not have choices. Jem had children. He wanted to put food on the table, grow old and see them grow up. Do you know what his other options were? To be snuffed out in a copper mine. Or survive the mine and die coughing his lungs out. He had no education or chance of education.'

'So that excuses crime?' he asked in that arrogant tone.

'No, but it makes it understandable. You are rich. You have so much money, you can gamble it away.'

'I did not know that you were so personally acquainted with my activities and financial situation.'

'Have you ever been in the mines? Have you ever been so deep in the earth that you are freezing, with air so dusty you cannot breathe and so little light that you cannot see? It makes smuggling seem the better alternative.'

'And you?' he asked. 'Are they now employing gentlewomen in the mine? Is that your excuse also?'

They stared at each other over the chest with its dangling broken lock and damning contents. They were only a foot from each other. She could see the dark intensity of his eyes.

'I do not need an excuse. I do not need to explain myself to you, but if you must know, I want to save my sister from marriage to Harwood.'

'Harwood? Lord Harwood?'

'Yes.'

'Why would she marry him?'

'Apparently my brother owned him money.' She stepped towards the door. 'Right, shall we go?'

Sam followed Millie as she led the way, skirting the low land. The rain had stopped, but the clouds were still heavy, the mists tangled in the few trees, obscuring the sun except for its glowing disc.

Millie's every movement, the way her hands formed tight fists, her quick steps and hunched shoulders spoke of her anger. Sam hurried after her.

Lillian Lansdowne should not marry Lord Harwood. No woman should marry Lord Harwood. Harwood was middle-aged. He was not accepted in polite society, frequented brothels, abused his mistresses and was diseased.

'Miss Lansdowne? Millie? There must be another option. How much is owing?' Sam asked.

'A thousand pounds,' Millie replied, without stopping or slowing.

'And it is authentic? Not a forgery?'

'I do not know.'

'What do you mean "I do not know"?'

'I do not have the information. Clear enough for you?'

'Why not?' he asked.

'His chose to talk to my mother and I did not see the note proving the debt.'

'A predator always goes for the weakest.'

She turned, briefly pausing. 'Very wise, Mr Garrett, but when I rescued you from the sea, it was not an invitation into my family's business.'

'I want to help.'

'Well, you cannot. Tom gave Harwood a promissory note. Now, he will throw Mother into debtors' prison if Lil doesn't marry him.'

'Do you have a solicitor?'

'Yes.'

'Then he needs to look into it. Have you spoken to him?'

'No, I was somewhat preoccupied with rescuing a drowning man and being kidnapped.'

She turned, starting to walk briskly again.

'It might have been a better initial first step. I mean, instead of smuggling.'

'A solicitor cannot find money that is not there. He will merely charge for the privilege. Besides, I needed to do something, not listen to some fusty man tell me there was nothing I could do.'

Her voice was thick with emotion.

'I'm sorry,' he said. 'I sounded judgemental.'

She shrugged. 'Obviously, my smuggling idea was not my crowning achievement.'

This much was true but he could understand her near panic. 'Harwood is…' he paused, trying to find the words '…unpleasant.'

No woman deserved such a fate. He realised he had no right to judge her or dead men.

Besides, his harsh words had been less about anger or judgement, but more about his own vulnerability. There was something about this woman which made him feel a complexity of emotion he did not begin to understand. She had such spirit and humour. What other woman would seek to save her sister by smuggling? Or be able to walk for miles, shoeless, and without complaint?

She was so different than most women of his acquaintance. He felt more in her presence. She attracted him in a multitude of ways. She intrigued him. His thoughts circled back to those moments by the fire. He remembered the touch of her lips and how physical desire had trumped sense.

She engendered a raw neediness, marked by a lack of control, and made him want to throw caution away.

But he'd done that before, immersed past, present and future into his adolescent love for Annie Whistler.

And then everything had disintegrated.

He pulled himself back from the past, focusing on the woman in front of him. She strode forward, her spine stiff, irritation almost bristling from her. She must love her sister very much to try smuggling in the middle of a gale.

'Miss Lansdowne, about Harwood—he is known to be ill and I have heard his behaviour is erratic. Why would he suddenly produce this promissory note, six months after your brother's demise? I do not know anything for certain, but a solicitor should be involved. Will you let me get my solicitor to look into it?'

She paused, glancing back at him and studying him with her intent gaze. 'Very well.' She turned away and they continued to walk for several minutes. Then she stopped again. 'Thank you,' she said.

'Over there. Look!'

Millie had stopped. Roused from his introspection, he squinted towards low hills.

'See! A road and a building. I think it is a tavern. Indeed, we are quite close to Fowey. I do not think I have been more glad to see human habitation before.'

He saw now the road winding through the countryside and a stone building, half hidden behind a cluster of trees. The harshness of the moors had lessened. The sparse grass and bent trees had given way to more habitable greenery and the patchwork of fields. Even the air smelled better, less peaty, laced with fresh grass and salt air.

'I have never been more famished,' he said.

She turned to him, her forehead puckered into a worried frown. 'But we have no money. Indeed, given the state of us, we'll likely be sent away as beggars.'

'Except I do,' he said.

'What?'

'Have money.' He pulled out a gold guinea, laying it flat on his palm.

'Where did you get that?' she asked sharply. 'The cottage?'

'Yes.'

She stood quite still, staring at the coin, before looking up with her dark brows pulled into an angry frown. 'People gave their lives for that. I'd prefer to go hungry than use that money. And you judge me and Jem? How much did you take?'

'A few guineas. I did not want you wandering about this moor with criminals tracking us.'

'So I am the reason? You would be quite happy to be tracked by any number of homicidal felons if you were alone? You blame your moral lapse on me?'

'You are being overly dramatic,' he said.

'And you are being a hypocrite. Besides, I am not your responsibility. Men always make poor choices and then blame women, as though we had somehow engineered them into it.'

They stood, glaring at each other. 'Fine,' he said. 'I made a choice. I am uncertain if it was honourable, but I wanted to make sure we are both safe. And stop the wreckers before they do more harm. If you are so vehemently opposed, we will not use the coins and continue walking without food or transportation.'

Her frown became more formidable, but after a moment she shook her head. 'No, that would be foolish. I just hope that you will recognise that the moral high ground is a luxury more easily afforded by the rich.'

'You can be appallingly smug,' he muttered.

It took longer to near the building than she had hoped, but eventually the foot path reached the road and, after some more trudging, they came to the cross road and a small hostelry.

'So what is the plan exactly?' she asked as they neared the courtyard. 'Are you going to give the landlord money and hope he will think us good gentle folk merely down on our luck?'

'We have had an accident. I generally find that a combination of gold and arrogance works to get one out of many situations.'

He spoke with that easy confidence that Tom had always wanted, but never quite attained. She glanced down at her own rags.

'And what of me? I am quite certain they will think my character questionable...as an unaccompanied female.'

'I would not advertise that.' He looked over her slim figure. 'Tie up your hair. Fortunately, you'll pass easily enough for a street urchin.'

'You are fulsome with your compliments.'

Millie kept her smile in place. She refused to even acknowledge that momentary hurt that she could be so easily dismissed. Indeed, any flicker of emotion was due to the fact that she was famished, fatigued and therefore less rational than usual.

Naturally, that kiss had meant nothing to him...or her. It was an aberration, having much more to do with circumstance than any emotion. The kiss had been a celebration of survival, nothing more. Or perhaps the result of proximity.

Whatever the reason, he doubtless greatly regretted the embrace. As did she, of course.

The gate whined as they stepped into a small courtyard. It smelled none too clean, a pig and several chickens apparently having free range. She also noted a rather disgruntled-looking donkey, a horse and a cockerel. The latter seemed to have lost several tail feathers, but made up for this with the volume of crowing and by taking several aggressive runs at the donkey.

The tavern was a stone building with a cobbled path leading towards the front door, as though it had once aspired to greater grandeur than currently demonstrated.

She halted, biting her lip nervously. 'Is it possible that the inn or landlord is involved?' she asked. 'I have heard that inns play a role in smuggling.'

'I do not know. We will keep our wits about us. And try not to arouse suspicion.'

'That's your plan?'

'Here!' He pulled a strip from the lining of his jacket. 'Tie up your hair.'

She took the rag. 'Thank you.'

They crossed the courtyard and approached the building via the cobbled path. Millie had not thought her feet had the capacity for more pain, but the stones cut into them so painfully that she found it hard not to wince.

Sam did not take the back exit as she'd anticipated but instead strode to the front, with a brazen swagger. Millie followed. There had been a shift, she realised. In desperation, there had been equality. Sea, hunger and the desolate bogs cared little for wealth or position. But even without clean clothes or money, he had that air of superiority.

He pushed open the thick oak door and they found themselves in a narrow entrance, which seemed dark after the daylight outside. She had not often been in a tavern and found the onslaught of smells—ale and sweat and food—almost overwhelming.

A round man with red cheeks fringed with white whiskers looked up from the behind the bar. His expression soured as he scanned both visitors.

'What are you doing in here?' he asked, his tone sharp.

'Good day. I am Mr Garrett and am pleased to make your acquaintance. I suffered an accident and require sustenance,' Sam said, with that strong imperious voice.

The landlord paused, eyes narrowed. Millie watched his gaze scan Sam's person, lingering for a moment on the tattered suit jacket.

'And how will I be paid then?'

Sam pushed forward the guinea. 'I will send my boy around with additional money when we get home.'

Millie glared, squashing the strong desire to pull a face as an urchin might. The landlord looked at the guinea so dubiously that she half expected him to bite it.

'We will need food and transport,' Sam said and again she noted that autocratic tone, as though privy to some private script.

'Very well.' The landlord folded his plump fingers about the guinea, pocketing it his trousers. 'There is a private room behind the tavern. Go there if you've a mind. The boy can eat out back.'

'I—' Millie started to protest, but Sam gave her a quelling glare.

'The boy can eat with me,' he said.

Perhaps it was Sam's manner, the hope of more guineas or a desire to avoid more people in the kitchen, but the landlord merely nodded. 'Follow me then.'

'Thank you.' Sam's tone was polite, but with no great gratitude, as though the landlord's compliance was only to be expected.

'I'll take you through and get Doris to bring you something to drink and eat.'

They followed him into the back room which had a collection of threadbare furniture, a table with several chairs, a multipaned bay window, and a fire. The landlord poked at the lacklustre blaze before turning to leave. 'Right then. I'll send Doris in,' he said.

They heard his retreating footsteps. 'The boy can eat out back,' Millie hissed, as soon as the door closed. 'Really?'

'Well, you do look a bit of a ragamuffin and smell a tad off to boot.'

'You're none too fresh either,' she muttered.

Sam sat somewhat gingerly on one of the straight back chairs. 'I feel like I have had ten rounds at Jackson's. Thank goodness we are getting fed. I believe I am hallucinating about roast beef.'

Millie smiled, the thought of food soothing her lingering irritation as she sat on the chair opposite, propping her elbows on the table. 'And I have been smelling fresh baked bread for the last hour.'

'With nary a bakery in sight. In a few moments you'd be dreaming of Brussels sprouts.'

'What a fate. I am indebted.'

'I rather like that,' he said, with that lopsided smile. Something in his tone sent a tingle down her spine, making her catch her breath.

Just then, the door opened and the landlord's wife

entered. She proved to be a round woman rather resembling her husband with florid, apple dumpling cheeks.

'I'm Doris,' the woman said, putting bread, ale, cheese and cut meat on the table. Millie felt herself salivate, her hands almost vibrating with the need to grab the food, stuffing it into her mouth, manners be damned.

Indeed, by mutual consent, neither Sam nor Millie spoke. Instead they ate steadily as Doris poured out a tumbler of ale for each and departed.

'I do not think food has ever tasted so good,' Millie said, at length, leaning back in her chair and sighing with deep contentment.

'I do not think I took the time to taste it.' Sam also stretched out his legs towards the fire. 'I wonder if I have enough guineas to convince them to provide us with a bath and fresh clothes.'

For a moment, the length of a heartbeat, she imagined him naked. His skin gleamed with moisture. The muscles of his shoulders and arms moved under the skin. She could even see the dampness of his hair at the base of his neck where the golden glow of the lamplight cast intriguing shadows.

'I…um…' She gulped the last of her ale. 'It seems unlikely that even your charm could achieve a new wardrobe.'

'Do not underestimate my charms.' He gave that half-smile, one lip twisting upwards and a dimple flickering.

She knew he meant nothing more than his ability to use his manner and his privilege to convince the landlord but, even so, she was conscious of her cheeks flushing as she moved uneasily within her chair.

'I hear the landlord or his wife coming so you can try your luck,' she said, keeping her tone brisk and clipped.

The door swung open and the landlord appeared. 'All done, then?'

'Thank you,' Sam said. 'That was delicious.'

'Aye,' he agreed. 'We make our own bread, cheese and sausage here.'

'Then you are to be commended. As soon as I get back to Fowey I will ensure that your kindness is recognised.'

'Fowey is it, then?' the landlord said, bending over to pick up the coal shovel. He added a lump of coal to the fire, stoking it with the poker. A flurry of sparks flew up the chimney.

'Yes, my sister lives there.'

'Aye. And who be that, then?'

'My sister is Mrs Ludlow.'

'Ludlow, eh? You do not say?' The landlord put down the poker with a clank, his increased interest and curiosity obvious.

'And would she be married to a Mr Jason Ludlow?'

'Yes.'

The landlord went to the door, moving with increased speed as he shouted into the nether regions of the inn, 'Doris, this is Mrs Ludlow's brother. What do you think of that, then?'

Doris appeared so fast that Millie wondered if she had been waiting outside or whether the news had made her run along the hallway. Either way, she seemed to bristle with an unexpected pent-up excitement.

'You do not say?' Her eyes grew round, like bright buttons set within the pouches of her skin. Again, Millie felt that Doris displayed an interest and eagerness which did not seem sensible in the situation.

Sam must have thought that, too, because his body stiffened. 'What is it? Are you acquainted with my sister or her husband? Have you some news?'

'It is not like us to gossip...' the landlord said.

'Indeed, no, we always keep our customers' confidences...'

'Except neither Mr or Mrs Ludlow are your customers, at present,' Sam said, leaning forward. 'And I am.'

Husband and wife glanced towards each other, although Millie did not know if they were hesitant to speak or merely engaged in a competition to see who would speak first.

The landlord apparently won. He straightened, cleared his throat and threw back his head as though about to recite a Shakespearean monologue.

'Mrs Ludlow is currently arrested,' he said.

Chapter Six

Whatever Sam had been expecting, it was not this. He stared at the man for a moment, not quite comprehending the words. He felt a chill that began inside and seemed to paralyse his muscles so that he could not breathe.

'Arrested? That is not credible. What for?'

'The murder of Mr Ludlow.'

'Murder? Jason is dead?'

The cold tightened, vise-like. It gripped at his heart and his lungs so that each exhalation hurt and felt like an effort of will. His dream, the blurred image of his brother-in-law, flickered before him.

'In a manner of speaking,' the landlord said.

'Well,' his wife corrected, 'more precisely he disappeared.'

'Disappeared?' Sam asked.

'His body has not been found,' she explained, adding ghoulishly, 'Yet.'

'But several of his personal effects have washed up on shore,' the landlord added. 'Leading people to think that 'e's dead.' To emphasise this point, he lifted his plump finger and made a movement across his throat, much as a school boy might.

'And they think his wife was involved?' Sam managed to ask, pushing out the words.

'Their relationship had been...' The landlord paused as though gauging Sam's reaction.

Sam lifted one eyebrow. 'Yes?'

'Fraught.'

Sam stood, the movement so **abrupt** that his chair banged into the wall behind him. The need to escape the curious eyes of the landlord and lady overwhelmed. Indeed, their earlier gossipy nosiness now seemed laced with malevolence. The smells of ale, food and tobacco no longer comforted, but seemed to suffocate.

Throwing down a guinea, he strode from the room, pushing open the door and almost sprinting down the narrow corridor and outside, into the fresh air beyond. The outer door clattered behind him. He leaned against the stone wall, staring blindly at the small courtyard, while gulping the air like a man drowning.

The stone exterior felt rough and bumpy against his spine. Dazedly, he watched the cockerel strut in a circular manner about the yard and the donkey gaze at it apprehensively.

What had happened that night? Why couldn't he remember? And would he ever?

'Frances couldn't murder or hurt anyone,' he muttered. 'They are all mad.'

But then what had happened to Jason? Where was he?

Again, Sam remembered his dream and Jason's face twisted with anger. He swallowed, fearing he might cast up his accounts. Could there be truth to his dream? Was it indeed not a dream, but a memory? Had they fought? Had some accident occurred? He could not have hurt his sister's husband in cold blood—he had never hurt a fellow human—but it was only logical that he might have had some involvement. It was too much of a coincidence that he had almost drowned and Jason had disappeared on the same night.

He pushed his head against the wall. What had happened? Anything, however awful, must be better than this blankness—this endless, awful questioning.

'But Frances could not have done it. She couldn't have done it,' he muttered, so oblivious to his surroundings that he was shocked by Millie's brisk response.

'Indeed not, I can think of many others with greater motivation,' she said, bracingly.

He turned around, staring at her strong features, the firm jaw and straight brows as though confused by her presence.

'And what about me? What if I did something to him?'

'You are a man beset by violent rages?' she asked.

'No.'

'Then it is entirely more likely that you both fell into the water doing something foolish or that you were attacked by someone who bore a grudge against him.'

'He was so angry in the dream.' He squeezed his eyes tight shut to block out the image.

'If you were both attacked, I presume he *was* cross.'

Again, he was struck by the woman's unflappability. She seemed as calm as she would have been discussing seasonal vegetables. There were no hysterics and no disposition to fall into the vapours, merely a bracing common sense.

'Thank you,' he said. 'You are right. There is no point jumping to conclusions.'

The door opened and the landlord emerged, his wife behind him, curiosity evident in their expressions. He wanted to avoid them, but also knew a sudden desperation to learn more or, at the very least, everything they knew.

'Thought I should tell you, the coach should be here in fifteen minutes, or so. Stops regular like,' the landlord said, ambling forward with the rolling gait of a sailor.

'It took two of you to deliver this message?' Millie snapped.

Sam ignored her, stepping forward almost as though motivated by a force beyond his control. 'What—why— what items washed up? Why do they think him dead?'

'His monogrammed handkerchief,' the landlady said.

'That is hardly conclusive,' Millie said. 'I have dropped my handkerchief a thousand times and I am still alive and well.'

'Aye,' the landlord agreed. 'Aye and so I can see. Except his pocket watch was also found. Besides, the big difference between you and 'im is that you're here and he ain't.'

'Lord have mercy!' his wife interrupted, her rosy cheeks flushing to a more hectic hue and her button eyes sparkling. She bustled past her husband, stepping close to Millie and waving a finger in her face. 'Lord have mercy. I knew as soon as you started talking about handkerchiefs that you ain't no lad. Running around in trousers. Spending time with gentlemen what have murderous relatives. I have never seen the like. This is a respectable place, I'll have you know!'

Sam watched the rhythmic wag of her finger. The words washed over him, waves of sounds, negligible against the discord of his own thoughts. The beat of his heart was like a tuneless chant. Dead…dead…dead…

And then, sharp against the blur that was his mind, Sam remembered that Jason had been wearing a gold watch. At dinner. Sam was certain of it. He could see the gold chain bright against the waistcoat.

'He had a watch,' Sam said.

He felt three pairs of eyes turn to him.

Jason had also been drenched in his dream. Sam pictured his angry face. He saw the dark hair and lank, sodden strands.

'He was wet,' Sam said.

Thoughts chased and bounced through his mind. A fight? An accident? Again his brother-in-law's image flickered before his mind's eyes: angry, drenched, hair plastered to his forehead.

'He was angry at me. I—I am sure of it. I must know something. It cannot be a coincidence. I saw him...'

Millie lunged at him, pressing a kiss on his lips. The move was so unexpected, he lost his balance, stumbling back against the wall while clutching her tight to him.

'Heavens above! I'll not have this! This is not to be tolerated. We run a respectable house and I'll not have goings on. Dressed like a man. And then carrying on! Off with you. Wait out front. I'll douse you with water if I have to. A respectable house this is. A respectable house!' After this rush of speech, Doris flapped her apron, making a clucking sound.

Millie stopped kissing him and Sam dazedly straightened from the wall.

'Off with you!' Doris gave another flap of her apron. The hens which had approached, hoping for scraps, scuttled away, while the cockerel darted towards her apron.

On any normal day, Sam would find the landlady funny, he thought, with that detached part of his brain. Indeed, this whole scene, complete with donkey and rooster, had an element of humour.

But this was not a normal day.

'We'll go,' Millie said, taking his hand and Sam found himself following her because compliance was easier than resistance. They walked to the front of the inn, skirting the chickens and donkey who stared at them with unwarranted malevolence.

'What was that kiss about?' he asked at last as they reached the road, just in front of the inn's bay window.

'It seemed the only way to shut you up before you confessed to something you cannot even remember,' Millie said.

'I was not confessing, but you must concur that it cannot be coincidence.'

She shrugged. 'Maybe, but that does not mean you had any responsibility. Surely it is more likely that you both met with an accident. Besides, those two were looking for a good gossip. I know their type. Doris would dine out on the tale for a month of Sundays. You'd have accosted him with the Spanish Armada by the time she'd finished. Besides, we do not want them calling in the constabulary. The most important thing right now is that you get back to Manton Hall and talk to your sister.'

'Yes,' he said. Indeed, his first priority must be to make some sense of this situation. Poor Frances must be out of her mind with worry. He certainly could not risk delay with unnecessary interrogation. 'That is true. Thank you.'

'Do not mention it. I seem in the business of saving you.'

Millie saw it first. The vehicle appeared little more than a small dot, visible on the road some distance away.

'That must be the carriage the landlord mentioned,' she said.

They watched as it grew in size, meandering through the fields. Sam paced beside the inn's stone exterior as though this would accelerate its progress. Millie sat on the inn's cobbled path, leaning against the wall. Her feet hurt too much to bear her weight for any longer than was strictly necessary. Besides, she looked sufficiently like an urchin to sit like one.

The vehicle was, Millie realised, a mail carrier which meant she was likely to know the driver and while this would guarantee them a ride, it might well end any last vestiges of her reputation.

Of course, given her prolonged absence, it was entirely possible her reputation was already in tatters and the option of marriage to Mr Edmunds gone with it.

'Millie,' Sam said. 'Who knows about you meeting *The Rising Dawn*? Anyone in the village?'

'Just Sally.'

'Do not say anything.'

'Because of my reputation? It seems cowardly,' she said. 'Besides, the damage is likely irreparable.'

He shook his head. 'It's not just about your reputation. Right now, the wreckers do not know anyone witnessed what happened at the beach. But if they know we were there and survived, they will worry that we know their identity.'

'I did not see anything except the movement of the light up the path.'

'But they do not know that. If they do, they may try to silence us.'

Millie nodded. There had been a ruthlessness in the men's execution. She had no doubt that the shooter would take any steps necessary for self-preservation. 'I won't say anything. But we must stop them and get Jem justice.'

'We will.'

The clip-clop of hooves heralded the coach's arrival as it turned around the corner and, with a rattle of wheels, pulled to an abrupt stop. It was Dobbs. Millie knew him quite well and pulled her cap lower.

'You two had best not be up to no good. I'm not having any trouble. I have my blunderbuss and will make good use of it,' Dobbs announced to them, brandishing the weapon.

'We require a ride,' Sam said.

'No doubt. And what will you pay me with?'

Sam produced another gold guinea. 'I am staying at Fowey. You go that way?'

'Aye.'

Dobbs's gaze shifted, moving to Millie. His eyebrows pulled together as though knowing he should recognise her, but not yet finding the name. She looked down, hoping her cap might further obfuscate her identify.

'Good Lord! Miss Lansdowne? What are you doing? And in that there customary?'

She sighed. 'You mean costume. It is a long story, Dobbs. Please, can you give us a ride?'

'I can hardly leave you, now can I? But good gracious, what would your mother say? Or your father, God rest 'is soul? And poor Master Tom?'

She did not say that if her father had not been drawn to disastrous financial investments or if Tom had not given promissory notes to despicable individuals, she might not have ended up on a smuggling mission disguised as a street urchin.

'Perhaps we might spare my mother's feelings by not—um—mentioning this,' she said. Dobbs was generally a decent type and everyone knew that her mother suffered greatly from nerves.

'Thankfully, we have no passengers, otherwise I do not know what they would say. Or what tale you could possible devise to explain your current situation.'

'I would ride outside with you and chat like in the old days,' Millie said. She had fond memories of child-

hood rides and had found him a source of useful information, a window into the lives of people living outside
her small village.

'Hmph, you're a tad too old for such foolishness.
You're a lady, in case you have forgotten. I do not know
what your mother would say.' Dobbs gave a sorrowful
shake of his head.

'She would be struck dumb which, if you know my
mother, is not necessarily a bad thing.'

'The cheek of you,' Dobbs said, in a tone which tried
to sound condemning but, instead, was laced with respect. 'Well, I'll have to change the horses, but we'll be
off soon enough.'

Although warmer, the interior was less pleasant than
the air outside and Millie rather wished she was perched
on the driver's box with Dobbs. Inside it smelled musty,
the atmosphere laced with the memory of a dozen jour-
neys, of bodies crammed too close and sodden footwear.

Moreover, her travelling companion seemed particularly morose. Sam sat opposite her, hunched, his forehead pulled into a frown as he massaged his temples as
though this might help him to better remember or make
sense of events. His distress was palpable.

'I am certain you will remember soon.'

'I wish I shared your certainty,' he muttered. 'It is as
though a whole piece of my life is missing.'

'Your mind may be clearer after you have rest.'

'I cannot rest until I see Frances.'

He turned away from her and seemed uninterested
in further conversation so she fell silent, watching the
scenery pass. There was an oddness about the journey.
When one was in danger, the future did not matter. One
lived in that moment, determined to survive from second

to second. Now her future crowded in on her. She feared both what she must do and also that her impulsive rashness might have made that duty impossible.

While Millie was hardly thrilled with the idea of marriage to Mr Edmunds, she'd recognised its merits, even before Harwood had made his odious proposition. Her mother and Lil would be allowed to remain in their current house. She could stay in Cornwall and gain some financial stability.

Harwood's unwanted advances only made marriage to Mr. Edmunds the more necessary. And yet, she appreciated a heavy, hopelessness which weighted her shoulders and tightened her abdomen.

The thought of this loveless marriage felt all the more abhorrent.

She glanced towards Sam. She had never considered that she might have an interest in a more passionate relationship. Indeed, even the thought made the heat rush into her cheeks. And, obviously, they had no future. He was a fashionable gentleman who lived in London. She was an unfashionable, poverty-stricken woman who lived in Cornwall.

But she had felt things she had not thought possible. Lillian might believe in love and happy endings but, for Millie, such things belonged in the foolish novels her sister so frequently enjoyed. However, for a brief, wonderful moment, she had felt something. And while she obviously did not believe in romantic notions, it had made her wonder whether she might be missing something if she married Mr Edmunds, for whom she could not summon even the smallest particle of desire.

She pushed the thought away. Mr Edmunds was middle-aged and already had five children and she sincerely hoped had no great desire to add to his family.

Moreover, she realised her feelings towards Sam were likely heightened by the danger they had experienced, the close confines or a myriad of other reasons, none of which impacted the present.

Laying her head against the glass, she looked at the passing scenery. One could not see the cliffs or ocean and it had none of the desolate windblown danger of the moors, nor the more picturesque beauty of the cottages closer to home.

However, as they progressed the land started to gain familiarity. The road became narrower, branches and leaves sometimes brushing against the window.

She'd be back with her family soon. She wondered if the memory of this experience would even seem real. She wondered if it would be better if it lost the sharp edge of reality, more closely resembling a dream.

Gradually, the carriage started to slow. She straightened, looking at Sam. His worry was evident in the tense lines of his body, but so was his isolation. He seemed to have aged within the last hour. Waiting was always the most difficult. She remembered that well enough with Tom. One's mind always went to the worst-case scenario.

Doubtless Sam was experiencing that now; lurching between worry that his sister had hurt Ludlow and fear that he, himself, had done so.

'Sam,' she said softly.

He turned.

'I spent rather a lot of time with Tom, and even my father, when they were in their cups. I found that their essential character did not change. I do not know what happened to you, but I do not think either you or your sister would have done anything out of character or wrong.'

'You have known me for less than forty-eight hours.'

'During which time we have experienced more than

people endured in lifetime. Though you have been irritating at times, you have always been decent.'

'High praise,' he said, his sober expression lightening just slightly with a tiny lopsided smile.

'Likely we won't see each other much after this so I just wanted you to know that.'

'Thank you. And, Millie?'

She nodded as the vehicle pulled to a stop.

'Find out how much Harwood is owed. I have a solicitor and money. No woman should marry Harwood.'

Again she felt that mix of emotion—a flash of angered pride because they were no charity case, but also gratitude. For the first time in for ever, she did not feel entirely alone. 'Thank you.'

The vehicle shook with Dobbs's movements as he clambered down. He pulled open the door and cool air whistled inside.

'I anticipate that you'd prefer to go in *sotto voce*, so to speak,' he said, thrusting his head inside, his face reddened from the wind.

Millie blinked in the dim, momentarily disoriented, before realising his meaning. As always, he had an interesting way with words.

'Er…yes, thank you.'

'Right, well, we're just down the drive. You walk up and I'll take this gentleman home and you…' Dobbs fixed Sam with glare '… Miss Lansdowne is one of ours and I do not want no gossip flying about.'

'Mr Dobbs, I owe Miss Lansdowne my life.'

'Hmph,' Dobbs said, as though finding this statement dubious.

Millie shifted forward, pulling her tattered clothes more closely about her as she slid across the seat towards the door. She glanced at Sam. His dark hair fell across his forehead and his eyes were shadowed with fatigue and worry. He was a young man and yet he looked oddly old and she knew a desire to run her fingertips across his hair and push the heavy locks back.

Swallowing, she pulled her gaze away. 'Be careful.'

'You, too.'

Chapter Seven

The final moments walking up the familiar path home seemed odd, painful, exhausting. How many times had she walked this same path? How many times had she walked from the village and heard the rustling branches and, in the distance, the waves crashing? And there was that wonderful mix of smells that seemed the essence of home: fresh mint from the kitchen garden, peat and that essential ocean scent of salt and fish and seaweed.

And here she was again, but she was not remotely the same person. Indeed, it was oddly disconcerting that the brick house, overgrown rockery and untended lawn should be so unchanged. How could everything be the same while her world had been tossed and shaken like a baby's rattle?

Afternoon was drawing to a close and the light dimming. She stepped on the paving stones, now overgrown with weeds. She went to the conservatory, which jutted from the solid brick façade like an afterthought of glass. She touched the door handle and it twisted easily.

She was home.

With an exhalation of relief, she slipped into the damp, earthy air, which even in this season was heavy with fragrance. They always called it her mother's conservatory although really her mother had spent little time in it. Flora and Lil were responsible for the plants that still occupied almost every ledge.

Much of the furniture in the rest of the house had been stripped and sold, but no one had wanted either the plants or the shabby rattan chairs so the conservatory looked as it always had. The tiles felt smooth to her feet. The long lacey fronds of an overgrown fern tickled her arms as she passed through, entering the main body of the house.

As always, the hall felt cold, dry and lifeless after the conservatory's air. Millie had no clear plan and her stealthy entry was motivated by the instinct of an injured animal seeking its lair. She wanted only to find her bedroom and rest.

Of course, this was not sensible. One doesn't disappear for days without disturbing one's family and within seconds of her entry into the hall, the parlour door was flung open.

Her mother appeared immediately, a lamp held high, the beams flickering on her face, haggard and creased with worry.

'Millie, oh, thank goodness. I thought you were dead. Indeed, I did not know what to do. Sometimes, I think this family is cursed, although Flora tells me this is not possible.'

Her words summoned Lil, who flew down the stairs, several paper curlers falling from her hair like leaves in autumn. She engulfed Millie in a tight, orange-blossom-scented hug.

'Mils, I am so thankful. So very thankful,' she said, her tones interrupted by hiccupped sobs. 'I was—so—so worried. Flora was ever so strong and said how you had a good head on your shoulders and would be back right as rain. Except I remembered how awful it was when Tom died and I feared the worse. Good heavens, you smell!'

This last sentence was uttered with a hiccupped sob, which morphed into a hysterical giggle.

Just then Flora came from the kitchen, bustling forward while simultaneous drying her hands with her apron. As always, Flora brought with her that calm competency and the innate feeling that everything would be well which had always made her the backbone of the Lansdowne family.

'There you are, miss. We were that worried. Now, Mrs Lansdowne, you get some rest. A little lie down and then I'll bring up a light supper for you in your room. I will prepare Miss Millicent a bath. That'll have you feeling better in no time. And I have some soup heating in the kitchen that will go down a treat.'

'I am sorry you were worried. I am quite unharmed,' Millie said.

'But whatever made you take your boat out on such a dreadful night?' her mother asked, dabbing her eyes with her handkerchief. 'It was not sensible and you are usually sensible.'

'I know and I am sorry. I never expected the...the weather to get bad. I thought I might catch fish for supper.'

'Truly, miss, you did not need to go to such extremes,' Flora said in her firm, bracing tones. 'Now, up you get and into the bath.'

'I am sorry I caused you all so much worry.' Millie rubbed a hand across her eyes, conscious of the tears welling up and trickling down her cheeks.

Her mother stepped forward. 'There, there. Fortunately, I had the forethought to tell Mr Edmunds that you were dangerous ill, which has likely only served to increase your value to him. One always values that which one might lose.'

'Um… Thank you… I think,' Millie said.

'Excellent forethought, Mrs Lansdowne. But time enough for that in the morning. Right now, Miss Millicent is dead on her feet. She will be much more coherent after a bath, supper and a goodnight's sleep and that you may tie to. Up you go and I will bring hot water.'

Flora said these last words to Millie and it took every last ounce of remaining energy to follow these directions. Indeed, her every step felt weighted and each movement Herculean in nature.

Like everything about her home, her bedchamber also seemed unchanged to a disconcerting degree. Her bed and night table were still as they had been throughout her childhood and the room was warm and pleasantly lit by the amber glow of the fire. She stepped to it, crouching down and leaning into its warmth. It was extravagant to light a fire. Her mother must have ordered it. She found that touching.

Millie and her mother had frequently disagreed. Mrs Lansdowne had spent little time in Cornwall during Millie's childhood, always preferring London. When they'd lost their money, her parents no longer kept the London house, moving permanently to Cornwall.

Mrs Lansdowne had not approved of Millie's friendships with the villagers, her fishing or long walks. In turn, Millie had not fully understood the extent of her mother's loss: the lifestyle, friends and social status. Indeed, these losses, followed by her husband and son's death, had crushed her.

Millie leaned against the chair, staring into the amber flames and watching the sparks flicker up into the chimney. After Tom's accident, her mother had retired to bed, leaving Millie to comfort her sister, work with the solicitor and resolve a myriad of other details that had kept a roof over their heads. Millie had been patient. She had been understanding...at least until Harwood's visit.

Somehow that had unleashed an anger and frustration that had been building since Tom's death. It was fear for Lil. It was anger that her mother had been in bed day after day but had struggled up for a man with a title. It was bewildered fury that such a marriage should even be considered. It was despair that Millie had just gained headway in the family's financial affairs only to be struck down.

They had fought. Millie closed her eyes as though this might help block out the memories and sharp unkind words on both sides.

'We are your daughters, not your sacrificial lambs. I will marry Mr Edmunds, but Lillian cannot marry Lord Harwood. I do not care what Tom owned him. I do not care if he has money or a title. There must be another way and if you cannot find it, I will.'

Except she hadn't. She had merely almost killed herself, which would have made Lil even more vulnerable to Harwood.

For a moment, as she listened to the crackle of the fire and felt its warmth, she could almost convince herself that she was back in the tiny cottage where past and future hadn't mattered. There was a freedom in living only for the present.

And then she thought of Sam. Even now, it seemed as though she could feel where his fingers had touched. As if, even through the cloth, her skin was still imbued with that peculiar, shivery, tingly, needy warmth.

From the corridor, Flora's footsteps could be heard trudging up the stairs. The door opened with whistle of cooler air as the maid stepped into the room, lugging a huge kettle of water, and placed it down with a heavy thud. Tendrils of steam rose upwards. Flora poured the hot water into the tub by the fire, then added cold water from the urn under the mirror—or rather, where the mirror had once hung. Now all that remained was the faded shape, like an imprint of a former life.

'There you are,' Flora said. 'Let's get you undressed.'

Millie stood compliantly, much as she had as a child, while Flora removed her shirt.

Lil came in with a second kettle of water, which she added to the bath. The curlers had been removed and her hair now hung about her in loose waves. Her face had flushed from the steam, or perhaps it was the excitement or the exercise of walking up the stairs.

'Millie,' she said in a hurried rush. 'Tell me what happened? We searched for your boat. Flora's family helped. We looked everywhere. Poor Mother has been frantic.'

'Now, miss,' Flora intervened firmly, 'like I told your mother, enough time for that later. You can catch up with your sister tomorrow.'

'But…'

'In the morning,' Flora repeated, half pushing Lil from the bedchamber.

Turning, Flora walked back to Millie. 'Right, miss,' she said in brisk tones. 'We'll get off those trousers and camisole and get you cleaned and tucked into bed. You'll be feeling as right as rain soon and that you may tie to.'

Millie was only too thankful to take direction and absolve herself from thought. Willingly, she let Flora remove her soiled clothes and lead her to the tub. Her feet stung, but the heat comforted and, with a grateful sigh, she sank into the warm water.

It smelled of lavender. Flora washed her gently, asking no questions. She wiped away the grime, making soft tutting sounds when she noted a bruise or abrasion. Flora always comforted first. When they were children, Tom and Millie would get into a scrape and Flora would feed, bandage and console before demanding explanation or restitution.

When she was little, she had admired Tom. It had seemed as though his impulsivity brought with it adventure and excitement. She had followed him like a shadow. They had been mischievous imps. Once they'd even brought goats into the main house. Millie couldn't remember why. Of course, the poor animals had run amok, butting the cook and eating several nice pillowcases hanging on the line. Tom had disappeared while Millie had chased the goats for the better part of an hour. Sal had helped—

Sally! Millie bolted upright so abruptly that water splashed from the tub.

Did she know? Did she know about Jem?

'Sal—Jem— Does she know?'

The image of Jem's face flickered before her mind's eye, bringing with it a wave of nausea.

'Yes. His body was found. I imagine we need to be thankful you were not also on that beach?'

Flora's tone was brisk, her sentence ending with a disapproving 'tsk', but Millie saw the worry etched on the older woman's face.

'You knew?'

'Aye. And it was a heavy burden not being able to tell anyone my suspicions.'

'Thank you.'

'What made you do it, miss? I thought I'd hammered more sense into you.'

'I am a work in progress, I suppose.' Millie hugged

her knees, one hand trailing in the sudsy water as she spoke reluctantly. 'Mother told me that Tom owed Lord Harwood money… Harwood will forgive the loan if Lil will marry him. Mother wanted that.'

She was angry also that, after all her sensible scrimping, saving, and strategizing, her mother had not even turned to her, asking for help, ideas, suggestions.

Something to save Lil.

'Harwood.' Flora exhaled, pressing her lips together. 'Well, that explains a lot.'

Millie glanced at the older woman, her worn face as familiar as her own. 'Does nothing shock you?'

'I find shock an unhelpful emotion not conducive to sound reason. You should have told me. I might have come up with something a mite more sensible than smuggling.'

'Does anyone else…know? About the smuggling? I mean, about me doing it?'

'I told my family that you'd gone out fishing and were caught in the storm. And I told Sally not to breathe a word. I'll get word down to her that you're safe.'

'I never meant to go on board the ship. I was only supposed to go to the vessel and be given the merchandise. Then I was to head straight back to shore and hide it.'

'Do not say something went wrong with your foolproof plan,' Flora said, wringing out the flannel, as though holding personal animosity against it.

'I found a man drowning and pulled him out.'

'You what now? One of the smugglers?' Flora asked.

'I thought so, but it was actually Mr Garrett.'

'Never heard of the man.'

'Mrs Ludlow's brother.'

Flora sat back on her heels, as she took in this new information. 'And now Jason Ludlow's gone missing. That cannot be a coincidence. There's speculation about Mr Ludlow. Some says as he's up to his eyes in nefarious doings. Likely this drowning victim might know summat about it.'

'No, Sam wouldn't,' Millie said with more heat than she had intended.

Flora raised an eyebrow, giving the flannel another twist. 'Sam, is it? And this Sam convinced you to run off with smugglers?'

'No, and I did not run off with them. They made us come on board. They pointed a pistol at us and then all manner of other awful things happened and... Anyway, I did not run off with them. I did not have a choice.'

The strength of this last statement was marred by the tremble in her voice.

'Hmm. A choice would have been to stay on dry land,' Flora said. 'But we can talk about that later. And mind you do not be telling your mother and sister about smugglers or this Sam character. Your mother would likely require smelling salts and your sister would find it romantic and tell all and sundry.'

'Lil does like stories involving pirates and princesses,' Millie said, which reminded her of her conversation with Sam. To her irritated mortification, she started to cry. Almost angrily, she wiped her eyes with the flannel, which was soapy, and only served to make her eyes sting further.

'There, there,' Flora said, providing her with a fresh cloth. 'You're alive, that's the main thing. Who knows? Like as not, this may have knocked some sense into you. Life is not all adventure and romance.'

Millie said nothing. Certainly, the last two days had not been romantic. They were too hungry and smelly and cold for romance. And her feet had hurt too much.

Blisters were not romantic. But it had been something. Those moments with Sam had made her feel as though her whole body was more alive. She had felt as though she had briefly glimpsed something unknown and unchartered.

She knew she had to marry Mr Edmunds, now more than ever. And she would. Nothing in the last few days had changed that. But her reluctance to do so felt stronger. She did not want to marry Mr Edmunds with his sausage fingers, his rotund figure and quest for land.

She closed her eyes. For a moment, she could picture Sam's strong, regular features and firm chin. She remembered his smile, the crease in his cheek and occasional humour in his eyes.

'Anyway, one way or another, we won't let your sister marry Lord Harwood. Your mother likely doesn't know his reputation. And I dare say once things are all sorted with Mr Edmunds, he'll have a suggestion or two. He is a decent man, hard-working and kind. You could do worse.'

'Yes,' Millie said. 'It's just he is not…'

Her words trailed into silence and she felt a sting under her eyelids. Flora took Millie's hand. The touch, her palms slightly roughened by hard work, was familiar.

'He is not…?' Flora prompted gently.

Millie remembered again the touch of Sam's lips and the way her body had felt about him.

'Mr Edmunds is not…' she paused '…young.'

'Oh, miss,' Flora said, her voice soft with sorrow, reading between the lines as she always had. 'I am that sorry. But you cannot be running off with some ne'er-do-well you've met on your adventures.'

'No, indeed not.' Millie spoke briskly. 'Besides, I am not acquainted with any ne'er-do-wells desirous of running off with me. I have learned my lesson. I will be sensible. I won't let Lil or Mother down.'

The butler opened the door of Manton Hall. Sam remembered him from when he had arrived in Cornwall… whenever that was. Time was a foreign concept. The servant was too well trained to betray any shock at Sam's appearance, merely swinging the door open and stepping aside.

'Mr Garrett,' he said in neutral tones, as though well used to guests arriving in rags.

Sam stepped in. 'Is my sister at home?'

'She is currently out, my lord.'

'Out? Where?'

'I do not know if I should—'

The butler's words were drowned by a sudden screech and the hurried patter of feet descending the stairs. A middle-aged woman rushed down so quickly that he almost feared she would tumble over her own flying feet. He recognised her as Marta Shingle, his sister's longtime maid, although she seemed much changed from the prim and proper woman he recalled.

'Mr Garrett,' Marta said, before Sam had even greeted her. 'Thank goodness you are here! I am that relieved. The magistrate has taken her off. As though the poor lamb would hurt a fly. I did not know what to think. And what with you visiting friends.'

'What? I did not…' He paused. 'What friends?'

'My poor lamb,' Marta repeated, not answering his question. 'I just did not know what to do. At my wits' end, I was.'

'I am here now,' he said bracingly. 'I can help.'

'I hope so. But Mrs Ludlow thinks—' She stopped herself, her eyes round and her lips pressed into a tight

line, as though to force herself into silence. Indeed, she
did not seem entirely sensible. All colour had drained
from her face except for her eyes, red rimmed from crying. Her hair was in wild disarray and her hands were
clasped together while her teeth worried at her upper lip.

'Perhaps if you tell me what is happening...'

'Not here.' Marta rolled her eyes towards the butler
in a manner which made him worry again for her sanity.

'Indeed,' he said. 'I take your point. Besides, I need to
bathe. Marta, you must calm yourself. Please go to the
library and wait for me. I will talk to you before going
to the magistrate and I am certain we can sort the matter out.'

His firm tone had the desired effect. The woman's
breathing slowed somewhat. She nodded, taking out a
handkerchief to wipe her eyes.

'Northrupt.' He turned to the butler, inordinately
pleased that he had recalled the man's name. 'Perhaps
we can arrange for a calming cup of tea to be served in
the library? And get Banks to come up to my bedchamber immediately.'

His valet proved more coherent, but no more enlightening. Sam peppered Banks with questions while he prepared the bath, but the answers were not entirely helpful.

'You had given me the evening off, sir,' Banks explained.

'Very generous and not particularly good timing,' Sam
muttered, throwing the tattered cravat and soiled shirt
into a corner.

'You wanted me to see if I could find any local gossip about Mr and Mrs Ludlow. You were worried about
Mrs Ludlow.'

'And?'

'I went to the tavern. Apparently, Mrs Ludlow hardly leaves the house. Mr Ludlow, on the other hand, leaves the house frequently. He spends much time drinking, gambling and spending.'

'Any rumours about criminal activities?'

'I am afraid the locals are somewhat tight-lipped on that subject,' Banks said.

'So Jason is currently presumed dead. What did they make of my own disappearance?'

'Nothing, my lord. No one knew you had disappeared. Mr Northrupt merely told me as how you was up early requesting a horse to visit friends.'

'But I was not up early. I never went to bed.'

'No, sir, I did not realise that until yesterday morning. I will admit I drank too much and overslept, which as you know is not my wont, but you had been kind enough to say that you wouldn't be needing me early. When I arose, Mr Northrupt said you had gone riding. I was distressed by this, given that I had not provided you with your usual shave. Indeed, I was uncertain if I had even packed suitable riding clothes given that you had not mentioned a plan to ride during this visit,' Banks said in injured tones.

'Because I did not have any intentions of riding and I did not go riding,' Sam replied. 'So no one noticed I was gone?'

'I saw your bed had not been slept in, sir, but everyone was at sixes and sevens looking for Mr Ludlow. The maid, Marta, had hysterics which was very hard on my head.'

'It sounds quite chaotic.'

'Yes,' Banks agreed. 'And I thought I'd get a message from you. I was just about to discuss the matter with Mr

Northrupt when he mentioned that you'd sent words of
your imminent return and here you are.'

'Indeed,' Sam said. 'However, given that I never sent
word to anyone, either Northrupt is psychic or he knows
more than he lets on.'

Sam sat silent in contemplation on this point while
Banks washed and shaved him.

'Try to find out why Northrupt said I was coming
back soon,' he said.

'Of course,' Banks said, touching his finger to the
side of his nose and looking more confident of his in-
vestigative powers than Sam was. Banks might be quite
excellent with cravat and collar, but certainly lacked any
great skills of deduction or investigation.

Indeed, Sam felt more confused than ever. He would
just have to hope that either his sister or his own mind
provided some help as neither Banks nor Marta appeared
insightful.

The magistrate's office and house was located in the
centre of town. By the time Sam had bathed, dressed
and talked to Marta, it was late and he was bone weary.
Marta still did not seem entirely sensible, merely saying
that the magistrate had come mid-afternoon and, moments later, the nursemaid, baby and Frances had left.

'I would have gone myself, but they had no room and
then Mrs Ludlow was most unpleasant and refused to
send for the carriage.'

'Mrs Ludlow? Frances?'

'No, Mr Ludlow's mother.'

'Of course, where is she now?' he asked.

'She is resting,' Marta said.

'Good, let's not delay getting over to the magistrate. I
have my own vehicle and can drive you. I hope to bring

Mrs Ludlow home, but in the event that I cannot, I am certain she can make use of you.'

The trip to the magistrate's house was short, which was fortunate given that the weather had forced him to raise the head of the curricle and Marta apparently required smelling salts frequently, a smell he had always abhorred.

The butler opened the door, and directed Marta to the servants' quarters while leading Sam down a narrow corridor to the study.

'Sir Anthony, may I present Mr Garrett,' the butler announced in sombre, well-enunciated tones.

A small, balding man sat behind a desk. He looked up when Sam entered, pale blue eyes shining from behind gold-rimmed spectacles.

'Good Lord, Giles, you make announcements as though we are at a ball. Come in…come in…good to see you, Mr Garrett, I must say.'

Sam entered the small chamber. A fired burned pleasantly in the hearth. There were several bookcases and the walls were decorated with a plethora of paintings depicting horses, hunting or hounds.

'Mrs Ludlow is my sister. I understand she is being held here. I would like my sister to be released into my care,' Sam said.

'She is not "being held" exactly and I would love to release her, but there is a problem with that,' Sir Anthony stated somewhat incoherently, pushing his gold spectacles further up his nose.

'What might that be?'

'Please, do sit down. A brandy?' Sir Anthony suggested, lifting a decanter conveniently located on his desk.

'No, thank you. This problem with Mrs Ludlow's release?'

'Yes, well, the fact is she refuses.'

'Refuses?'

'Yes, sir. She won't leave.' Sir Anthony's forehead shone with perspiration and he dabbed at it with his pocket handkerchief.

'Why?' Sam sat, trying to process this new information.

'I...um... I am not exactly sure.'

'Then can I see her?'

'Again, there is another problem. I certainly would never prevent you from seeing your sister, but the thing is, we had to get Dr Acton. She was rather upset and he prescribed a sedative.'

'That was necessary?'

'Yes, she was distressed, but she is now resting. I invited my sister, the rector's wife, to stay to ensure propriety. Her child is also here. I mean Mrs Ludlow's child, not my sister's, as she is old—not that she would like that description—and the child's nursemaid.'

'Gracious, you have a full house. She would not return home?'

'No. Indeed, she was quite insistent. Actually...' The man blinked rather rapidly from behind his round spectacles, then placed his plump fingers together in the shape of a steeple. 'I had not wanted to bring her here. I merely wanted to ask her a few questions at her house.'

'She asked to come?'

'She was most insistent. And brought her child. I must say I did not know what to make of it. Anyway, the whole thing quite upset me so I decided it best to consult Dr Acton. Nice fellow, you know. You're certain you won't take a brandy?'

Sam again shook his head while Sir Anthony poured himself the libation. Frowning, Sam leaned heavily back in the chair, recognising his own exhaustion as he tried to take in these new details. 'Does she feel unsafe at home?'

'She…um…did not say so.'

'Did you ask?'

'Well, no, one doesn't like to pry, what.' The man swallowed.

'Given the situation, it might have been relevant. So what were her reasons for staying?'

'Mrs Ludlow is experiencing a somewhat strained relationship with her mother-in-law. High-strung creatures—women, you know. Never married myself. Do not have the stamina.'

'Do you know the cause of this strain?' Sam asked.

The man paused in obvious discomfort, again dabbing at his forehead. 'Mrs Ludlow senior feels that your sister might… I mean, that it is possible…that she could be involved in her husband's…um…disappearance.'

'Her own mother-in-law thinks that? It is ludicrous. My sister is physically and emotionally the most unlikely person to do anything to harm anyone. What motive would she have?'

'I do not want to be indelicate.' Sir Anthony pursed his lips as if even speaking the words was distasteful.

'You are suggesting my sister harmed her husband. I do not think you need to worry about delicacy.'

'Not me…would never accuse—' Sir Anthony stopped after meeting Sam's impatient gaze. 'Mr Ludlow was known to enjoy the company of other women,' he concluded.

'Good Lord. If that was all that was required for murder, half the wives in London would be guilty.'

'Except…' Sir Anthony paused again as though unwilling to continue. 'The other wives you speak of have husbands who are still hale and hearty while your sister's…isn't.'

'We do not currently know whether Jason Ludlow is hale and hearty or not.'

'True enough. Indeed, it is my greatest hope that he returns, healthy and hearty. It would be one less thing for me to do. I would never have become a magistrate if I had known the work involved.' Sir Anthony reached for the decanter again, pouring another drink.

Sam rubbed his temples. There was little point, he supposed, in rousting his sister and child, particularly if she had had a sleeping draught. Moreover, he could hardly drag her back to a place she did not want to live. Sir Anthony seemed a pleasant enough fellow, if somewhat inarticulate, and he felt certain Marta would ensure that every measure of comfort was provided.

'Very well,' he said. 'I will return in the morning. I brought her maid with me and would like her to stay. I am certain she could help her mistress and provide comfort.'

'Yes, of course, very happy to oblige,' the magistrate said. 'This is all very troubling, I must say.'

Sir Anthony rang the bell, his eagerness to finish the unpleasant conversation quite palpable. The butler arrived promptly and they all moved into the hall. Sir Anthony directed the butler to ensure that Marta had accommodation and that every comfort was provided for both mistress and maid.

Sam exited, thankful to sit back in his vehicle. Although, as the vehicle headed towards Manton Hall, Sam had to admit he would not have minded also imposing on Sir Anthony's hospitality. The idea of staying at the hall was not enticing. Its owner was presumed deceased. His own absence had, apparently, been covered up by the butler with some ridiculous story about dawn horse rides, and its mistress was in such fear that she refused to remain there. Meanwhile, the other Mrs Ludlow was throwing around foolish accusations. Sam could only hope he escaped to bed and did not have to interact with her tonight.

Indeed, respite at Manton Hall seemed more a recipe for a melodramatic play than a goodnight's sleep and, for a moment he wondered if he should find an inn. However, he dismissed the idea. He would not find anything to stimulate his memory within the smoke-filled walls of a tavern or the bottom of a tankard.

Chapter Eight

Millie woke late the next day with a confused disorientation as she stared about her bare bedchamber. Her every muscle ached and she had the feeling that she had slept for days, although she could scarcely claim to be rejuvenated. She had not even dressed or drunk her chocolate before her mother knocked at her door.

'I really think tomorrow might be preferable? Do not you?' her mother said, as soon as she had entered the bedchamber.

'That rather depends. What for?' Millie said warily.

'Why, for Mr Edmunds's proposal, of course. He asked me if he might propose to you, which is only right and proper. And, of course, I said "yes". However, he is under the impression that you are ill so I think another day to recuperate would be wise. You look remarkably peaky which goes well enough with the subterfuge, except I do not know how we will explain that bruise.'

'Perhaps I walked into a door in my delirium.'

'Indeed,' her mother agreed, crossing the room and pressing a kiss against her cheek. 'But that does make you sound rather clumsy. And we do not want to mention delirium. You do not want him to think that any form of madness runs in our family or that we have a weakness for delirium.'

'Heaven forbid. We come from a long line of gamblers, but let us draw the line at illness or poor co-ordination.' Millie was tempted to add that Mrs Lansdowne's refusal to even rise from her bed for weeks after her son's death might also make someone question the family's stability, but bit her tongue.

'Millie,' her mother said, sitting rather heavily on the chair opposite. 'How can you speak about your father and brother in such a way? Dear Tom would have grown out of it eventually.'

'Perhaps.' Millie agreed doubtfully. Millie had adored her brother, but she was uncertain if the passing years would have brought any maturity.

'Anyway, marrying dear Mr Edmunds is for the best.' Her mother nodded emphatically to add credence to the statement.

'Very likely.' Millie agreed. 'But are we going to ignore the other issue?'

'The other issue?' her mother asked vaguely.

'Do not prevaricate. I have experience with amnesia and you do not have it. Lil cannot marry Lord Harwood.'

Her mother frowned, standing and pacing nervously about the chamber. 'He will put me in debtors' prison. He said so. And he was polite when he visited.'

'Threatening to put you in debtors' prison is hardly polite.'

'I know he doesn't have a reputation as a pleasant man.'

'He is a middle-aged cad with a fondness for dairy maids and more illegitimate children than a dog has fleas.'

'Millie, I do not know where you picked up such expressions,' Mrs Lansdowne said. 'They are quite dreadful.'

'My expressions are the least of our worries. And Lord Harwood is dreadful. He wants to acquire Lil for her beauty. I think her very lack of sophistication appeals to him. He will dress her up like his own private doll. Besides, I question whether he is even offering her legitimate marriage. And did you properly examine the note? Are we certain that it is not a forgery?'

'I am not a detective. However, I am sure the offer of marriage is legitimate. He is unmarried and wants a legitimate heir, I hear.'

'That is a distasteful thought. Anyway, that doesn't even matter. He would hurt Lil. You know he would.'

'I know. I know.' Her mother paced again. 'I just do not know how I will survive in prison.'

'Better than Lil would with Harwood. We still do not know if the note is authentic, so let us not get ahead of ourselves. I will ensure a solicitor looks at it. Rest assured, I will marry Mr Edmunds and do what is necessary to fix this. For now, do not tell Lil about any of this. I do not want to worry her.'

Sam had lain wide awake for most of the night, only to fall into a deep slumber close to dawn. He woke midmorning with a thudding headache, made worse by the bright light as Banks drew the curtains.

'I presume Mrs Ludlow senior is still in residence?' he asked his valet somewhat glumly.

'Indeed, sir. However, she has not risen yet.'

'One good thing, I suppose. Best get up before she emerges. Order the carriage for about an hour from now,' he instructed.

* * *

Sam had managed to eat and dress while still avoiding the elder Mrs Ludlow and found himself driving towards Sir Anthony's house with a certain elation, much as a fugitive might.

The gentleman was again in his study. He smiled pleasantly, still peering from behind gold-rimmed spectacles, his fingers pressed together as though contemplating a metaphysical dilemma, though it was more likely he was in deep contemplation about lunch.

'Very nice to see you,' he said, although Sam rather thought Sir Anthony would likely say that to the devil himself, a lapse of manners being worse than any other offence.

Sam nodded. 'And you. Might it be possible to see my sister now?'

'Absolutely. Her maid stated that she slept well and is relieved that you have returned. I believe she is in the breakfast room at present.'

Sir Anthony rang a bell and Sam was taken into a small, pleasant parlour. A fire warmed the room and he saw his sister seated, a small bassinet at her feet.

'Frances, thank goodness.' He hurried to her, taking her hand in his own, again struck by her gaunt expression and the thinness of her hand.

'Sam, I was so…so relieved when I heard you were back.' Her voice trembled, tears already visible.

'Should I bring tea, ma'am?' the butler asked.

'Tea?' Frances looked confused, as though the familiar beverage was foreign to her.

'No tea,' Sam said sharply and the man bowed, taking his leave.

He had thought his sister changed when he had arrived from London, but he had not fully appreciated her weight loss or pallor. Everything about her now seemed subdued, as though bereft of a life force. Dark shadows circled her eyes and her skin was pale to the point of translucence. Her gaze moved jerkily around the room, as if for ever anticipating an enemy just outside the scope of her vision.

'What happened?' she asked. 'Do you know where Jason is?'

'I do not know.' He sat heavily in the chair opposite.

The tears brimmed over, tracking down her cheeks. 'I was hoping you would know. You weren't with him that last evening?' She lowered her voice to a whisper, although they were quite alone within the chamber.

'I do not know. I had an accident and my memory is gone.'

'Gone? What sort of accident?' She reached forward, clutching his hand once more, her grip tight.

'I am fine. And I remember everything except for a few hours in the evening. My hope is that if you tell me everything that happened after dinner, it might help.'

She released his hand, her fingers twisting nervously in the cloth of her dress. Her eyes again scanned the room. Her foot moved the bassinet in a rocking motion too quick for comfort. 'We had dinner. You and Jason drank port. Then Jason and I fought—after dinner—in our bedchamber. And he went out. That is the last I saw of him.'

'What did you fight about?'

She shrugged, the rocking movement of her foot increasing. Her gaze jumped between the furniture as if uncomfortable with looking at any one object for too long.

'I—I angered him frequently. We fought a lot. He said I had not looked sufficiently happy at dinner. Over port you had asked him about me and why I was unhappy.

You wanted me to go back to London. Do you remember?' She spoke quickly, the words jerky.

'No. I do not remember that conversation. I am sorry if I caused a fight between you. I have a fuzzy recollection of dinner, but nothing more. I only know that I ended up almost drowning in the sea.'

'Drowning?' she gasped.

'I was rescued.'

'You were in the sea? With Jason?'

'No. At least he was not there when I was rescued.'

'I hate the sea,' she said, rather oddly. Her gaze had briefly stopped moving between objects, but now focused on him with too much intensity.

'Yes, well, I cannot say that I am an enthusiast either. What happened after you fought?'

'He went out. He often goes out. But his mother thinks that…that…she thinks…that I followed him…and hurt him.' Her voiced dropped so low on these last syllables that he could scarcely hear them.

'That is nonsense. You would never hurt anyone. I do not care what his mother—'

'Shhh.' She placed her fingertips to her lips. Her breathing had quickened, her fear palpable, her eyes wide and taking on an odd appearance. 'Do you think they listen at doors?'

'No,' he said. 'Sir Anthony would see it as a breach of manners.'

It was the right response. She blinked, her expression softening with a tiny half-smile. She dropped her hand and took a tiny inhalation, as if suddenly remembering to breathe.

'Sir Anthony is not a bad man, although he does enjoy his brandy,' she said.

'He said you need not stay here. I have my carriage.

Perhaps we should get you both home?' He nodded to the sleeping child.

This was not the right response. Her eyes widened again and she pressed her spine back into the chair, as though expecting a physical attack. Two bright spots of colour appeared on her thin white cheeks and she shook her head too quickly. 'No. I cannot go back. I cannot. She will take Noah. I know she will. You…you cannot make me.'

Her distress frightened him and he understood now why the doctor had been called. He also knew that this behaviour was, or would be seen as, irrational.

'Of course not,' he said. 'I would never make you go somewhere you did not want to go.'

She stared at him as though trying to discern if he might be lying before allowing herself to relax into the chair.

He was silent for a moment, looking at his sister, noting the movement of her foot and the nervous rubbing of her fingers against the cloth of her dress. This was a dilemma. Obviously, she could not go back to a place which caused her so much fear, but she also could not stay here. Sir Anthony had been kind and accommodating, but he was a bachelor and would not want Frances, Marta, a nursemaid and the rector's wife imposed upon him for ever. As magistrate, he might decide that Frances, or at least Noah, must return to Manton Hall, where there was a grandparent eager to provide care.

'Frances.' He reached for her hand, again conscious of its fragility and the movement of the thin bones under dry, papery skin. 'You must have a female friend? A local family of good repute. Someone you could stay with?'

She shook her head, again the movement jerky and

too swift. 'I do not know many people here. Jason did not encourage me to go out.'

'The rector's wife?'

'No. No. She wants to get home and is well acquainted with Mrs Ludlow. She says I am unstable and that it is likely the influence of the devil. The devil is very active in her world.' These last words ended with a stifled sob.

'Then London? We have Aunt Tilly. She is quite lovely, if a bit eccentric. A change would do you good. You and Noah will go up to her. Sir Anthony will allow it, I am certain, if he has the address. I will stay here, but follow as soon as possible. I am quite sure that a change in scene will help.'

'No. No. No. Mrs Ludlow—she said that I mustn't. It would look as though I do not care about Jason. She would say that I am fleeing the country and she might take Noah and I couldn't bear that.'

'London is still England and, as far as I know, Mrs Ludlow is not the law of the land.' But his curt response evoked no smile or flicker of relief, only the continued shaking of her head with such energy that he feared she would give herself a headache.

'No. No, I cannot. She will say I am trying to run. This will make me look guilty. I am afraid she will take Noah. She has already been here, saying that I am not a—a fit mother. She believes that I hurt Jason. She says that Noah should be home with her. I heard her telling that to Sir Anthony.'

Sam fell silent again, watching his sister's jerky movements as she rocked the bassinet. At this rate the poor child would get seasick. Indeed, Frances was so greatly changed from the sister he remembered that he felt oddly at a loss.

He stood, walking to the window and staring at the

drive as though the paving stones might provide some solution. Frances was unravelling. He could almost understand Mrs Ludlow's concern for the child, but return to Manton Hall would be his sister's undoing. She needed a safe place, with kind people whom she did not fear.

'I have it,' he said, speaking before he had fully formed a plan.

Frances looked up, brows raised.

'Millicent Lansdowne. You will go to her.' Even as he said the words, he had a feeling of deep relief, as though the weight of his burden had shifted. The image of Millie's firm expression and competent movements flickered before him.

'I—I cannot. I do not know them.'

'I do,' he said.

The rap on the door made the three Lansdowne women startle. They were sitting around the parlour fire, which was small and giving little heat. In fact, the chimney was smoking, likely because it had not been cleaned in donkey's years.

Lil was attempting to do needlepoint to while away the long afternoon while their mother pretended to read. Millie stared into the fire. She would have read except she felt certain it would bring on a headache. Every square inch of her body hurt.

The atmosphere in the house had not been entirely comfortable since her return. Millie was worried, tired and disheartened. The promissory note loomed and she could still sense tension with her mother. Indeed, she even felt irritation with Flora and Lil. With Flora, it was her complete surety that marriage with Mr Edmunds was best, while Lil's very beauty irritated. If she hadn't had the blonde perfection, Lord Harwood would not even be interested in her. And underneath this thought, there was the knowledge that if she had more of Lillian's beauty, manners and social ability, she might be the right sort of woman for a man like Sam Garrett. Not that she was interested in Mr Garrett, who obviously had sufficient worries of his own.

The brisk knock on the outside door caused Millie to straighten, lowering her feet from the stool on which they had been raised. She winced. Her feet still hurt.

'Perhaps it is Mr Edmunds?' her mother said with too much enthusiasm. 'Perhaps he could not wait for tomorrow.'

'Mr Edmunds does not strike me as the impetuous type,' Millie said. 'Indeed, I am certain he weighs the pros and cons before even choosing which shirt to wear.'

Lil giggled. Their mother made a tutting sound.

'Mr Edmunds is a lovely man.'

'His moustache makes such a description quite inaccurate,' Millie said.

'It isn't Edmunds,' Lil announced, having flung aside her needlepoint into an unhappy muddle of silks and dashed to the window.

'Well, that is likely a good thing. Your sister is not looking her best, bruised and scratched as she is. Now come, Lillian, it is quite gauche to be staring from the window.'

'It is a fancy curricle with two horses,' Lil interjected.

Just then, Flora opened the door. 'You have visitors. Mrs Ludlow and Mr Garrett,' she said, her eyes round and, although usually unflappable, obviously impressed and somewhat disconcerted.

Millie stood and then sat again because she did not wish to seem overly enthusiastic. As well, her knees had peculiarly buckled. Besides, standing was more painful than sitting.

Sam entered, followed by a woman. For a second, Millie scarcely recognised him, he was so changed. She had looked through Lil's magazines often enough to know that his clothes were of the latest fashion, the collar high and his coat of an impeccable cut.

Indeed, everything about him seemed larger within the small confines of the room, while his sophistication made the bare dinginess of their home all the more obvious. He was followed by a woman, also tall, but while his stature provided him with an air of authority, hers only gave the impression that she had outgrown the strength of her willowy body. Indeed, her shoulders were bowed and her physique so thin as to be unhealthy.

Millie's mother rose to the occasion so that one would scarcely suspect that she'd been bedridden mere weeks previous. 'Why, Mr Garrett, it is so lovely to see you again. I remember you when you visited us in London as Tom's friend. Please, sit down.'

'Mrs Ludlow, do make yourself comfortable,' Millie added, instinctively wanting to include the woman who seemed somewhat separate from the scene—as though her thoughts were many miles away—and looked likely to keel over.

Mrs Ludlow took a seat, but made no effort to converse. Instead she sat with unnatural stiffness, her hands clasped tightly within her lap.

'Millie, I did not realise you were acquainted with Mrs Ludlow and Mr Garrett,' her mother said. 'May I order tea?'

Sam sat beside his sister. 'Thank you. Tea would be lovely.'

'Flora, could you—' Mrs Lansdowne said, but her words were interrupted by an infant's cry.

'Noah!' Mrs Ludlow said, immediately bolting upright despite her brother's restraining hand.

'Your son is here? He does not have a nursemaid?' Mrs Lansdowne asked.

'Yes, but…' The woman's gaze darted about the room like a hunted creature.

'Do not worry. Flora will make certain your maid has everything necessary for your baby's comfort.'

Millie stood, stepping towards the other woman, softening her voice and speaking in measured tones. 'I will go and tell the nursemaid to bring your son in here immediately. Doubtless, he is missing his mother.'

'Thank you,' Mrs Ludlow said, her voice soft and low.

'I will go now to do that while Flora makes tea. Mr Garrett, might I have a moment of your time?'

Sam followed her out into the corridor and, after quickly directing Flora to make tea and have the nursemaid bring the child to Mrs Ludlow, she turned to Sam, brows raised in question.

'Frances needs a place to stay,' he said bluntly.

'To stay? As in "remain for the night"?'

'Yes.'

'I—' She paused, for once uncertain about what to say. 'I was not expecting that.'

'I know this is unusual.'

'Somewhat,' Millie agreed. 'We also have limited furniture, although we still have a guest room. However, we cannot offer Mrs Ludlow her familiar comforts.'

'I do not care if she has fluffy pillows, I just want— I need her to feel safe.' Worry was etched in his face, lines bracketing his mouth and deepening the crease between his brows.

'She feels unsafe?'

He rubbed his temples, stepping further away from the parlour door and glancing about as though worried they might be overheard.

'I do not understand it myself. Jason is still missing. Sir Anthony brought Frances in to ask questions, but he did not arrest her. However, she is unwilling to return to her own home.'

'Why?'

He pushed his hand through his hair in the way that had become familiar to her. 'She is nervous, as you may have noted. She seems quite convinced that her mother-in-law sees her as an unfit mother. Apparently, Mrs Ludlow is positive that her son is dead and Frances is... involved.'

'Would Jason's mother not want to hold on to every hope that he is alive?'

'One would think. Maybe it is harder to hold on to hope in these situations.'

'Do you think she would harm Frances?'

'I am sure not. However, proximity to her will harm Frances.' He stopped, the worry for his sister touching. 'And I fear for my sister's sanity. I think she will become very deeply distressed if she spends more time at Manton Hall.'

Millie nodded. 'I have feared sometimes for my mother's sanity, although she is doing better now.'

'Will it distress her? Having Frances to stay?'

'No, likely she will be happy to provide hospitality to a woman of superior social status. And, yes, of course she can stay.'

'Thank you,' he said.

'And has your memory come back at all? Did seeing your sister help?' she asked quickly, needing to fill in the quiet.

'Not with my memory.'

'I'm sorry.'

'Did you find out anything about Harwood?'

'Mother confirmed that we owe a thousand pounds.' She felt the smart of tears in her eyes.

He took her hand. 'I will help. I will get my solicitor on it. Harwood will not marry your sister.'

Even the light touch of his hand seemed to sear through her so that she felt the contact throughout her body. It seemed her heart beat faster while her breath became uneven. For a moment, Millie had that feeling of time standing still and everything and everyone becoming distant and unimportant. Only she and this man existed. Her body felt that peculiar feeling as though her skin and every part of her had developed a tingling sensitivity as her vision narrowed and she heard the pounding of her pulse against her eardrums.

In that moment, it seemed that the fancy clothes and dingy house did not matter and they were as they had been in the cottage.

'Thank you,' she said. 'Truly, I thank you.'

In that tiny pause he seemed very large in the entrance hall and very close. Indeed, it took willpower and inordinate physical effort to turn away from him.

'Now I must assist Flora in the kitchen. If you will excuse me,' she said as she hurried down the hallway, needing to find a larger space, their small entrance way having become claustrophobic, the air sucked from it.

'By the way, Miss Lansdowne?'

She turned back. He had moved towards the parlour door, but paused, his hand on the knob. 'You clean up quite delightfully.'

Chapter Nine

Millie flushed. She was already partway down the corridor towards the back of the house, but even from that distance Sam could see the pink stain her cheeks.

There was an excitement in seeing her again which even his worry over Frances couldn't quite negate. He had not realised his own eagerness to see her again until she'd greeted him in that dismal threadbare parlour. There was a thrill in seeing her as the proper young lady in her plain, well-cut dress with her hair tidy. It was not only that she looked attractive, but also that he knew that other part of her, as though they shared an intoxicating secret.

He watched as she walked briskly towards the back of the house. The evidence of the family's poverty was everywhere: in the bare floors, the pale square of lighter wood where a grandfather clock had once stood and the rectangles bereft of pictures. He must talk to Banks and ensure that any food or additional coal required by Frances was provided.

On entering the parlour, he was pleased to see that Noah now slept in his bassinet while the three ladies appeared to be conversing pleasantly. Millie's younger sister was detangling a mess of silks while Mrs Lansdowne discussed hairstyles and the delight of the classically inspired modern looks. Frances still appeared abstracted, but seemed to be paying some attention.

Indeed, the scene was so entirely normal he almost wanted to laugh. It was the first time anything had been even a little 'normal' since he had regained consciousness on that pirate's ship. Indeed, even thinking the phrase 'pirate's ship' made him almost chuckle because it was so bizarre and completely discordant with this scene of pleasant domesticity.

He was about to sit down when he heard footsteps outside. The door opened and Flora and Millie entered with a tea tray. This was placed on a table and Mrs Lansdowne moved forward to pour the tea. She handed a cup to Millie, who placed it beside Frances with a reassuring smile.

'Mother, I have delightful news. Dear Mrs Ludlow has been finding the sea breezes too brisk. Manton Hall is dreadfully windy at this time of year and we are so much more sheltered. She would like to stay here for a day or so and, naturally, I said we would be delighted.'

'I...' Mrs Lansdowne, briefly put down the teapot. 'Yes, of course, we always enjoy company. That would be very pleasant.'

'Thank you,' Frances said.

'We are so very happy to help,' Millie said. 'Truly.'

'But you will be very cramped. We live quite simply, being in mourning. Perhaps we could clean out the nursery,' Mrs Lansdowne suggested. 'Flora, could you—'

'Please, that isn't necessary,' Sam said, noting his sister's increased agitation, the movement of her hands as they twisted nervously within the fabric of her gown.

'I insist. It will cheer me up. I have been lachrymose lately. It is a nice enough room, quite large with a bay window facing the sea so that one can see it in the distance. I will have the servants clean it out immediately.'

'No, please—' Frances tapped her foot. She worked her mouth as though chewing words she seemed unable to say. Fear flickered across her face as her gaze darted jerkily. Sam was so strongly reminded of a cornered animal that he half feared she would bolt from the room.

Just as he was wondering how he could possibly intervene in the domestic arrangements of another family, Millie spoke in her competent manner.

'It is a lovely idea, Mother, but we no longer have servants, only Flora, and she has not yet mastered the art of duplication. Moreover, much of the furniture has been removed. Mrs Ludlow, would you mind most awfully if we leave the nursery closed? Perhaps Noah could sleep in your bedchamber or with your nursemaid?'

'With me,' Frances said quickly. 'That would be much preferred.'

'Really?' Mrs Lansdowne said. 'How unusual. I was an absolutely doting mother, as my girls can attest, but I was quite glad to hand them over to the nursemaid. I have a sensitive disposition and suffer greatly from my nerves, you see.'

'Indeed, but having a guest will be a tonic. It will be lovely to have you to stay,' Lillian Lansdowne said, smiling at Frances. 'Mother and I always love talking about fashion or London.'

'I have not been to London for a while,' Frances said, softly.

'No matter, we have not either.'

Sam had not really noticed Millie's younger sister previously. He saw now that she was beautiful, the type of beauty that portrait painters would like: blue eyed, blonde-haired and with that vaunted English skin. He could see why Harwood would be interested, although he also hated the thought. She had a classical beauty, combined with a fresh-faced innocence, of a type not usually found among concubines or harlots.

Millie was quite different from her sister. Her hair was dark and even now had an untamed quality with several strands falling free. Her skin was also pale, but her eyes were a deeper blue. The effect, therefore, was not that of a China doll, but rather that of the mystic. Despite the demure dress, there was still something different about her. It was as though she was privy to a cosmic secret which allowed her to view society's conventions, the trappings of this life, with an amused indifference.

These musing were interrupted by the unpleasant recognition that everyone appeared to be looking at him, as though expecting some response.

'Er...pardon? So sorry, my thoughts must have wandered,' he said.

This comment produced a rather disconcerting smirk from the younger sister and a disapproving glower from the servant who, as far as he knew, he had never wronged.

'I was merely asking,' Mrs Lansdowne said, 'how you and my daughter are acquainted?'

'Ah...well...we met...' Sam paused and was again relieved when Millie swiftly intervened as his mind seemed to be working in a slow, pedestrian manner.

'Mrs Ludlow and I have met at church and she promised to introduce us to her brother.'

'Really? I do not recall you going often to church, dear,' Mrs Lansdowne said.

'It was when you were not feeling quite yourself.'

'Yes, my nerves. I was better when we lived in London. I do not like the sea, you know,' Mrs Lansdowne acknowledged to the company in general.

'I hate the sea!' Frances said suddenly. The fierce words jarred through the room. Her voice was too loud and her hands too tightly clenched in her lap.

There was a momentary pause and everyone felt a certain relief when Noah broke it with a wail of hunger, requiring a sudden bustle of movement. Frances immediately picked him from the bassinet, holding him and rocking him while Millie stood, stepping to the door.

'Mrs Ludlow, let me show you upstairs so you can make yourself comfortable.'

'Thank you.' Frances stepped towards the door. Noah's sobs had lessened as, still rocking him against her, she followed Millie out of the room.

This resulted in a general exodus. Millie's sister picked up the bassinet, following the other women out of the room, and Sam went outside to organise Banks and the nursemaid to unload Frances's few belongings while Millie took Frances and Noah upstairs.

As Millie led Frances to her bedchamber, she had the feeling that she needed to tiptoe as though any loud noise might startle her companion.

She stopped at the door of the east bedchamber, pushing it open. 'I hope you will be comfortable. There is a small sitting area where the nursemaid could sleep if you would like.'

'Noah must sleep with me. We cannot be apart,' Frances said in an anxious rush of words, her hands wrapped about the infant as though fearing someone might physically remove him from her.

'Of course, Lil is just behind us with his bassinet. We are happy to change anything you need to accommodate you.'

'Thank you. And—and you will not allow visitors?' Frances asked.

'We do not get many visitors,' Millie said. 'And we will ensure you are not disturbed.'

'Thank you,' Frances repeated.

They entered the bedchamber, and Millie was glad to see that Flora had already lit the fire so that, although bereft of paintings or rugs, the room was not without welcome. The curtains were a pretty blue, matching the bedspread, and Flora had also provided hot water and towels, a cot for the nursemaid and even some flowers from the conservatory.

'I hope you will be comfortable,' Millie said gently.

Frances stood, cradling Noah, as her gaze scanned the small room. Millie touched the woman's arm to guide her further into the room and was startled by her instinctive flinch as she jerked away.

What had her husband done to her that had made her so frail and frightened? Millie had not liked Jason, but largely because he drank and gambled and always encouraged Tom to do likewise. She had not previously realised that he was a cruel man.

Lil put the bassinet by the bed and then left to show the nursemaid the way. Still cradling Noah, Frances went to the window, pressing her face to the glass.

'You cannot see the sea,' she said.

'No, we are further from the coast than Manton Hall, though you can get a tiny glimpse from some of our rooms.'

'I do not know if I am sad or relieved.'

Millie stood beside her. 'I have always felt that the sea was the most wonderful, beautiful part of my life here, but also cruel and unpredictable. I felt that particularly...' she paused '...during the last few days.'

'It takes so many lives. I think about them. I think about them all the time, you know, the people that do not come home.'

The image of Jem and the other men flickered before Millie's eyes. She pushed it away. 'I am certain that your husband will be found safe.'

Frances did not appear to hear her, still staring through the pane. 'Sometimes, I think I can hear them. Crying and asking for help.'

'It is the sound of the wind and waves, Mrs Ludlow,' Millie said. 'I have often thought that the wind sounds like a cry. You will hear it less here. It is more sheltered than Manton Hall.'

'Could you call me Frances? Mrs Ludlow sounds like my mother-in-law.'

'Of course, and I am Millie.'

Just then, Flora and the nursemaid entered and Noah, likely unimpressed by the delay in his feeding, cried again, his face scrunched up with anger and his tiny fists and feet kicking.

Millie turned to depart—the time for confidences had passed. She paused at the door. 'Please, let us know if there is anything you need. We eat quite simply as it is just my mother and sister and I, but even so... I am wondering if you would prefer a tray in your bedchamber? I sometimes find too much socialising tiring.'

A flicker of gratitude flashed across Frances's face. 'Yes, I would prefer to eat here.'

'Then we will make it so. I am afraid it will not be anything fancy. To be quite honest, our financial circumstances are not what we would like. Hence the lack of furniture and pictures.'

Frances smiled, as though finding this confidence reassuring. 'Truthfully, my entire circumstances are not what I would like.'

'Then we have much in common.'

Sam got into his carriage with a surge of gratitude. The family had their own challenges, but they had offered hospitality instantly and without question. It had been the right choice and Millie had a strength that reassured him. She would not be easily swayed by the senior Mrs Ludlow.

Speaking of whom, he realised that he had best get to Manton Hall and collect Marta, who had been packing up more of Frances's belongings. Besides, there might be some news of Jason.

When Sam exited his carriage at Manton Hall, he had a vague and unrealistic wish to enter and depart without the elder Mrs Ludlow being any the wiser. Unfortunately, his plan was scuttled the moment he saw Northrupt, who announced that Mrs Ludlow had left the sanctuary of her bedchamber.

'She asked if you would see her in the parlour, sir, on your return.'

'Of course,' Sam said, as he could hardly refuse. It would be rude and, more practically, she had attended the dinner prior to Jason's disappearance and conversing with her might stimulate his memories.

Before his recent trip to Cornwall, he had met Mrs Ludlow at the wedding and a few times in London. She had been known as having a clever wit and a glamourous sophistication that even middle age had not fully eclipsed. However, with her husband's death a few years previous, her influence had lessened and she had spent more and more time away from the capital.

The butler led him into a well-appointed room which seemed too full of items and had a new shininess that was discordant with the house's older exterior. The paint was fresh. The windows were large, the ceilings high and decorated with rubicund cupids and ornate gold filigree. A fire burned brightly, providing considerable warmth, and Mrs Ludlow sat near it in a comfortable wing chair.

He remembered her dimly from the dinner two nights previous, but he was struck again at how changed she seemed from the sophisticated woman he remembered from London. Her hair was simply arranged, her clothes circumspect to the point of dullness and her forehead puckered into a frown. Only the rings glittering in the firelight spoke of wealth or glamour.

She looked up quickly and he wondered if she might be hoping that he was Jason. She must be on tenterhooks, desperate for news.

However, if disappointed, she covered it well, her expression softening into a smile. 'Sam, I am pleased to see you. Everything is so incredibly worrying.'

Sam took her outstretched hand. 'Northrupt says there is still no news of Jason.'

'No. Do you know anything?'

He shook his head. She slumped into the seat as though some integral strength had been lost to her.

'I wish I could remember something that would help,' Sam said, weighing his words with care. 'I must have drunk too much. I do not remember much of anything from that night.'

'You do not remember the evening?'

'I remember bits about dinner, but nothing later,' Sam said, sitting in the chair beside her.

'You went to bed early.'

Except he had not...or he had gone to his room and

had then gone out for a seaside stroll during a bloody storm.

He wondered if he should explain, at least what he knew. It might serve to exonerate Frances. Except, any mention of smuggling or his rescue would then implicate Millie, damaging not only her reputation but possibly jeopardising her physical safety.

'And did you hear that Sir Anthony is questioning dear Frances? Have you spoken to him? Are you able to bring Frances and Noah home?'

'No,' he said. He knew the one word was inadequate and that he should clarify, but did not know what to say or how to explain Frances's aversion to coming home.

'They are with Sir Anthony, I presume. He is a dear man. I know he will do his best, but I am still concerned.' Her anxiety appeared genuine, her eyes glazed with tears.

'You mustn't worry. They are…' He hesitated. It seemed unkind to delude her. 'Quite safe.'

'Sam,' Mrs Ludlow reached again for his hand. 'Frances and Noah need to come home. She needs familiar objects and care at such a time. Please help Sir Anthony to understand.'

Her hand was cold and slightly clammy, and he had to ignore the instinct to snatch his own hand away.

'I am certain Sir Anthony would understand and doubtless Frances would be more eager to return if you did not suspect her of wrongdoing,' he said, more sharply than he had intended.

'Is that what she said?' Mrs Ludlow tightened her grip on him, shaking her head to emphasise her denial. 'She misunderstands. I know she would not hurt a fly in her right mind. But, well, you must see that Frances is different.'

'Her changes are not sufficient to enable her to emotionally or physically hurt a man twice her size.'

'Not on purpose. And truly I hope you are right. Gracious, do you think I want to suspect my own daughter-in-law of hurting my son? And I know Jason is no angel, but…'

The words trailed away as she let his hand go, finishing the sentence with a mute shrug.

'What exactly do you suspect?' he asked.

She clasped her hands together. 'I am uncertain. We know they fought. They do quite often. The servants heard them. Jason's fault, no doubt. He can be…unkind. But Frances has become obsessed with the sea. I think she ran out into the storm and he followed her and…and some dreadful accident occurred. I do not mean that she did anything on purpose, but she knows more than she is admitting.'

'Frances is not obsessed with the sea. We grew up in London, so she likely finds this place desolate, but you make her sound unhinged.'

Mrs Ludlow stood. He stood also. She turned so that they faced each other. 'She doesn't leave the house except to walk down by the ocean. She paces back and forth across the shale. And she takes the child everywhere, even out into the bleakest of weather.'

He said nothing, going across to the window. He remembered Frances's jerky movements as she rocked the bassinet and her near desperation at any threat of separation from the infant.

'Women can become out of sorts after the birth of a child. It is likely nothing more than that,' he said.

'Indeed, Jason has not been the best husband. I know that all too well. I just want Frances to tell us anything that might help us determine what may have happened.

I—I fear the worst. I worry for Noah's safety. I cannot lose both my child and grandchild.'

'Noah is quite safe.' Sam looked across the bleak grey ocean, pressing his fingers against the sill as though the hard pressure against the wood might help him remember or ground him into some sort of reality. The window opened on to a terrace of red brick. Beyond this, the green lawn stretched towards the grey waters. *I hate the sea.* He remembered the way she had spoken the words, her eyes and her distracted movements. *I hate the sea.*

'I am worried for my son,' Mrs Ludlow said softly. 'And terrified for my grandchild.'

'Frances adores that child. She would protect him with her life. She would never, ever hurt him or allow anyone to do so.'

He heard the movement of her gown, the rustle of cloth as she approached the window, standing beside him so they both stared out at the grey day. She smelled of lavender. Lifting her hand, she pressed her finger to the glass so that it covered the shoal beach. Slowly she moved her finger back and forth against the pane, with the slight squeak of flesh against glass.

'I counted once. Frances paced that beach at least one hundred times. One hundred times, back and forth, back and forth. Are you really willing to stake your nephew's life on her sanity?'

Her hand dropped to the sill, the gems glinting in the dying daylight.

'Yes,' he said.

Sam stood by the fire at Lansdowne. The room was small, ill-furnished and the chimney did not draw properly, making the atmosphere smoky. Yet, he had never in his life felt more thankful to be somewhere. It felt safe. It felt wholesome. It felt, ironically, like a breath of fresh air away from the chill sophistication of Manton Hall. He'd stayed there longer than anticipated. Mrs Ludlow had asked him to dinner and he could not refuse. Besides, he still hoped something might jar his reluctant recollection.

But his memory remained blank as ever. To do her justice, Mrs Ludlow tried to make the repast as pleasant as possible, given the situation. They dined quietly and, by mutual consent, did not talk about Jason or Frances, instead sharing recollections about opera and theatre productions in London.

She had, he realised once again, circulated in high circles. Her husband had been many years her senior, apparently doting on her, and for some years she had reigned in political and fashionable circles. It seemed that this power had diminished with her husband's death, her fading looks and a son who lacked the political acumen of his father.

Sam did not rush dinner, despite his impatience to return and see Frances was settled, as he knew Mrs Ludlow must find company a welcome break from worry about her son. Indeed, he felt a sympathy for her. She must always be straining to hear the knock which might bring news, her emotions perilously balanced between hope and fear.

Therefore, it was quite late by the time he and Marta arrived with the remainder of Frances's belongings. Flora answered the door and stated that Mrs Frances Ludlow, Mrs Lansdowne and Miss Lillian had retired to bed. However, Miss Lansdowne was still up if he wished to speak to her. Her tone did not sound as though she encouraged this option.

Despite the maid's sour looks, he'd accepted. He needed to thank Millie for her hospitality and the thought of seeing her held appeal. He trusted Millie. At times, he doubted his own mind, his sister's sanity and whether Mrs Ludlow was friend or foe, but his trust in Millie remained constant. She was a source of sanity in a world gone mad.

He stood close to the fire, warming his hands. The mantel was made of sturdy wood, its centre darkened by the smoke accumulated over the centuries. The wallpaper was yellowed, except for a square where a portrait had likely once hung.

Perhaps it had been of Millie's father. Mr Lansdowne had been a pleasant enough fellow. Sam had met him several times with Tom during that wild year when he'd thought his heart shattered following his broken engagement with Miss Whistler.

Mr Lansdowne and Tom had similar personalities. Both had been individuals of impulsivity and extreme moods. Often Mr Lansdowne had been wildly elated about an investment, only to be cast into deep despair following the scheme's failure.

'Sam? Sorry I took so long. You wanted to see me?'

Millie's soft tone startled him and he turned quickly. She stood in the doorway.

'I wanted to thank you,' he said.

'I am glad I could help.'

'I did not know where else to turn. She doesn't seem to know anyone locally.'

'She seldom left her house,' Millie explained, stepping further into the room.

He sighed. 'She used to be quite outgoing. She has changed. Very much. Anyway, thank you.'

'Umm—did you want to stay here?' She looked up, flushing, as if uncharacteristically unsure. 'I mean to talk. I mean…if you need…to talk?'

'Thank you.' He was in no hurry to return to Manton.

She nodded, sitting on the chair and inviting him to sit opposite with a wave of her hand.

'We seem to spend a lot of time sitting around fire,' he said.

She smiled. 'At least we are no longer walking. I do not think my feet will ever recover. Besides it is somewhat warmer here than in that cabin.'

Her words made him remember the intimacy of the cottage, their shared confidences and kiss. Maybe she thought of it, too. She glanced down, her lashes forming fans against her cheeks. The fire crackled. There was no other sound, not even the ticking of a clock.

'You still do not remember what happened that night? I—I mean, the night of your accident?' she asked jerkily, the colour in her cheeks deepening.

'No. I'd hoped being at Manton Hall would help, but… nothing.' He rubbed his temples. He must ask Banks if he'd found out anything to do with his fabricated dawn ride.

'He must have encountered an accident. I am certain that Frances would not have done anything to her husband on purpose. I have only met her briefly but I find that quite impossible.'

'Thank you.' Her words comforted. It was wonderful to hear someone else, an unbiased source, affirm his sister's goodness. His conversations with Mrs Ludlow had shaken him more than he cared admit. 'Mrs Ludlow feels she has become unstable. She even suggested that Fran might hurt the baby.' He pushed out the last words with effort.

'She wouldn't,' Millie said.

Again, her firm, confident words reassured. There

was no wavering, no 'buts' or hesitation, just a firm statement of fact.

'That is the most comforting thing I have heard all
day.'

She reached forward, clasping his hand. There was
strength to her grip and reassurance. 'I know Frances
would not hurt anyone and certainly not her child.'

'I know it, too.' He pushed his hand through his hair,
rubbing his temples. 'It is just—she is so much changed
and Mrs Ludlow was describing her behaviour and, even
to me, she sounded…erratic.'

The word did not seem entirely sufficient to describe a
woman pacing a deserted beach in Cornwall in January.

'I think your sister is vulnerable and not entirely well,
but I do not believe she would have the capacity to hurt
anyone and certainly not Noah. Why do not you tell
the authorities about the smugglers and our experience?
Surely it would deflect suspicion from Frances.'

'I'd sooner confess myself. I will not ruin your reputation or put you at physical risk.'

'I do not need your protection.' She stood, as if to emphasise her point.

He stood also so that they were facing each other.
He saw the stubborn lift of her chin. It reminded him of
those moments in the cabin. Indeed, everything in this
moment—the soft flickering firelight, the rain outside,
the solitude—reminded him of those moments. Her hair
was now almost entirely undone. Her lips were parted,
softly pink and with a gleam of moisture. The neckline
of her gown was demure, but even so he could see the
swell of her breasts. The lace trimming made a tiny, delicate, intricate shadow against her pale skin. A loose curl
had fallen forward.

'You do not have to look after everyone,' he said.

A lock of hair had fallen forward into her face. He stepped forward, gently reaching to tuck it behind her ear. His finger grazed the soft skin of her cheek. He felt her start at his touch. He heard her gasp and saw her eyes widen.

He should leave.

Slowly, and with deliberation, he stepped even closer to her, so that there were mere inches between them. He ran his fingers along her jawline. He touched her chin, tipping it upwards. He bent forward to kiss her pert, upturned nose, her high forehead, soft cheek, the delightfully stubborn chin and, at last, her lips. Her response was instant and spontaneous. Her hand reached up, touching his chin and the nape of his neck, winding her fingers through his hair to pull him closer to her.

He heard the rustle of her clothes as she shifted towards him. The kiss deepened. His grip tightened, his fingers splayed against her back, pulling her tighter. He could feel her pressed against him, swaying into him. A need, a desire, like a primal life force, engulfed. He wanted this woman. Her eager innocence threatened all self-control. Everything intensified the feeling: the tentative touch of her tongue against his, the instinctive, unschooled arch of her body, her muted groans of need and the soft husky breathiness as she whispered his name.

His fingers ran up her spine. He felt the fine cloth, the soft skin of her neck and the silk of her hair. The muslin slipped from her shoulder, exposing the creaminess of her skin. He ran kisses down her neck and her collarbone. They inched backwards towards the sofa and she sank into it, half lying. He knelt beside her, undoing the top button of her gown so that her bodice loosened. He pushed it lower, revealing the chemise. Through the thin cotton, he could see the darker outline of her nipples.

'Sam,' she breathed.

The need, the desire pulsed through him. He stared down at her flushed countenance, her huge magical dark blue eyes and parted pink lips.

'Millie,' he groaned. 'I— We...cannot.'

She smiled, as always her expression slow to build, but then transformative. 'Why not?'

'You are an innocent.'

'Maybe I do not wish to remain so.'

The calm, husky words were more arousing than anything he had ever heard. Shock mixed with a tidal wave of lust.

He cupped her face with his hands. 'You are entirely different than anyone I have ever met.'

With exploratory fingers, she reached up to his face. She touched his chin. She ran her fingers along his jaw, her movement unschooled and spontaneous. He touched her lips and she teased his tongue. His kiss was no longer tentative. He plundered her mouth, his hand pushing up the fabric of her skirts, feeling the shape of her legs through the cotton pantaloons. Then he kissed the smooth line of her jaw, her neck and the sweet spot on her collarbone where he could feel the beat of her pulse. Her skin had a dewy softness. He slipped his hand under the thin cotton fabric of her chemise, exposing her breast. He kissed the rosy tip while his hands bunched at the fabric of her skirts.

Millie felt beautiful. She felt wanted. She had never felt like this before. She felt like a woman—a woman who was desired. Instinctively, she pressed herself closer so that she could feel every inch of him. She revelled in the strong, hard lines of his body, his quickened breath and the urgency of his movements. She revelled in the intoxicating power that she could make this tall beautiful man murmur her name and pull at her gown with a driving need.

His touch ignited her skin with a heat that connected to the very core of her. Her fingers moved under his jacket. She could feel his skin through the fine cotton of his shirt. The muscles were hard, but their movement fluid. His hair fell forward across his forehead. She reached up, pushing it away, allowing her fingers to trace across his jawbone, feeling the slight roughness of stubble on her skin.

Her own pulse drummed against her ears. Her body became molten, no longer composed of bone and muscle, but rather she was liquid, sensuous and fluid. She moved without thought, instinctively responding to the driving heat, pulsing throughout her body. She arched against him. Her hands gripped at his shoulders. Exaltation, sensation and primal need dwarfed all other thoughts.

The rattle of carriage wheels on the drive outside sounded loud and discordant in the quiet room. Millie and Sam froze in the tumbling return of reality.

He jerked away from her. 'Millie— My God—I am sorry. I—I apologise.'

Millie sat upright, gripping her clothes about her. Confusion, hurt, loss and a raw vulnerability flooded her. He turned away from her, adjusting his jacket as she hurriedly straightened her clothes. Her nipples felt painful against her chemise as she quickly did up the buttons with trembling fingers. Her cheeks burned. Her lips felt swollen by his kisses and her hair fell about her face in long tangles.

'Who would be visiting us at this hour?' she gasped.

'Whoever they are, thank goodness they are here. I am so sorry. That should never have happened.'

She stiffened. The words struck a chill in her. She felt the hurt, that raw neediness morphing to anger. Her confused thoughts circled about that one phrase: *That should never have happened.*

Of course, it should never have happened. She was not destined for desire or love or happily-ever-afters. Did he think she did not know that? Except she'd wanted to feel something before she dutifully married Mr Edmunds. Did that make her a fallen woman? Or just stupid? She supposed it was yet more proof of the family failing—to risk without thought of consequence.

That should never have happened.

Somewhere outside, a carriage door slammed.

With efficiency verging on viciousness, she twisted her hair into a bun, jamming pins into it. Then she smoothed down her skirts, staring at the parlour door with apparent fascination, if only to avoid his gaze.

'Again, I apologise,' he said stiffly.

'I would not worry about it, Mr Garrett. We all make mistakes.'

'I was irresponsible.'

She paused at the door, her fingers resting on the knob. 'Then it is fortunate that we both returned to our senses. Doubtless the foolishness was brought about by our misadventures and the danger we experienced. Indeed, I do not know what came over me given that I anticipate a proposal of marriage in the near future.'

'What?' She heard his movement behind her and felt the clasp of his hand on her shoulder as though to swing her around. 'You are to be married?'

She glanced back at him and saw an expression of his face which was not anger. She wished she could pull back her words or, at least, say them better and less harshly. 'Sam, I— It is not—'

A loud knocking reverberated through the house. Flora's hurried footsteps sounded in the hallway outside.

'Why did not you say something?' His tone was hard with anger, his expression closed and jaw tight.

'Perhaps we were too busy running from pirates.' She turned, walking into the outer hall, forcing her expression to be calm.

Married.

The word had struck him with an almost physical force, leaving him feeling winded. How could she have let him kiss her and hold her and lust after her if she was promised to another?

For a moment, he could not follow her. He was not a man of emotional extremes and yet in the last thirty minutes he'd swung like a weather vane in a storm. Had it happened again? Had he again missed the truth staring him in the face? He thought of Miss Whistler with her vows of eternal love until the advent of the wealthy duke with his land and title.

Married!

So much for Miss Lansdowne's blunt talk about honesty. He'd thought her different. She'd *seemed* different. Did all women hide the truth? His own mother could not admit she was dying. Annie could not admit she was on sale to the highest bidder and Millicent Lansdowne could not admit she was engaged.

Loud voices from the hallway stirred him into action. Forcibly squashing down the muddle of emotion, he opened the parlour door. The entrance way was surprisingly crowded. Sir Anthony and Mrs Ludlow stood within the hallway while Flora was on one side of the front door with Millie at the base of the staircase, blocking access to the upper storey.

'Miss Lansdowne,' Sir Anthony was speaking to Millie, his face puckered with concern. 'I am sorry to intrude. This is Mrs Ludlow. I am sure you are acquainted.'

'I understand that my dear daughter-in-law is staying here,' Mrs Ludlow said, interrupting any response Millie might have made. 'I wish to speak to her.'

'She has retired for the evening,' Millie said.

Sam stepped into hallway, facing Mrs Ludlow. 'Why are you here? How did you even know to come here? Did you have me followed?'

'I am so sorry, Mr Garrett. I did not want to do it.' Mrs Ludlow clutched her long grey cloak about her, as though needing to keep herself together, crossing her arms more tightly. 'Perhaps I shouldn't have done so, but when I learned that Frances had left Sir Anthony's I had to know where she was. You see, I am so worried for my son and, now, my grandson. She is not well. You must see that.'

'I—' Sam paused, momentarily uncertain, the image of Frances's face and darting gaze flickering in front of his inner eye.

Millie spoke, stepping into his confused silence. 'Mrs Ludlow, I quite understand your worry. However, both Noah and your daughter-in-law are quite safe under this roof.'

Mrs Ludlow's worried gaze shifted to the younger woman. 'Please, Miss Lansdowne, I only want what is best for the baby. Mrs Ludlow may have…may have hurt my son. I hope not, but it is possible. I would like to take the child home.'

'The child's home is with his mother and I am not waking my guest and her child at this late hour and in such inclement weather. It would hardly improve Mrs Ludlow's health or that of the child.'

Mrs Ludlow's gaze focused on Millie with sudden intent, as though she had not properly studied her until this moment. She straightened, her aspect suddenly more closely resembling the woman Sam remembered from London. 'I must insist that you allow us to remove the child.'

'Absolutely not.' Millie's firm tone and air of command was at odds with her small stature. 'That will not occur unless Sir Anthony has a warrant for Frances Ludlow's arrest. Do you have such a thing?' Millie turned towards that gentleman.

'No, Miss Lansdowne,' he said, looking very much as though he hoped the floor would open and provide him some escape. Or, failing this, a bolt of lightning would not be unwelcome.

'Then it will be best for everyone if we allow Mrs Ludlow to rest,' Millie said.

'Miss Lansdowne, I may have lost my son, but I will not lose my grandchild. I will proceed with a warrant, tomorrow, as you give me no other choice.'

'You won't,' Sam said.

'Pardon?'

'You will not get a warrant or disturb my sister tomorrow,' Sam said.

'I cannot see how you can prevent me. I am quite certain that Sir Anthony would agree there is sufficient evidence to suggest that your sister has some involvement in my son's disappearance. They fought and she was the last person to see him alive.'

'She was not,' he said.

'How would you know?'

'Because I was.'

Chapter Ten

Everyone turned and stared at Garrett, the movement happening almost in unison. There was a moment of stunned silence when Millie thought she could hear each person's breath and even the blinking of their eyes.

'That—that is ludicrous,' Mrs Ludlow said, her jaw slackened. Her hair was threaded with grey and dark shadows ringed her eyes. For a moment, she shifted from middle-aged to old.

'It isn't. I fought with Mr Ludlow and we both fell into the sea. My sister was nowhere in sight.'

'You are confessing to my son's murder?'

'I am confessing to a fight and to the fact that my sister was in no way involved.'

Sir Anthony stepped forward, belatedly attempting to take control of the situation. Millie had known him for all her life and he was seldom able to control anything, even his household staff. This level of absurdity would be totally beyond his ability, she thought, oddly dispassionate.

'Right, well, indeed,' Sir Anthony said, as though by throwing out enough exclamations he might pretend some command. 'Indeed, in this event, Mr...um...um...'

'Garrett,' Sam provided helpfully.

'Yes, I... I feel I should question you on the specifics, don't you know.'

'I quite agree,' Sam said. 'I will accompany you now. You have your own carriage? I can direct my groom to take Mrs Ludlow back to Manton Hall while I travel with you for any interrogation you would like, if that is convenient to all.'

Millie felt her own jaw slacken. Good lord, the man had just confessed to murder or manslaughter...and he was organising transportation as though co-ordinating an excursion to a village fête.

'This cannot be true,' Mrs Ludlow said, her tone almost accusatory. 'You said you had no memory of that night.'

'A temporary disability.'

At that moment, with the timing a playwright might have envied, Millie's mother appeared at the top of the stairs, holding a candle. This low flickering light oddly shadowed her features while her voluminous white dressing gown and nightcap provided a sharp contrast to the dim corridor. Rather like a poorly dressed ghost, Millie thought. She felt a giggle bubble in her throat and wondered if she was slipping towards hysteria.

'Flora? Millie? Dear Sir Anthony, is that you? And Mr Garrett? Good gracious, what is happening? Is there an emergency? An accident? My poor nerves!'

'Mother.' Millie stepped forward, shaking off the numbness and pushing away her rising hysteria. 'I will explain everything tomorrow. Everyone will leave as soon as the vehicles are brought to the front, so you have no need to worry.'

Her mother descended the stairs, still somewhat dazed. 'But what happened? I am sorry to be in dishabille.'

'A risk people must take if they visit at odd hours,' Millie said. 'Let us invite Sir Anthony and Mrs Ludlow into the parlour while they wait for the horses? Flora, if you could ensure that the carriages are requested?'

Flora nodded and hurried towards the back of the house while Millie's mother, surprisingly rising to the occasion, stepped down the stairs, ushering her guests into the parlour.

'Would anyone like tea? I am sure it could be arranged,' she said with admirable aplomb.

'A brandy would be most welcome,' Sir Anthony muttered, following in his hostess.

As quickly as possible, Millie shut the door behind them, grabbing Sam's arm and urging him down the narrow, dingy hallway so that they were positioned midway between the parlour and kitchen.

'You remember that night? Your memory has come back?' she asked.

'No,' he said.

She stared at him, stunned into silence. 'You just confessed to murder for a lark?'

'I confessed to a fight which is not the same as murder and is, indeed, the most likely explanation of events.'

'Most likely explanation? But you do not know what happened? You still cannot remember?'

'No.'

'You cannot confess to something you do not remember. I mean, if you do that, the die is cast. It becomes fact and no one will believe you even if you later recall events,' she hissed in a harsh whisper.

'Very theatrical.'

'Except it isn't theatre. It is real life and could get you hanged,' Millie retorted.

'And what if they'd returned with a warrant for Frances?' he asked with sudden intensity. He stood close to her, his dark greenish-grey gaze catching her own. The limited lamplight somehow emphasised the squareness of his jaw and the angry determination of his countenance.

Millie took an involuntary step back. 'She would be questioned again and you could still investigate and help—'

'Do not you see? There would be no help for Frances. Separation from her child, even for a moment, would destroy her. You can see how vulnerable she is. She would likely confess to a murder she did not commit.'

'A characteristic which seems to run in the family,' Millie said.

'Millie, I let her down. I stayed away too long. I am afraid for her.' He took a step nearer, again standing so close that she could hear his breathing and the rustle of his shirt.

'I understand, but you cannot pretend to remember something you do not.'

'And I cannot let her take responsibility for something I may have done. Isn't it more likely that I physically fought with Jason than that Frances did?'

'Or neither of you fought and you are obscuring the truth,' she said.

'Since when have you been so keen on the truth?'

Millie stepped away from him. 'I have always adhered to the truth. Are you referring to my possible engagement? Nothing is official. And the situation is entirely different.'

'Really? How can you claim to adhere to the truth when you went on some crazy smuggling expedition without telling your family and kissed me without telling your fiancé?'

'He isn't my fiancé yet. And as for kissing you, that mistake will not happen again,' she snapped.

'I am relieved to hear it. However, I would suggest that you are still not in a position to lecture me on the truth.'

The door of the parlour opened and Millie and Sam swung quickly about as light spilled into the front entrance way. Her mother exited, followed by Mrs Ludlow and Sir Anthony.

'It would seem the carriages are out front,' Millie said to him, stepping towards the front entrance.

'Millie?'

'I do not think we have anything more to say,' she said, glancing back.

'Thank you for providing my sister accommodation.'

'Of course,' she said stiffly as she turned to walk briskly towards the front door.

Millie flung herself on her bed. She felt the sting of tears. She was angry with herself, with Sam, with Tom, with her father, her mother, society.

Why did men always make foolish choices? Obfuscating fact with fancy? Her father had misled her mother, stringing tales about fortunes made. Tom had misled them all, promising to drink and gamble less.

And why did women lack choices?

Truthfully, she was equally angry with herself. Why had she allowed Sam Garrett such liberties? She condemned her brother and father for taking risks, but she was a hypocrite. She was as foolish as the heroines who proliferated Lil's favourite reading, but with no kind author to mandate a happy ending.

Had she wanted to experience desire before marrying the dull Mr Edmunds or had some foolish part of her hoped that Sam would tumble into love with her?

Sam belonged to a set of gentlemen who divided women into strict categories: mistresses and wives. She fit neither category, although she was apparently apprenticing for the former. There was no future in developing feelings for Mr Garrett. She did not have the looks, manners or wit necessary. Mr Garrett was from London and occupied a station in life too dissimilar to her own. Her duty lay in sensibly marrying Mr Edmunds.

Despite her exhaustion, rest would not come. Images flickered in front of her eyes. In one moment, she could feel the warmth of his skin, the touch of his fingers, her need and urgency. In the next, she would hear his apologies and see his stricken face and later condemnation. In one second, she would convince herself that she was well rid of him. In the next she would break out in a cold sweat for fear that he would be found guilty and hanged or imprisoned.

Then her thoughts would bounce to Mr Edmunds and she would see her life stretch into dull drudgery. A moment later, and with equal intensity, she would fear that Mr Edmunds would have learned of her smuggling exploits and refuse to marry her.

Indeed, she did not know which scenario was worse.

At last, dawn's light shimmered through the curtaining and she rose, unable to stay still any longer. She walked to the window. Everything hurt: feet, head, arms, legs, chest. She felt weighted, as though lead lines like those used by the fishermen had been hung on her limbs.

She paced across the bare floor, feet padding softly. How often had she paced this room? She knew the exact number of steps and the moment when the floorboard would creak. She'd waited up for the doctor after Father had collapsed. She'd waited up for Tom night after night.

She'd waited up with her mother for the sleeping draught to take effect. She hated waiting and worrying.

A tentative knock sounded at the door. 'Mils?' Her sister's voice was soft and hesitant.

'Come in,' she said.

Lil entered. Even in her simple nightgown and with her hair pinned into curls she had stature, elegance and well-proportioned beauty. She moved with a fluidity which often made Millie feel uncoordinated or slap-dash.

'I heard you pacing and knew you were awake.'

'Sorry,' Millie said. 'I did not mean to disturb you.'

'Come back to bed. Keep me warm like we did when we were children.' Lil scrambled under the covers.

Millie joined her, lying down and shivering despite the blankets and her sister's warmth.

'Mils, Flora told me everything.'

'What?'

'She told me about Lord Harwood wanting to marry me.'

'She shouldn't have,' Millie said.

'Why not? Why shouldn't I know? It's me he wants to marry,' Lil said pertly.

'Because I did not want you to worry. I am certain I can determine a solution,' Millie said.

Lil turned, her head rustling on the pillow as she took Millie's hand under the covers. 'You do not have to solve everyone's problems alone, you know.'

'You sound like—' Millie stopped, biting off the sentence. 'That is the second time someone has said something like that in the past twenty-four hours.'

'As well you should not marry Mr Edmunds. Mother and Flora seem to think that it's a perfect solution, but there must be another way.'

Millie glanced across to her sister's profile, her perfect nose, the sweep of blonde hair lying so smoothly on the pillow. 'It is definitely preferable that I marry Mr Edmunds than that you marry Lord Harwood.'

'I won't marry Lord Harwood. I'll go with Mother to debtors' prison first.' The firmness of her sister's tone surprised Millie.

'I am glad. I was worried that Mother might pressure you.'

'She might try,' Lil said. 'But it won't work. And I wrote to Aunt Carol.'

'You did?'

'Yes, she will let us stay with her. Likely as unpaid companions, but it would be better than Harwood.'

'Yes,' Millie agreed. 'Why didn't you tell me?'

'I did not get her response until a day ago.'

'Mother hasn't spoken to her for a decade. They had that dreadful row when Uncle Taylor invested in one of Father's schemes. I am surprised she would help.'

Lil sat up, hugging her knees against the early morning chill. 'I appealed to her sense of pride. I know it is not the whole answer. Tom owed Harwood money and we do not have a solution to that yet, but it's a start.'

'It is,' Millie agreed.

'Millie,' Lil said, still hugging her knees, but glancing back at her sister. 'I am not ungrateful. I know that since Tom died, you have been trying to save us.'

'Not entirely successfully.'

'Without you, it would have been impossible. You arranged to rent our land. You sold the livestock we did not need. You paid bills. You organised everything. I am grateful. It felt as though I'd lost everyone: Father, Tom and even Mother, in a sense. But I am stronger now and if we work together, we'll figure a way through this.'

Millie glanced up at her sister's face, visible with the

early morning light. She realised that she had thought of her sister as a child for too long. 'Come back under the covers,' she invited. 'I am glad Aunt Carol will let you live with her. You will meet someone in London. Indeed, if you marry someone important, it might add to Aunt Carol's social status, which was always close to her heart. Perhaps that will motivate her to provide you a modest debut.'

Lillian snuggled back down. 'We will both live with Aunt Carol. That way you need not marry Mr Edmunds.'

Millie gave her sister's hand a squeeze. 'We cannot both land on Aunt Carol's doorstep. Besides, it would take considerably more effort to marry me off than you. No, Mr Edmunds is still the best option for me. And he isn't an unkind man.'

'But you do not love him.'

'Lil, you have read too many books. Love as a basis for marriage is highly overrated. Besides, I love Cornwall and Mr Edmunds is safe and reliable.'

'You sound as though you are talking about an old horse,' Lil grumbled.

'Horse or man, safe and reliable is a good thing. Mr Edmunds will not engage in some crazy escapade. He will die at an old age in a respectable manner in the comforts of his own home.'

'What heady goals you have for him. So why have you looked so sad since your return?' Lil asked.

'Blisters on my feet. They have a deleterious effect on the spirit.'

Lillie giggled. 'Millie, you can joke about it, but you must dream of more than Mr Edmunds?'

It was Millie's turn to laugh although she noted a bitter note. 'In the last few years, I have had too many nightmares so I have rather given up on dreams.'

'Do not,' Lil whispered. 'You have to have dreams. Besides, what of Mr Garrett?'

'Mr Garrett? What has he to do with anything? We hardly know him. We are merely providing accommodation for his sister, as good neighbours should. I doubt very much that he cares for our domestic arrangements.'

'Well, you're twitchy as a cat every time I say his name. Moreover, this sudden acquaintance with Mrs Ludlow is questionable. I am quite certain that I have seen her at church only once. So how does she suddenly know you so well that she brings over her brother and invites herself to stay?'

'I do not know. We already agreed that she was odd.'

'I think that you and Mr Garrett met when you had your "fishing trip", which was not a fishing trip,' Lil said. 'And when he realised that his sister had some sort of hysterical condition he sought your help because you have developed a close bond.'

'You should write all this stuff and sell it,' Millie muttered.

'But I would much prefer for you to live it.'

'Lil, I love you. And I love what you are trying to say. But even if your far-fetched story is correct, Mr Garrett has no interest in me. Moreover, he has more important issues on his plate, given that he recently confessed to causing his brother-in-law bodily harm.'

'He what?' Lil jerked upright again, twisting around and sending a blast of cold air under the blankets. 'When?'

'Yesterday evening. You were asleep. Jason Ludlow is still missing. His mother thinks Frances is involved so Sam—Mr Garrett—decided to say they'd had a fight and that Jason had fallen in the ocean.'

'And did he?'

'Mr Garrett doesn't know. He doesn't remember. He

was drunk or injured or both on the night Jason Ludlow disappeared.'

Lil bounced on the bed with a creak of the springs. 'I knew you knew more about Sam Garrett than you let on! And are you saying that Sir Anthony and Mrs Ludlow came in the middle of the night and I slept through it?'

'It was in the evening. Late in the evening.'

'Of course I sleep through the only exciting thing that has happened around here for ages.' Lil's look of consternation would have been comical in other circumstances. 'Anyway, I am quite certain Mr Garrett had nothing to do with Jason's disappearance.'

'Based on your five-minute acquaintance?'

'Based on the fact that my sister would not fall in love with an individual of bad character.'

'Good Lord,' Millie said, also sitting up. 'I am definitely not in love with anyone and certainly not Sam Garrett. Besides, marriage to Mr Edmunds is a good option.'

'Marriage to Mr Edmunds would be boring as mud. You cannot just give up.'

'I have not "given up". You do not know…' The image of the smuggler's ship, broken, on fire and sinking into the sea flickered before her mind's eye. 'I am ensuring we have a decent life. You, me and Mother.'

She had risked everything and lost. She had gambled like her father and played with danger like her brother.

And had lost.

'I know, you think your "fishing trip" was a mistake. But maybe you should think less about the mistake and more about your indomitable will, which helped you to survive.'

Millie glanced at her sister, her heart full. '*You* helped me survive. Thinking of you helped me to survive.'

'Then make good use of your second chance.'

* * *

As soon as it was a decent hour, Millie went to see Frances. She knocked softly, but, even so, Frances jumped at her entrance, fear and worry evident in her face.

'I have brought you some tea,' Millie said, stepping carefully around Noah's bassinet, which had been placed to the left of the bed.

Frances was sitting upright, propped by pillows. She smiled tentatively as Millie passed her the cup. 'Thank you.'

'May I sit with you a minute while Noah is sleeping?' Millie asked.

Frances nodded. 'You are kind. You must think me very weak.'

'I think nothing of the sort,' Millie said firmly. 'You obviously care for your child and are determined to keep him safe.'

'Yes.' Frances glanced towards the bassinet. 'Yes, he is everything to me.'

'I can tell that…' Millie paused, as she sat beside the bed, smoothing her gown as she tried to find the right words.

Frances glanced towards her, anxiety evident in her eyes, which appeared oddly magnified in contrast to her thin face. 'You are worried. Do you want me to go? Does Sir Anthony have more enquiries? My mother-in-law— has she come for Noah?' The questions were rattled off in quick, nervous succession, the cup rattling so much that Millie worried it would spill.

'No.' Millie reached for the saucer, taking it from the woman's trembling hand and placing it on the night table. 'No. Do not worry. No one is coming. You are quite safe.'

Millie waited, watching carefully as the other woman

took in this information, gradually allowing herself to relax. 'I need you to be calm so that we can talk things through. I think that is the best thing we can do to figure things out. Can you do that?'

Frances nodded, the movement slight and her expression still one of apprehension.

'Thank you,' Millie said. 'First, you need to know that your brother is talking to Sir Anthony. Mr. Garrett thinks that he and Jason may have fought and worries it resulted in Jason's disappearance.'

Frances stiffened. 'Sam is saying that to Sir Anthony?' she asked in breathy whisper.

'Yes. You see, Sir Anthony and Mrs Ludlow came here last night.'

Frances's fingers gripped at the fabric of her blanket so tightly that Millie could see the white of her knuckles. She swallowed. 'For me?'

'Yes.'

'Sam took the blame for me? To protect me?'

'He wanted to protect you, but I think he also believes that he might have some involvement.'

'He shouldn't have told Sir Anthony.' Frances's fingers picked nervously at her nightgown, finding a loose thread and twisting it about her finger

'Perhaps not, but he did,' Millie said. 'So the best thing we can do is to determine what really happened.'

'You'll help us? Why?'

Good question, Millie thought. Because she'd saved him once and did not want her good work undone? No, that was not true. It was too flippant. The reality was that the thought of Sam's conviction hurt in a deep, all-encompassing way.

'Because you need help and Sam is…nice,' Millie said lamely, before continuing more briskly. 'Can you tell me anything you can remember from the night Jason disappeared? Anything that would help?'

Frances continued to pluck nervously at her nightgown. Millie could hear the scratch of her fingers at the cloth. 'Sam arrived earlier in the afternoon. I did not know he was coming, but I was glad to see him. Jason had never wanted him to come so I'd made excuses to keep him away. Anyway, we had dinner, all of us, me, Sam, Jason and his mother. And then I went to bed.'

'You last saw Jason at dinner?'

'No.' Frances fell silent and then spoke in quick bursts of staccato speech. 'He came up later. I do not know what time. He was angry because I had not looked happy enough. He said I looked like a miserable old hag. He said that Sam wanted me to go with him to London and that Sam thought he was a monster.'

'And that was the last time you saw him.'

'Yes.'

'And you do not know if Sam saw him after that?' Millie asked.

'No.'

'Or where Jason went after your fight?'

'No.' Frances paused again, looking at Millie, eyes shimmering with unshed tears. 'I was just glad he had gone. Is that awful of me?'

'Not at all. In fact, it was very practical in the situation.'

Frances gave a wan smile, even as the tears brimmed over, trickling down her cheek.

'Why did he marry you?' Millie asked.

Frances startled at the question. 'I thought we were in love.'

'That is why *you* married him. Why did *he* marry you?'

'I thought he was in love, too. But I have an inheritance. Sam is only my half-brother. My birth father left money in trust to any male children I might have.'

'So Noah is wealthy. But not you?'

'I am comfortably placed, but I do not have a lot. Jason was…angry…when he found out.' Frances spoke slowly, the words stilted. Millie felt sure there was a world of horror behind the simple phrase.

'And do you have any idea why either Sam or Jason would go out to the sea in the middle of a storm?'

Frances shifted, her fingers clenching the blanket, scrunching the fabric into tight bunches of cloth.

'What is it?' Millie asked gently, clasping the other woman's hand. Her fingers were cold and thin, her nails bitten low. Frances swallowed. Her gaze flickered about the room. 'I do not know why Sam would be outside, but Jason…he has rough friends.'

'Rough?'

'Smugglers,' she said, dropping her voice.

'He was involved with the smuggling?'

'And…' Frances paused, biting her lip. Outside, Millie could hear morning birdsong, the drip of water from the gutters after the night's rainfall and the rustle of branches against the eaves from a tree too near the house. 'And worse,' she finally said.

Frances's voice was so low that Millie had to bend forward to hear the word. She clutched at Millie's hand, her grip surprisingly strong, but with a wiry desperation.

Millie felt herself stiffen, as though the paralysis of her body was making up for the lightning-speed movement of her thoughts. 'Can you tell me what you mean?' she asked, holding her breath as she waited for the answer.

Frances swallowed, leaning even closer. 'I… I do not know anything for certain, but he talks when he is drunk.

I cannot understand everything that he says. But…it…it is bad.' Frances's words came out in a trembling, stammering rush.

She released Millie's hand, drawing her knees to her chest and hugging them tightly. The baleen springs creaked with her movement. There was a wildness to her face that was both frightening and pathetic.

'Is Jason involved in wrecking?' Millie asked.

Frances's gaze darted about the bedchamber, while hugging her knees even more fiercely. 'I… I… I think about them…the people on the boats. I think about them all the time. I go down by the ocean and I think about them. I see their faces. I wonder if it is true. Sometimes I think it is. Sometimes I think it isn't. I feel I should tell someone…but who would believe the ramblings of a mad woman…?'

'Frances,' Millie said gently but firmly. 'You are not mad. You are very brave to have told me this. And I believe you.'

'You do?' The quick movement of her gaze stilled to rest on Millie's face.

'Yes, and I also think you are a wonderful mother to have taken Noah from that house. I want to talk to Sam, but rest assured that you will be safe here. I am going to leave both Flora and Marta to look after you.'

'Will you tell?'

'I will tell Sam. We will find proof. We will stop this and then the faces won't worry you.'

Frances leaned back, allowing her legs to straighten on the bed and her hands to unclasp, as though finding some comfort and relief. 'Please help Sam. He would never hurt anyone, but I worry he will take the blame.'

As do I, Millie thought.

'We will find the truth and clear both you and Sam of any wrongdoing,' she said.

'You look very determined.'

'To the point of stubbornness,' Millie said with a grin.

Sir Anthony had not interviewed Sam when they'd stumbled into his home the night previous. Instead, he'd ordered that a room be made ready for his guest, stating that the whole matter would make more sense in the morning.

In the morning, Sir Anthony provided a pleasant repast and then announced a delay in the interview.

'I think it would be better to investigate the matter in London,' he said. 'They have greater expertise in such matters.'

After learning this plan, Sam requested pen and paper and wrote to Frances, Millie and Banks, apprising them of the situation. In these missives, he assured them that they need not worry, while requesting that Banks pack and follow them on the five-day journey as quickly as possible.

In Millie's letter he apologised for his rudeness the evening previous and requested that she allow Frances to remain at Lansdowne and to keep her safe. He added also that he would still do everything possible to ensure her sister need not marry Harwood.

As he signed and sealed the notes, he realised that, in some ways, he trusted Millie to an extent greater than any other. Mysterious fiancé or not, he felt an absolute certainty that she would shelter Frances. He trusted not only her willingness, but also her practical efficacy in doing so.

However, he could not so easily dismiss this almost or 'unofficial' engagement from his thoughts. Indeed, he continued to ruminate to a degree which was not sensible to the situation. What had she meant by that anyway? Why hadn't she mentioned this before? How had he been so oblivious that this woman was promised to someone else?

And why did it feel as though the bottom had fallen out of his world? At no time had he consciously considered that they might have a future. Indeed, they had been too busy surviving the present. Moreover, Millicent Lansdowne was not the sort of individual he had envisaged marrying. Of course, he'd imagined marriage with only one individual, Miss Annie Whistler, who now appeared to him as vapid and entirely lacking in wit. He had learned the hard way that attraction was a fickle emotion.

Still, Millicent had made him less lonely. Briefly, he'd felt as though he had someone at his side. Indeed, he supposed this was true, at least with Frances.

However, he had been reminded that nothing lasted for ever and that he had learned long ago that life was a solo occupation.

Sir Anthony's conveyance proved to be a large, cumbersome vehicle with a musty scent that suggested an aromatic history of all the shoes and cloaks it had housed. Sir Anthony proved considerate, offering him every courtesy—even suggesting a hot brick or blanket—so much so that Sam feared Sir Anthony had mistaken him for an elderly maiden aunt.

Still, as they rattled forward, Sam decided that going to London might not be a bad idea, even if it would be tiring. In Cornwall, he trusted no one, worrying that anyone could be connected with the wreckers or, if not conspirators themselves, might tip off the guilty party.

In London he might be better able to seek justice without inviting risk.

As for Jason, his disappearance remained a mystery and Sam still worried about his own involvement. Perhaps he had seen his brother-in-law leave the house after his fight with Frances. Had he followed him, wanting to talk? Had they come to blows? Or had one of them merely tripped and the other had not offered assistance?

All scenarios seemed improbable, but then, half-drowning in the sea and being rescued by a female smuggler seemed improbable.

They were barely forty minutes into their journey when Sam noted the horses slowing and saw they were approaching a tavern just up the hill from Fowey.

'It is convenient that we are here,' Sir Anthony said, raising his stick to bang on the roof of the carriage. 'Let us go in. I must chat to the landlord.'

The carriage stopped and Sir Anthony got out. 'You might as well come, too. I rather think a brandy might be in order. Make the journey more pleasant.'

Sam followed. He was surprised that they were breaking their journey already, but was in no position to object. Besides, Banks would be better able to catch up with him this way.

Sir Anthony was served a generous brandy and consequently nodded off by the blazing fire. Sam watched the magistrate and was just considering waking him, when he heard a commotion in the hallway and the innkeeper's raised voice. 'Really, miss! I must protest. You cannot just stride in—'

The door was flung open and Miss Lansdowne entered the chamber, bringing with her a chill draft.

'I am glad you have not left. You are still going to

London?' she asked, glancing towards Sir Antony, who was snoring sonorously.

'Yes.'

'Do not.'

'Not exactly up to me,' Sam said.

The conversation roused Sir Anthony, who straightened, blinking owlishly at Millie through his spectacles.

'Miss Lansdowne,' he said. 'I did not expect to see you. You have news of Jason?'

'No, sir, I just wanted to assure you and Mr Garrett that we will look after Mrs Ludlow and, of course, write to you in London if there is any news.' She beamed at Sam. 'Banks also requested that I provide you with an additional portmanteau, which I have left at your carriage.'

'How is my sister?' Sam asked.

'Making progress. I know Marta and Flora will look after her and, of course, she can stay with us for as long as she would like.'

'Very considerate, Miss Lansdowne.' Sir Antony beamed. 'Sorry for our swift departure. I thought it better to involve the professionals, you know. A bit out of my bailiwick.'

'So wise,' she agreed.

'Anyway,' Sir Anthony said, placing his hands on the arms of the chair and inhaling deeply, as he prepared himself for the effort of rising. 'Mustn't linger, long journey ahead, you know.'

'Indeed, although it is after luncheon and I worry that you will both get hungry. Still, I suppose you can get something to eat on the way. Although the smell in the hallway suggests that the landlord must have brought in Mrs Bridges today to make her roast beef. My mother always says Mrs Bridges's beef is the best.'

'That is true,' Sir Anthony concurred. He pulled out

his gold pocket watch, glancing down. 'Good Lord, I have been snoozing a while. Perhaps we should have something to eat here; I mean, if you do not mind?' He posed this last question to Sam.

'I—'

'I am certain he wouldn't mind,' Millie said. 'And poor Banks is so very anxious to catch up to you.'

Sam studied Millie. Her dark blue eyes looked extra wide and her entire expression was one of sweet innocence. This made him completely convinced that she was up to something.

'I am at your convenience, Sir Anthony,' he said, knowing there was little harm in delaying. Banks would arrive. Possibly Jason would appear magically and solve all their problems. Or some of them. Or his memory would return.

'Good.' Sir Anthony rang the bell and the serving girl appeared. 'Betsy, we'll have the beef. Miss Lansdowne, will you stay?'

'I would be delighted.'

'Three beef dinners,' Sir Anthony said. 'And another brandy would be pleasant. Really, I do not think there is any need for a great rush to London. Perhaps the powers that be might even despatch someone down here. And really, Mrs Bridges's beef is too good to miss.'

'I do agree,' Millie said. 'And after your late night yesterday, it is little wonder that you are feeling fatigued.'

Betsy returned with the brandy while Sir Anthony and Millie discussed the climate which concluded with mutual agreement that Torquay enjoyed quite the most moderate temperatures on the British Isles. After this enlightening conversation, Millie rose.

'I should see the innkeeper. I was rather rude when I burst in and must apologise,' she said.

Sam raised a brow. 'Unusual.'

'I know; I am hardly ever rude.'

'That is not quite what I meant.'

Millie returned some moments later and Betsy brought in the beef shortly thereafter. She put down the tray as Sir Anthony and Sam sat at the round table within the centre of the room. Millie passed around the plates, also pouring wine from a crystal decanter. She handed glasses to both gentlemen.

'Thank you, miss,' the maidservant said. 'Though you do not need to bother.'

'It is no trouble. Betsy, why do not you put some more coal on the fire and make it lovely and warm?'

Betsy did this, although Sam did not think it necessary as it was already burning brightly and the room was warm enough to be considered tropical. Sir Anthony ate his beef with enthusiasm, drank his wine and, after several muffled yawns, retired to a chair close to the fire. Within seconds they could hear his heavy breathing, followed by his rhythmic snores.

Sam glanced towards Millie. 'You are determined to make the room so hot that we all fall asleep?'

'No, only Sir Anthony.'

'I cannot see the point. We will have to wake him sooner or later.'

'I'd suggest not,' Millie said. 'I have every confidence he will sleep well tonight.'

Sam had picked up his fork, but laid it down again. The woman looked suspiciously demure. 'What exactly do you mean?'

'Only that he will get very adequate rest.'

'What did you do?' Sam asked. 'I do not want a man's poisoning on my conscious. Along with everything else.'

'Nonsense—I merely gave him a small amount of my mother's sleeping draught. He will be absolutely fine.'

He stared. 'You cannot go around drugging people.'

'I do not intend to make a habit of it,' she said airily. 'Now, did you want to discuss my moral compass or make use of the delay I have arranged?'

'I— What do you have planned?'

'We are going to see Sally and her father,' Millie said.

'Why?'

'Come on, we can talk about the "whys" and "wherefores" later.' Millie was already at the door to the corridor, looking at him with some impatience.

With a shrug, he followed. Sir Anthony did not appear likely to wake any time soon. They exited into the hallway, which was narrow, close and fragranced with roast beef. Indeed, he was quite glad to escape the muggy warmth and get into the brisk air outside.

'So why are we seeing these people?' he asked as they exited, the door closing behind them with a heavy *thunk*.

They stood to the left of the courtyard, facing the cliff, the silvery shimmer of the sea visible within the distance.

'I spoke to Frances. She says that Jason told her things when he was drunk.'

'Things?'

She scanned the courtyard. It was empty save for a donkey, a cart, Sir Anthony's carriage and a lone lad, sweeping the straw some distance away. 'He may have been involved in the smuggling and Frances suspects he was part of the wrecking.'

The words sent a shiver of cold shock through him. 'Why did not she say?'

'She did not know anything for certain and she was afraid. He spoke when he was drunk. She guessed the rest. I think that is why she is so obsessed with the sea.'

They looked at each other, acknowledging the unspoken words.

'And these people, Sally and her father, will talk to us?' he asked.

'They want to get to the truth.'

'And Sally's father is a smuggler?'

'Not any more, but he used to be. He knows a lot. People trust him,' Millie said.

'You do not owe me this. You have done enough.'

Briefly, her body stiffened. 'I am not doing this for you.'

She started towards the clifftop. Despite the stubborn set of her shoulders and quick pace, she looked slight and vulnerable in her sombre skirts, starkly outlined against the sea.

He followed, more slowly. 'Another cliff? There must be a road?' He'd scrambled down enough cliffs to last a lifetime.

She glanced back towards the donkey. 'I left the horse and gig at home and I used up Jeremiah's limited good will getting here. Anyway, this is a shortcut.'

'Of course it is.'

They started down the steep path, walking with care, their footsteps sending occasional tinkling cascades of pebbles. It was not overly steep, tending to follow a switchback formation. They paused at a plateau where the trail levelled. The weather had cleared, for once, and the sea shimmered blue under clear skies.

'I am doing this because these people need justice. If Jason is the wrecker, it might have been him on the beach. He could be alive and you are unnecessarily covering for him by saying you fought and he fell in the sea.' Millie spoke in her calm, blunt way, arms crossed as she stared seawards.

'You still think I was wrong last night.'

'Yes.' She started walking again. 'I understand why you want to protect your sister, but, whether you believe me or not, I have faith in the truth.'

He remembered how his mother would say 'the truth shall set you free'. It was from the Bible, but she also knew it in Greek.

'My mother said she believed in the truth.' The words came out with a bitter twist and he wished he could reel them back.

'She did not live up to those words?' Millie asked.

'No.' They walked for a while in silence. That was the thing he'd noticed about Millie, she did not rush to talk. She did not fear silence. 'She chose not to tell me that she was dying.'

'That must have been such a shock.'

'I was eight. I should have known,' he said.

'We do not see things we do not want to see.'

'I remember wondering how I could not have known. She was wasting away, turning into a ghost. And why did not she tell me if she believed in "truth" so much? Did I not have the right to know, to say goodbye?'

'You had the right, but sometimes it is hard to do things, even when we believe in them,' she said. 'Knowledge doesn't always help. My father kept having chest pains. I'd make stupid agreements with myself, like if I was polite or always ate my crusts, he'd get better—' She stopped.

'We cannot keep the people we love safe,' he said.

'I suppose your mother wanted to keep your childhood safe, to protect you.'

'It did not help.'

'She gave you a few extra months of joy.'

This much was true. Those days before her death had

been joyful, halcyon times. But that had only made the pain worse.

'Millie?'

'Yes?'

He had to ask. 'Who are you marrying?'

Chapter Eleven

She stiffened, the question taking her by surprise. For a few moments, she'd felt a tentative connection not marred by reality. It had felt like the cabin again. 'A local gentleman, Mr Edmunds. But it is not official yet.'

'Edmunds? I know a Mr Edmunds from Cornwall. Must be his father. How did you meet him?'

He'd been sitting in the church pew since she was a child, dragged to church. 'It is a small town and there is only one Mr Edmunds from Fowey. Geoffrey Edmunds,' she said.

'But he is...' The words petered away. 'Why?'

'He would like our land. And wants a mother for his five children.' She continued to walk down the path.

'But why would you marry him?'

'Women do not have many choices,' Millie said. 'Lacking patience and sufficient education, I cannot see myself as a suitable governess or companion.'

'Is it to save your sister from Harwood?'

'In part, but this will also help me to ensure Mother has a home and secure some funds for Lil's debut.'

'But there must be someone else. I mean someone

other than Edmunds that would be more suitable for you,' he said.

Anger flashed through her; a sudden, unexpected, fiery emotion surprising her with its intensity. 'So it is fine to sell myself, as long as it is to someone young and with all his teeth.'

Fuelled by the emotion, she walked down the path more rapidly.

'Slow down, for goodness sake,' he muttered, scrambling to keep up with her. 'Edmunds is dull as ditch water. Good lord, I swear he counts his shillings for entertainment.'

'Better than gambling them away.'

'What if you had a come-out in London? I have a great-aunt. And you have done so much for me, I am certain I could finance—'

They had reached the base of the cliff. She pulled to an abrupt halt, turning to him, her face for once oddly expressionless. 'Thank you, Mr Garrett. While I appreciate and welcome your offer to help my sister, I do not require such assistance. I am entirely happy with Mr Edmunds. My hope is that Mr Edmunds will propose. We have many things in common.'

'Like what, for goodness sake?'

'We dislike the city and we are opposed to gambling, drinking or other dangerous pursuits.'

'But you cannot build a life based on what you both dislike. And Edmunds doesn't just hate the city, he hates anything that has life or any frivolity. You will suffocate. I do not see why you are throwing my offer to help secure you a debut in my face.'

'Because the anticipated arrangement is entirely satisfactory. Mr Edmunds is not mean. He will let Mother stay in the house and I can stay in Cornwall. Indeed, your offer of help is completely unnecessary.'

They walked in silence. Millie's back was poker straight and stiff, her shoulders slightly raised as though he had angered her.

He glowered. She'd thrown back his offer as though it was a personal insult, but had shown no hesitation in involving herself in his life. She'd drugged Sir Anthony and likely expected Sam to feel grateful, but his own admirably sensible solution was somehow unforgivable.

This unfriendly silence continued until she stopped in front of a small structure at the outskirts of the village. A light was visible in one of the windows and a whisper of smoke escaped from the chimney, twisting into the clear evening sky.

'Do they know we are coming?' he asked.

'Yes. I sent word with Flora.'

The door swung open as a woman stepped out. Her hair was without grey and her skin unlined, yet she did not seem young. There was something in her movements, the fatigue in her expression and rounded shoulders which spoke of age, or premature age.

'Sally!' Millie stepped up to the woman, arms outstretched.

The woman wrapped Millie in a tight hug while two children peered from the doorway, their faces round, flushed and curious.

'I am so sorry,' Millie said, holding the woman tight.

'I know. I know.'

After this tight embrace, the woman stepped back, eyeing Sam with hesitation. She was taller and plumper than Millie. Her eyes were rimmed red. She wore an apron and her hands twisted nervously in the cloth.

'This is Mr Garrett. May we come in?'

'Of course,' she said, leading the way into the small cottage. 'Flora said as how you were coming and wanted to speak to Da.'

The cottage was simple with small, high windows and a peat fire flickering within the hearth. The two children retreated into the back of the room, their eyes still wide, while a middle-aged man and woman stood in greeting.

'Mr Garrett, this is Mr and Mrs Aimsworth, and my good friend Mrs Strand and her children, Libby and Gerald,' Millie said.

'I am very sorry for your loss,' Sam said.

'Aye,' Mrs Aimsworth acknowledged. 'Well, come in then.'

They walked further into the room. The air felt warm after the chill outside and laced with the scent of herbs. The room was spartan, clean with a bare wooden table and a kettle hanging over the flames. 'Would you be wanting anything to eat or drink?' Mrs Aimsworth asked.

'No, thank you,' Millie said. 'We just wanted to talk with you for a moment.'

Sally turned to her children. 'How about if you two go out and feed the chickens table scraps?' Sally suggested.

They complied, with evident reluctance, leaving with a patter of footsteps, followed by a clang of the outer door.

After this exit, the adults faced each other with serious formality. Sam glanced about the cottage, realising how infrequently he had visited a working-class family. The smallness of the space and stark simplicity struck him.

'It is kind of you to come. Sit down.' Mrs Aimsworth invited.

They sat at little awkwardly at the table. There were

insufficient chairs so Mr Aimsworth pulled up a stool from the hearth, moving a much-used battledore—a book to help the children learn their alphabet—placing it on the table, the alphabet and a picture of some clouds visible.

'Thank you for allowing us to come,' Millie said. 'We are sorry to intrude, but we are hoping that you can help us. We want to get some justice for Jem.'

'Aye, we warned him to stay away from smuggling. These days it ain't the same as it once were. He never should have done it,' Mr Aimsworth said, shaking his head.

'Jem just wanted to give me a good life—' Sally spoke, her tone defensive and her face flushing.

Millie slid her hand across the table, touching her friend's arm. 'Jem was a good man. He did not deserve what happened to him.'

The other woman grasped Millie's hand, angling towards her with sudden intensity. 'There are rumours. I hear say that they weren't all drowned. That it weren't an accident and how the ship were wrecked on purpose. That it were—it was murder.'

'Yes,' Millie said.

'So it is true.' Sally's voice dropped so low, it was scarcely a whisper.

'Yes.'

'Wrecking's a bad business. The devil's game,' Mr Aimsworth said in the brusque tone that men often use when fearing they might display emotion.

Millie took both Sally's work-hardened hands within her own. 'We think that there are wreckers tied up with the smuggling here in the village. And we want to stop the wrecking. Anything you know could help. Anything.'

'And how do you fit it?' Mr Aimsworth posed this

question directly to Sam, his eyes narrowed with suspicion.

Millie looked as though she were about to speak, but Sam shook his head. Mr Aimsworth deserved a direct answer.

'Truthfully, I do not know. As Miss Lansdowne may have said, I am Frances Ludlow's brother. Jason Ludlow is my brother-in-law. As you likely also know, he is missing. I had an accident on the same night, but my memory of the event has gone.' He paused, running his fingers over the worn primer, so used the pages were disintegrating. 'I would like to find out the truth both to ensure there is justice for the men lost and that my sister is not blamed for her husband's disappearance.'

There was a silence after this statement. Mr Aimsworth eyed Sam for a moment, as though weighing him up. He reached up to the mantel, pulling down his clay pipe and studying it with some intensity.

'Right, so how can we help?' he asked at last.

'My understanding is that there has always been some smuggling here, but that, more recently, this has become lethal, involving wrecking. Are people from here—from this village—involved?'

'Aye, there are rumours,' Mr Aimsworth said.

'Who?'

'Some of the smugglers—'

Sally gave a gasp.

'Not Jem, mind. But I heard tell the Captain was involved,' Mr Aimsworth continued.

'The Captain?' Millie said. 'Of *The Rising Dawn*?'

'Aye.'

'But that doesn't make sense. The Captain was on the ship. He was killed.'

'Reckon he weren't the boss. Wrecking is different

than brandy running. There's jewels, watches, specialised cargo. You need connections. You need people in the big cities.'

'So you think someone else was involved?' Sam asked.

'Aye.'

'Who?'

The word hung in the air. It seemed like everyone in the tiny cottage was holding his or her breath. Even the fire's crackle was muted. Millie felt her own breath catch and hold.

'We do not know for sure,' Mr Aimsworth said.

'But you have heard the rumours?' Sam leaned forward. 'I'm guessing it is my missing brother-in-law.'

Mr Aimsworth refilled his clay pipe, his movements slow and careful, as though the task required his entire concentration. Again there was that sense of waiting, as though time had been suspended. 'Aye,' he said.

'But why wreck *The Rising Dawn*?'

Mr Aimsworth put the pipe between his lips, inhaling deeply. 'I have heard tell the Captain wanted out of the wrecking business. Didn't sit right with him. Plus they weren't going to get away with it for much longer.'

'Why not?' Sam asked.

Mr Aimsworth exhaled a cloud of smoke. 'Too many cutters. This Waterguard nonsense. Besides, your brother-in-law isn't best suited for a role requiring silence and subterfuge. He enjoys his drink and likes to talk.'

That much was true. Tom had occasionally brought Jason to Lansdowne House.

So had Jason plotted against *The Rising Dawn* or was there another person or entity involved?

She'd always considered him capable of violence, but not the cruel measured calculation needed to lure a ship to its doom. Millie remembered the steady shooting as the three half-drowned men had struggled from the water. They had been so utterly defenceless.

'I did not think him capable of wrecking,' she said.

'Jem did not know anything about this, so why? Why did Mr Ludlow or anyone kill him?' Sal asked.

'No loose ends,' her father said.

Millie tightened her clasp on her friend's hands, holding them between her own. She looked about the small, familiar cottage and felt the tears in her eyes. They had so little. It was so cruelly unfair that fate should have taken Jem.

With unspoken accord, they stood, chairs scuffling back.

'Thank you,' Millie said, again reaching to hug her friend. 'Let me know if there is anything you need. Anything I can do to help.'

'I will,' Sal said.

Millie glanced down at the well-used battledore. 'You're teaching them to read?'

'You taught me,' she said. 'Gerald is a bright lad. There has to be other choices than smuggling or the mine.'

Millie nodded. There was something brave in her friend's determination to help her children achieve a better life.

'I will send Flora down with some more primers or come myself, I promise.'

They walked towards the door.

'And we will send word if we learn anything,' she said.

'You have an idea where Mr Ludlow might be?' Sal asked.

Sam glanced at Millie. 'I do not know where he is, but I know where I will start looking.'

* * *

Sam and Millie walked into the cool chill air of evening. There was a relief in leaving. The atmosphere in the house felt weighted with grief. For a few moments they strode in silence, needing to distance themselves from the poverty and pain in the cottage.

'You're thinking of the hut? You think Jason might be there?' Millie asked, as they neared the base of the cliff.

'It's a good place to start,' Sam said. 'Sir Anthony could take the constables tomorrow.'

Millie shook her head, glancing towards the shale beach and the unusually calm sea. It would be a clear night. 'Tomorrow will be too late. If Jason is alive, he has done all of this to make us believe him dead. He wants to escape to the Continent.'

'You think he would go tonight?'

'The weather is good. He would be a fool not to.'

'So he has likely already left the hut?'

She nodded. 'He has likely taken the jewellery and coins and is hiding close to shore with a boat arranged to take him to France. We could rouse Sir Anthony and we could get a boat—'

'No.' He spoke sharply. '*We* are not doing or going anywhere. Not tonight, tomorrow or the next day. There is no "we".'

'Fiddlesticks,' Millie said. 'I am in this. Talking to the Aimsworths was my idea. Someone lured those men to their deaths. I cannot turn my back on them. I can be a witness—'

'I won't let you put yourself in danger. We still do not know if Jason was working alone. We may not even be right about Jason.'

'It is my choice. You do not need to protect me as well

as your sister. You are not the self-appointed protector of the vulnerable and hopeless. I make my own decisions.'

'Why?' He faced her. 'Why would you want to be involved? I thought you were all about honesty. You said you are sensible and not a risk taker. You cannot decide to be cautious one moment and marry Mr Edmunds and then decide to chase a murderer in the next.'

'Sally is my friend. I knew those men. They were lured to their death.'

'And your death will hardly be a comfort for her or any of them. Plus it would be mighty inconvenient for Edmunds at the wedding.'

'I do not know why you keep mentioning Mr Edmunds and my wedding.'

'And I do not know why you did not bring it up a tad sooner.'

'For goodness sake, it is not even decided yet. Mr Edmunds hasn't officially proposed. Anyway, I did not mean to keep it a secret. It just did not come up.'

'It did not come up? We were talking about everything else. I felt... Anyway, it seems a big item to omit.'

'Perhaps not when escaping a shipwreck,' she retorted. 'Anyway, you know now.'

'I do and I am certain your intended would prefer that you do not run around chasing criminals.'

'It isn't any of his business,' she retorted.

'It soon will be.'

This, of course, was true. It was why she would prefer never to marry anyone. 'A fundamental weakness in our society,' she said. 'Anyhow, I feel no need to consult him at least until the engagement is official.'

He glared at her and then turned, walking briskly. 'And I feel no need to involve you in the further pursuit of Mr. Ludlow.'

'But I am involved. I was there. I witnessed men murdered. Besides, you still need me.'

'I do not,' he said.

'Actually you are going up the wrong path to get back to the inn, so maybe you do.'

They hurried up the steep path in an angry silence, punctuated only by the scrabble of their shoes and ragged breaths. The sun was setting, its dying rays disappearing behind the horizon. The temperature had dropped and their breath formed small clouds of mist.

Once at the top of the cliff, they hurried across the grass towards the lighted windows of the tavern. Roast beef mixed with smoke, salt water and that peaty scent indigenous to Cornwall still perfumed the air. The landlord opened the door almost before they had knocked.

'I saw you out the window,' he explained as they stepped into the dimly lit passage way. 'In fact, Sir Anthony is wanting to see you. Most particular like.'

'He is?' They exchanged glances as the landlord led them down the corridor.

'Here we are then.' The landlord flung open the door, with almost theatrical aplomb, before shifting back.

'Thank you.' Millie smiled as they stepped forward into the warm, well-lit room.

Briefly, everything was disjointed, as though only seeing pieces of a disconnected scene, impossible to comprehend. She saw Mrs Ludlow. She saw her smile and soft violet gown. She noted the inviting fire and glowing lamps.

Mrs Ludlow's tone was calm, almost gentle, and the greeting gracious. 'Welcome, I have been expecting you.'

Millie's lips twisted into a smile of greeting as she heard Mrs Ludlow's words, even as her heart thudded like a wild thing.

Chapter Twelve

Millie tried to make sense of the dichotomy: Mrs Ludlow's smile of welcome and the pistol's barrel aimed at them.

'Mrs Ludlow? What are you doing?' Sam demanded, finding his voice first. 'Put that down before you hurt yourself.'

'Do not worry, I am quite skilled,' she said with that pleasant smile.

'Why?' Millie pushed out the one word through stiff lips.

'So I can look after my son. It is a mother's duty.'

'Where…where is Sir Anthony?' Millie stared at the comfortable chair. It was empty. 'Did you k-kill him?' She stumbled over the word, the simple one syllable hard to form.

'Of course not. He is quite fine. Cartwell put him upstairs to sleep. I will have enough bodies to dispose of as it is.'

You will? Millie said or thought she said. Goose pimples prickled her skin despite the room's heat.

Mrs Ludlow reached for the bell pull, while still keeping the pistol levelled at Millie. The landlord entered, holding on to a rope, which he twisted nervously within his hands.

'Good,' Mrs Ludlow said. 'I am glad you brought the rope. Miss Lansdowne, you look very tired. Come over here, dear, and sit down.'

Millie stumbled into a chair which was quite close to where Mrs Ludlow stood at the hearth.

'That's better. You must be exhausted. You have been walking your feet off these last few days. So very adventurous.' She moved so that she stood directly behind Millie's chair, placing one hand on Millie's shoulder. Even through the cloth of her serviceable gown, Millie could feel the hard tightness of the woman's fingers.

The pistol was pressed flush to her temple. She could feel the chill metal.

'Mr Cartwell, if you could tie them up, please? Start with him.' Mrs Ludlow nodded towards Sam.

'Cartwell, are you mad?' Sam demanded.

'No,' Mrs Ludlow said. 'I think not. It makes absolute sense as I am paying him well and I hold the pistol, a winning point in any argument.'

'Mrs Ludlow, please, you cannot get away with this. Do not condemn yourself to Jason's fate,' Sam said.

Millie felt Mrs Ludlow remove her hand from her shoulder and felt transitory relief, inhaling as though the clamp of the woman's cold fingers had impacted her ability to breathe. This sense of respite dissipated almost immediately as the older woman leaned over, so close that Millie could smell the cloying scent of lavender and the tickle of her hair against her skin.

'Isn't Mr Garrett kind?' Mrs Ludlow whispered against her ear. 'I thank you for your concern. Now, please, co-operate with dear Mr Cartwell as I do not want to become unpleasant.'

There was a rustle of cloth behind her and Millie felt metal at her throat. At first, she thought it was the pistol, but winced at the sharp prick of a knife's point.

'Do not hurt her,' Sam said quickly. 'This has nothing to do with her.'

'I believe you involved her when you invited your mad sister to Miss Lansdowne's domicile. Still, I won't hurt her now, if you co-operate.'

Sam put his arms behind him as Cartwell moved towards him.

'That's better. Isn't everything so much easier when you co-operate?' Mrs Ludlow said, moving the knife so gently that it tickled Millie's skin as she ran it up her neck and along her jawline.

The older woman bent forward, her tone becoming almost affectionate as she moved the cold metal tip of the knife over Millie's skin in an eerie caress. 'Poor Millicent is not considered the pretty sister, you know. They underestimate her, I think. Of course, society always likes blonde hair and blue eyes. I believe you were quite taken by a blonde, blue-eyed miss yourself once, Mr Garrett. Little Annie Whistler, as I recall, but I quite like Miss Lansdowne's looks and her skin is perfect. Not as pretty as Lillian, but more interesting... Society is not kind to women, you know. They discard us when our chins sag and our skins wrinkle.'

Her tone softened into melancholy. Millie felt the whisper of her breath and its smell mixed with the scent of lavender. She pressed her back into the chair, as though this slight movement might give her some respite from the woman's proximity.

Then, with lightening rapidity, Mrs Ludlow's mood changed. She straightened, prodding the pistol at Millie's temple with sudden irritation. 'Good heavens, Cartwell,

you're making a meal of it! Stop playing with the rope
and get the man tied. Feet as well, but not too tight. They
need to walk. And for goodness sake, do not take all day.'

The landlord bent, kneeling beside Sam, looping the
rope about his ankles, effectively shackling him.

'Much better. Now tie her up, too. Stand up, Miss
Lansdowne. You may be tired, but we cannot have you
sitting about all the time, you know.'

Millie stood, dazed. It seemed incongruous to be
bound within this snug room—*The Rising Dawn* had
provided a more appropriate location for such a misadventure. And the Captain, with his pockmarked face,
had been more suitable as a captor. This middle-aged
woman with her violet dress and salt-and-pepper hair
was wrong. She had walked into the wrong play and was
reading the wrong script.

Millie was jolted from her confused tangle of thought
as the landlord pulled her hands back, winding the rope
tight about her wrists.

'Feet, too, remember,' Mrs Ludlow said.

The landlord bent, squatting down and winding the
rope about Millie's ankles. He had a white fringe of hair.
It circled his head, leaving the centre shiny and bald.

'Very good,' Mrs Ludlow said. 'Now lead them out.'

'What? Me?' the landlord asked. He voice rose and
Millie saw apprehension flicker in his expression.
'Where?'

'Down to the ocean,' Mrs Ludlow said with a benign
smile, as though offering a child a weekend treat.

'Well, I…um… I have the pigs to feed. And the cows
to milk. I mean, Betsy usually does that, but you had me
send Betsy home.'

'The pigs and cows will have to wait. Unless, of
course, you want me to have that little chat with the ex-

cise men. Here.' The benign tone turned sharp as she
tossed a coin to the landlord. 'Any more concerns?'

'No, ma'am.'

'Good.'

They stumbled forward, walking through the corridor,
stuffy with the smell of stale food, and into the brisk air
outside. The darkness of night was broken by the silvery
luminescence of the full moon and the flickering light of
Cartwell's lamp. The air was cold. Millie heard her teeth
chattering as they moved across the courtyard, towards
the trail that they had so recently climbed. The heavy
ropes made walking difficult. Millie fell once, sliding
on to her rear, just able to save herself while a cascade
of rocks clattered downwards.

'It would be quicker and easier with our legs untied,'
she said.

'Yes, it would, wouldn't it,' Mrs Ludlow agreed eq-
uitably.

They did not take the path towards the fishing village,
instead veering to the left. This trail was so overgrown
that branches snapped against their faces, arms and legs.
Even with the lamplight they were constantly stumbling
over twisting roots threading the path.

At last they burst from the cover of foliage and on to
the shale beach. Millie felt both a relief and dread. There
was the thankfulness that the long, painful walk was
over, but also dread of what was to come.

It was a circle, one that had begun on the ship and
ended here. The ropes around her arms and legs felt
oddly familiar. The moon shimmered. It seemed more
beautiful than Millie had ever seen it, like liquid silver
splashed across inky waters.

'Took you long enough!' The strident male voice vio-
lently shattered the dark silence.

Millie jumped. She twisted, losing her balance and almost falling on to the pebbled beach.

Jason Ludlow strolled towards them. 'Rumours of my demise have been grossly exaggerated.' His speech was slurred, his movements unsteady. 'Mother, why the hell have you brought these fools?'

When Millie had last seen him, he had appeared the gentleman. Now, his clothes were dirty, his face unshaven and he looked every inch the hardened criminal he had become.

It was a circle and now they would die, not by fire or drowning, but by execution on the shale beach.

Jason came up to her, so close that she could smell the alcohol on his breath and the stink of his soiled clothes. 'Tom's little sister. Decided to join the party? Grown prettier, I see. But too serious. You were always much too serious. Do not like my women serious.'

'I am not your woman!' Millie snapped.

'Feisty, too. I remember that. I rather liked it...'

'Jason,' Mrs Ludlow said with more sorrow than anger. 'Jason, you couldn't stay sober even for a day? You did not go into the village to get more, I hope?'

He yawned. 'Good gracious, enough with the nagging, Mother. Always you nag and bother me with ludicrous rules and admonitions. No, Mother, I found your stash of food and beverage and, while not overly generous, there was a sufficiency. Did you find a vessel for me?'

'Yes.' Mrs Ludlow glanced towards the sea. 'It will be here soon and will take you to France.'

'And what of them?' He nodded towards Millie and Sam.

'Murder, then suicide, I think.'

'Jason, for goodness sake, this is crazy. No one will believe that,' Sam said.

He shrugged. 'I'll be in France.'

Sam looked towards Mrs Ludlow. 'Right now you have committed no irreversible crime. I can talk to the magistrate, plead clemency. You are desperate to save your son, that will be understood. But if you kill us, you will be guilty of murder.'

Mrs Ludlow gave an odd laugh. 'No irreversible crime? And what crime is exactly reversible? Haven't you realised that there are no criminals: just the rich and the poor, the winners and the losers, weak and powerful. I have it all worked out. It is not what happens that matters, but what people believe.'

'What do you mean?' Millie asked.

'Let me enlighten you.' she said, as though sharing a pleasant narrative. 'You see, we have dear Mr Garrett, the loving brother, who came down from London and was so distressed by the cruel treatment of his sister that he killed the cruel husband. The local magistrate is easily convinced that the death was largely accidental, a skirmish between men with unfortunate results. But the grieving widow stays with dear, sweet Miss Lansdowne and tells her that the brother, Mr Garrett, actually plotted to murder the cruel husband. You have such a sympathetic ear, dear. And nice skin.

'Miss Lansdowne accosts the loving brother. She accuses him of murder. A hangable offence. Furious, the brother kills the grieving widow's dear friend. Or maybe they have an argument and she falls off a cliff. Mr Garrett, tortured by guilt, commits suicide. Very tragic. It could be an opera. You like opera, as I recall, Mr Garrett?' She stopped again, her voice raised and at odds with the rest of the recitation, which had been spoken in a peculiar singsong manner.

'Do not!' Sam snapped out the curt command. 'No

one in their right mind is going to believe such nonsense.
It is a load of drivel.'

Mrs Ludlow gave a graceful shrug. 'Maybe. I do find
being in one's right mind limits creativity. And it is a bit
far-fetched, I'll grant you. However, the fanciful tale will
be believed long enough for dear sweet little Frances to
have a nervous breakdown. At this point, I will step in, as
the doting grandmother, and look after dear Noah. I have
already been working on my grandmotherly looks—less
glamorous, you will note.

'Naturally, I will feel the need of a warmer clime and
leave, with Noah, for Italy. I am not particularly fond of
children, but I am fond of trust funds. Jason will join us
and we will be comfortably settled in a delightful villa
before anyone questions—'

'No!' The one syllable shattered the night, silencing
the older woman.

A dark shadowed shape exploded from the shrubbery,
catapulting on to the woman with a primal force. For a
confused moment, Sam thought a wild animal had attacked as Mrs Ludlow buckled, falling to the shale beach.

Acting with pure instinct, Sam rammed his body
against Jason, despite his bound legs. The man crumpled, striking his head against a boulder and then lying
quite still.

Sam turned. Two dark figures struggled on the beach,
silhouetted against the moon's white disc. The pistol had
fallen from Mrs Ludlow's hand and in a blur of movement, he saw hands outstretched, fingers scrabbling over
the shale, reaching and grabbing for it. Then, for a split
second, he saw Frances's white face.

She grasped the pistol.

The two figures disentangled. Frances reared up and

swung the pistol wildly, striking Mrs Ludlow so that she collapsed to the ground.

There was a moment of silence, broken only by the waves and the sound of Frances's panting breath.

'How did you get here?' Sam gasped.

His sister did not answer. Instead, she weighed the pistol in her hand, cupping the handle almost lovingly and staring at it with apparent fascination.

'Fran, untie me and give me the pistol! We'll use these ropes to bind them. Where is Cartwell?' Sam asked.

'Ran away!' Millie shouted. She was kneeling beside Jason. 'He did not even leave us the lamp. Jason is still out cold, but we'd best tie him up, just to be sure. Frances, could you untie Sam so we can use the ropes?'

Frances still made no response. Instead, she walked quite slowly over the shale to where Jason lay, as though pulled by an inexorable force. Her footsteps made a rattling sound as the shale settled under her weight. She stopped with her feet inches from the man's body. Lifting her foot, she prodded him, her movement almost delicate. He groaned.

'He is not dead,' she said.

'We'll tie him up,' Sam said.

'You would have killed my brother and taken my child,' she spoke to the unconscious man, still cradling the pistol.

'Fran, untie me.' Sam felt cold apprehension. It tightened his throat, drying his mouth and making his breathing uneven.

Frances seemed disconnected from the scene, oblivious to their words with her entire concentration focused on the pistol in her hand.

'And now, I will take your life, Jason. That seems fair. You have taken so many lives. Men, women, children even. I still see them. They haunt me. Do they haunt you? Do they haunt your dreams? Do you see their dead faces ravaged by the sea? I see them all the time. I see them when I sleep. I see them when I wake. I see them when I walk along the shore.'

Very slowly, she lifted up the pistol, smiling slightly and almost caressing the barrel, as her finger reached for the trigger.

'Fran, no!' Sam said. 'Please, you cannot be judge and jury.'

'I can, actually.'

Slowly and carefully, Frances took aim.

Chapter Thirteen

'Frances, do not. Please,' Sam repeated.

Millie's heart pounded and her thoughts bounced about her head as she watched the woman's slow, almost drugged, motions. It was as though she was powered by a force outside herself.

There must be something she could say or do that would help.

Something...something...something...

Millie was on the ground, quite close to Jason. Looking up, she could see both the pistol and Frances's pale face, visible in the moonlight 'Please,' she whispered. 'Please, I know it feels as though we have no choice or control. But we do. We can control who we are. That is the only thing we can control.'

For a moment, Frances seemed oblivious to her words but then she spoke in slow rhythmic tones.

'He was cruel. He *is* cruel.'

'I know he is cruel. But you are not. You are kind.'

Frances glanced to her.

It was the first time her focus was moved from the man or weapon and Millie felt both hope and sick fear. 'Please,' she said, scared of saying the wrong word and desperate to prolong the tenuous connection. 'Please give Sam the pistol. Your son needs a mother and Sam needs a sister. He has lost so much. Please, please, do not take that from him.'

The moment felt long, endless. Everything stilled. The lapping of the waves, the rustling leaves, the crackling branches, singing crickets, everything became muted… subdued…slowed. Millie dared not exhale, fearful even of the sound of her breath. Thoughts and words filled her mind, but she squashed them. She'd said enough.

Very slowly, Frances lowered the pistol and walked to Sam, placing it into his hand.

'Thank you,' he said.

He turned his gaze to Millie. 'Thank you.'

It was Millie who saw Mrs Ludlow move to the water's edge.

Sam was bent forward, binding Jason's arms while Frances sat on a boulder, curved in upon herself, as though spent of every last resource.

Mrs Ludlow rose. Millie tensed, fearful of attack, but Mrs Ludlow did not turn to them. Instead, she gathered her skirts, stepping to the water's edge, her movement oddly graceful.

'Sam! Mrs Ludlow—she is going into the water,' Millie said.

Sam glanced up. 'She cannot go anywhere.'

'There is a boat out there. In the distance.'

'It's heading away. I'll use those ropes for her hands, when she gives up on the notion of walking to France.'

Millie watched as Mrs Ludlow stepped forward with a steadiness of purpose, moving with neither speed nor hesitation.

'We have to stop her. I do not think she is quite sane. Jason was likely cruel to her also,' Millie said.

Cautiously, she walked over the shale. 'Mrs Ludlow?' She raised her voice, but kept the tone kind. 'Please, come in, before you catch your death.'

Mrs Ludlow stood knee-deep in the shallows, looking into the distance. Almost to Millie's surprise, she turned, her expression startled, as though she had forgotten the presence of others.

'It went away, Miss Lansdowne,' she said. 'The boat. It went away.'

'I know, but come in now. The ocean is so cold. We do not want you to become ill.'

Mrs Ludlow smiled, as though privy to some secret knowledge. 'I do not believe catching my death will really matter, you know. They will hang me.'

'Please do not think that. They won't hang you,' Millie said. 'We are alive and you aren't responsible for Jason's choices.'

'Miss Lansdowne, Jason doesn't choose. He careens through life like a drunken blunderer. Rather like your brother, I suppose.'

Millie stiffened at the mention of Tom. It still hurt, that mix of pain and grief and a seldom-acknowledged raw anger.

'Come in, Mrs Ludlow, so you can get dry.'

To her surprise, the woman complied. She walked towards the shore, the water splashing with her movement. 'I had intended to take my own life, but I find it not as easy as I had anticipated. Likely, they will resolve the issue for me.'

Millie glanced towards Sam. He had finished binding Jason and rose, the ropes held in his hands. Frances was still unmoving with her arms hugging her knees, her eyes focused on the horizon.

The older woman moved steadily, displaying little haste, as she stepped further up the shale shore. Her skirts hung about her legs, clinging in damp folds. Her hair fell on to her forehead, wet and dishevelled. She looked at Jason where he lay, unconscious, but secured with ropes.

'Poor Jason. So inefficient. Never the brightest, you know. I told dear Jason to make you dead. But you are not dead.' She walked up the shore towards Sam.

'*You* told Jason to attack me?' Sam said.

'Not attack. Get rid of. A mistake, I know. I should have done it. If a job's worth doing... But I was needed somewhere...else.'

'Somewhere else?' He went up to her, the ropes held limply in one hand, the rocks and shale rattling under his feet.

An expression of horror and confused disbelief suffused his face and Millie knew that it was duplicated in her own.

'Some...where...else,' he repeated, pacing out the words. 'My God, it was you...on the beach. You killed those men. Not Jason.'

Out of the corner of her eye, Millie saw Frances move, uncoiling from her rock.

'Sam, you have surprised me,' Mrs Ludlow said, with that odd laugh. 'It is quite refreshing as I am so seldom surprised. You were there?'

'I was there,' he said and Millie knew from his tone that he was remembering the drowning men and the three who had made it to shore, only to be picked off like clay pigeons, staining the tidepools red with blood.

'I had wondered how you survived. The smugglers

picked you up. What humanity. I wouldn't have thought they'd have bothered.' She glanced again towards Jason. 'Silly boy, he should have killed you properly. Or kept his wife happy until we were ready.'

'You.' Frances had walked several feet so that she was on a line with Millie, facing her mother-in-law. Something in the way Frances said that single word made Millie shiver.

'Of course, I blame myself as well.' Mrs Ludlow spoke to Sam, not even glancing at Frances. 'I underestimated you when I chose her. I did not think you'd visit. You were drinking and hardly devoted to family.'

'You…did…this…to…me. You…chose. You plotted…' Frances now stood only a few feet from the other woman. Every part of her body seemed tight, her intensity in sharp contrast to Mrs Ludlow's peculiar nonchalance.

Mrs Ludlow shrugged. 'Do not sound so surprised. Jason has very few original thoughts. Besides, as I said, Jason doesn't choose, he careens.'

'You are worse than him,' Frances said.

'I am what the world has made me.'

'You planned this? You plotted with Jason to fake his own death?' Sam asked.

'But why?' Millie whispered. 'I understand that you wanted Jason to escape and you also wanted Noah. But why did you kill Jem and all those men?'

'Dead men cannot talk. The Captain knew too much.' Mrs Ludlow stopped, her eyes moving towards Millie with an expression close to animation. 'Why, Miss Lansdowne, how vastly amusing. *You* were there, too. *You* were on that smuggling ship. Indeed, I believe *you* rescued dear Mr Garrett.'

She smiled, her expression beatific. 'I find it satisfying. I prefer my original plot, of course. I always wanted a villa in Italy and money. However, it is interesting that it was you, Miss Lansdowne, who changed the narrative. Have you noticed, Miss Lansdowne, that women always play a role, but we never get to write the script?'

'I—' Millie paused, meeting the other woman's gaze. Mrs Ludlow stood in her wet clothes with her hair in tangles about her face and that oddly pleasant smile. She was mad, of course.

'I have noticed it,' Millie said.

Standing at the water's edge, time paused and Millie knew that these moments would be indelibly carved into her mind for ever. She would always remember every word, the dim outline of the older woman silhouetted against the moon's shimmer, the injured man sprawled across the pebbles, the seaweed scent, the lap of waves, the cold air and the rocks hunkered at the shore.

Then, as if to compensate, time started again, moving with an excess of speed, a blur, like the countryside during a fast gallop.

The beach, deserted moments before, became a veritable thoroughfare. With a burst of cracking branches, rustling foliage and shouts, Banks, Cartwell, Sir Anthony and two other gentlemen arrived, catapulting themselves onto the beach.

Millie turned at the noise. For a moment, it felt that while her eyes were able to discern and identify the figures, she could not comprehend or make sense of their presence. It felt, she thought dispassionately, as though the narrative had been switched, flipping from Mrs Ludlow's tragedy into comedic farce.

Oddly, she did not feel the relief that she knew she should feel. Instead, she watched with an exhausted numbness. She remembered thinking that Sir Anthony looked greatly in need of either a strong cup of tea or smelling salts. Likely he'd prefer brandy. Indeed, the poor man looked close to collapse, dabbing his forehead with a handkerchief while his gaze swivelled between the prostrate Jason and the elder Mrs Ludlow with a bewildered confusion.

Cartwell talked a lot, a confused mumble of words centred around how he had summoned assistance at the very first opportunity. He stated several times that he was very sorry for 'all the upset' while he mopped his forehead. He had come better prepared than Sir Anthony and had a small flask of brandy.

Banks appeared somewhat indifferent to the scene, examining his footwear with considerable concern and frowning at Sam, although whether this was in disapproval of his actions or the treatment of his clothes, Millie did not know.

Meanwhile, the other gentlemen, local constables, were of a more practical mindset. One removed the flask from Cartwell and administered it to Frances. She complied, but with detachment, as though compliance was easier than refusal. Her face held a dazed confusion and Millie wondered if a similar look was duplicated in her own expression.

Sir Anthony, Sam and the constables seemed to have a lot to say. She did not even try to follow the conversation, explanation and hand gestures. Then, one of the constables blew a rather piercing whistle. Instructions were shouted and the second constable bent over Jason, heaving him over his shoulder. Jason groaned. Millie was rather thankful as she had begun to wonder if the man was dead.

And thus the expedition left the beach, Jason dangling over the burliest man's shoulder while the other constable escorted Mrs Ludlow, trailed by Frances, Millie, Sam, Cartwell, Banks and Sir Anthony.

Nobody seemed much interested in conversation, although Cartwell continued to mumble until Banks requested, politely enough, whether a moment's silence might be possible.

'Likely to mourn my jacket,' Sam muttered to Millie.

The wry words made her giggle, a rather high-pitched chortle which, even to her own ears, sounded somewhat hysterical. She hurriedly subdued her laughter, resulting in a slight hiccup.

'How are you?' he asked, softly. 'You have not said anything.'

'I think I am fine,' she said uncertainly. 'I…um…do not really know. It feels as though everything is disconnected and I need to wait until things connect again to know if I am fine. Does that make sense?'

'Some,' he said. 'I do not know how to thank you enough for helping Frances, saying the right words.'

'I was so worried and so thankful when she lowered the pistol.'

They continued in silence. This was broken again by Banks, who shared that his investigation with Northrup about Sam's dawn horse ride had proved fruitful. Apparently, that gentleman had been told to say this by Mrs Ludlow, most likely to cover both Sam's absence and her removal of a horse from the stables.

Millie glanced at Mrs Ludlow and wondered if she was listening or if she had retreated into the madness of her mind. How had she thought that it might work, killing Millie and Sam? Indeed, the plot she had outlined seemed flimsier than the creations Millie and her sister created as children with playing cards and toothpicks.

Or the tree house Tom had built which had resulted in a broken arm.

But then, she'd likely only hoped for a short-term solution, long enough for Jason to escape and Frances to be declared incompetent.

The group continued to walk up the path towards the clifftop. It was long and tiring, but almost an anti-climax. It seemed that such a dramatic interlude should not be capped by this silent, exhausting walk.

At the inn, Sir Anthony announced that he and the constables would keep custody of the two prisoners and suggested that everyone go home, saying that Sam could come to his office tomorrow morning to make a statement. He would allow the ladies to wait for a day and follow up with statements later in the week.

After this announcement, he provided his carriage for Millie and Frances, while Cartwell secured a conveyance for Sir Anthony, the captives and one of the constables. Sir Anthony told Cartwell that he would also be in his custody until greater insight had been gained about his part in the evening's events. This resulted in several expostulations from Cartwell which were eventually silenced when Sir Anthony agreed to send a servant to request that Betsy look after the cows, pigs and chickens. The remainder of the party, Banks, Sam and the second of the constables took the smaller carriage to the inn in the village.

Indeed, Millie thought, as she sat in Sir Anthony's carriage, they had all switched conveyances in an odd game of musical chairs. How strange to be sitting on the crimson velvet cushions of Sir Anthony's rather stuffy coach as though they had done nothing more dramatic than attend church choir practice. Not that she had ever participated in a choir of any sort, as she was quite lacking in musical talent. Her lips twitched again with humour that was likely closer to hysteria than genuine amusement.

In the seat opposite, Frances sat with an unnatural stillness, her hands clasped tightly together and her teeth worrying nervously at her bottom lip.

'You will be quite safe now,' Millie said cautiously.

'Yes, thank you. For a while I was numb. I could feel nothing. Now I can feel almost too much. I am worried about Noah. I want to see him. Part of me wants to run from this coach, as though I could cover the ground faster.'

'It is a ponderous vehicle. However, if your feet feel anything like mine, I am certain the coach is moving faster than we could,' she said lightly.

'I just need to know he is safe. What if Mrs Ludlow did…did something…?'

'Do not think of it,' Millie said. 'She was too busy with us. And, remember, her intent was never to hurt him. She wanted to be his guardian to access his trust fund. Besides, Marta and Flora are in charge and they would both put their lives on the line to keep a child safe.'

'I know. I just need to see him.'

'You will. As soon as we get home.'

Despite Frances's nod of acknowledgement, Millie could see her abstraction and feel the circling of her worried thoughts. 'You were very brave to help us,' she said, hoping that conversation might distract the other woman.

'Was I? When I jumped, I did not even think. Was that really brave or just a crazed impulse?'

'Brave,' Millie said. 'But how did you know we were at the beach?'

It was odd, Millie thought, that she hadn't thought to ask earlier. Of course, everything had been so bizarre that Frances's sudden appearance was but another item in a long list of the miraculously bizarre.

'I wanted to tell Sam about everything I knew about Jason being a wrecker. I wanted to convince him not to take any blame. At first, I was not brave enough, but then Flora let me take your gig.'

'I'm glad I left it for you. Gracious, I forgot about Jeremiah. Our donkey. No doubt someone will bring him home. He has a somewhat unpleasant personality, so no one would want to keep him. Did you go first to Sir Anthony's?'

'Yes, the butler said they were going to London, but that Sir Anthony always stopped at the tavern.'

Millie reached forward, clasping the other woman's cold hands. 'And you went?'

'The place was deserted. There was no maid or cook. The cows needed to be milked. And Sir Anthony's carriage was still there. I knew something was wrong.'

'But how did you know to come to the beach?'

Frances shrugged. 'I thought that Sir Anthony had taken Sam down to the village. Then, at the fork, I heard voices and saw the bent branches.'

'And you saved us all. Do not ever say you are not brave again,' Millie said.

'I hardly remember what I did.' Frances paused, glancing downwards, her fingers pressing nervously against the cushioning. 'And, Miss Lansdowne, thank you for stopping me from doing something terrible.'

'I only helped. You made the choice.'

'There is a fine line between sanity and madness.'

'You stayed on the side of sanity.'

Chapter Fourteen

Millie woke up the next morning to a thumping head-ache greatly aggravated by her mother's strident tones. 'Good heavens! What have you done to yourself? You are black and blue and dreadfully scratched.'

Millie pulled herself upright. It seemed almost unbe-lievable that she was back in her bedchamber, staring up at the same cracked paint with the same yellow circle of damp centred over her bed. It was as though nothing had happened or changed. But then, of course, really noth-ing had changed for her.

The wreckers had been stopped. Frances would heal and, eventually, escape her marriage. Sam knew he was not responsible for Jason's death. Indeed, Jason was not dead. Mrs Ludlow would head to prison or the madhouse.

Everything was neatly fixed and tidied, but ultimately unchanged in the Lansdowne household.

In fact, everything felt worse. The thought of marry-ing Mr Edmunds felt especially worse. Last night had shaken her. Seeing the pistol pointing at Sam…endur-ing the certainty that her own life was going to end be-fore it had begun.

Now, she could not even pretend to herself that Sam

did not evoke unwanted emotion. Indeed, meeting him had opened her eyes to feelings and emotions she had not known possible.

Yet this awakening had only made everything the more difficult.

Whatever bond they had was forged from danger and circumstance. He was just grateful to her. If he helped with Lord Harwood, she'd be grateful to him, too. However, their worlds did not overlap. He belonged in London, in fashionable London places and, when he did marry, he would have a witty, fashionable, beautiful wife, willing to embrace the aimless life of an English aristocrat.

And her aspirations had always been that of independence...

'Good gracious, you still look half-asleep and it will soon be afternoon.' Her mother pulled the curtains back with a noisy rattle so that sunlight invaded the chamber.

Millie groaned. 'Must you be so loud?'

How was it possible that her mother had only weeks ago found the strength to get out of bed, at all?

'Yes, I must be loud,' Mrs Lansdowne said. 'I am in considerable distress. Goodness knows where you were last night. Likely fishing, hunting rabbits or visiting your village friends. And you, just getting over a cold...'

'Never had a cold.' Millie muttered.

'It was gone eleven when I went to bed and you were still out. I do not know how I got a wink of sleep. I strongly suspect that Flora gave me a sleeping draught. Now I come up here and you look as though you have been in a boxing match. And what will Mr Edmunds say? I am certain he will come today. Of course, I could postpone. I could say that you are still afflicted or perhaps that I or Lil have caught a chill and you must nurse us. A tempting option, except he might well decide that our family is sickly. Likely he doesn't want to lose another wife, having just lost one.'

'Indeed, people might consider him careless.'

'Millicent Lansdowne, this is no laughing matter—'

Just then Flora knocked at the door, entering almost immediately, a piece of notepaper clasped in her hand and an expression of subdued excitement visible on her countenance.

'A note from Mr Edmunds,' she said.

Mrs Lansdowne took it, reading quickly. 'He is going to visit us this afternoon, if convenient. Is the footman waiting for a response?'

Flora nodded and Millie groaned, flopping back against her pillow, then wincing with the pain of this movement.

'We cannot postpone again,' Mrs Lansdowne said. 'But what will we say about all these cuts and bruises?'

'A nasty side effect of catching criminals?'

'Criminals! I do not want to mention criminals. Indeed, it is very ill bred to converse about criminals. I will invite him to tea. That will give us sufficient time to think of something. Flora, tell the footman to wait a few more minutes.'

Flora left.

'Now, Millie...' Mrs Lansdowne paused, pulling her eyebrows into a frown and seating herself on the chair beside the bed. 'You must stop scrambling about the countryside all hours. You are no longer a child. I'll let you rest for now and hopefully Mr Edmunds will propose today. Indeed, I do not know why you are not more excited. I thought you quite approved the idea?'

'That was before...' Millie paused, biting her lip.

Before she had fallen head over heels with exactly the wrong sort of man.

She pushed her hand through her hair. 'Mr Edmunds has not even proposed.'

'Which is why he wants to come for tea. Promise me you will not be foolish.'

'Are you wanting a lifetime commitment to that?'

Sam did not visit. Millie knew he was likely busy making a statement or dealing with other legalities, but still wished she could see him. At the same time, she knew a strong irritation that she should feel this sentiment combined with the notion that she would likely find any visit awkward and painful.

Nor was there time to visit Sally, although she told Flora she would do so as soon as tea with Mr Edmunds was finished. She did not want Sally to learn the details of last night through the inevitable rumour mill. Although the events of last night almost seemed impossible. With Frances still in bed, Millie almost wondered if she had dreamed the night previous. Being bound at gunpoint seemed such a far cry from a day listening to her mother's concerns about tea, Mr Edmunds and the lack of flowers for any type of arrangement.

'It is not yet February,' she told her mother, with limited sympathy. She knew that she should be happy that her mother was no longer listless in her bed and taking an interest in daily living, but she rather wished Mrs Lansdowne could be somewhat less voluble about it.

Disgruntled and grumpy, she returned to her bedroom shortly before luncheon, leaving her mother to dust their remaining furniture. She sat heavily on the bed, feeling both physically aching and emotionally drained.

A small part of her hoped that Mr Edmunds would

take one look at her and run for the hills. Certainly the reflection within the looking glass left her in little doubt that she appeared pale and fatigued. Still, she doubted it would make a difference. Mr Edmunds's interest in her was purely pragmatic and he was not harbouring any romantic feelings.

Lil tapped on the door, which was ajar, entering before Millie had even responded. She sat on the bed beside Millie, angling her body in a manner suggestive of shared confidences. She looked particularly good with flushed pink cheeks and blue eyes positively sparking with excitement.

'I have been talking to Frances.'

'You have? I have not seen her today. Marta said she was sleep—'

'Yes, yes, I woke her,' Lil said with some impatience. 'I needed to talk to her. And I felt it imperative to do so prior to Mr Edmunds's arrival.'

'Why? What has Mr Edmunds to do with this?'

'We do not have to stay with our aunt. We are going with Frances to London.' Lil made this announcement with all the drama of a magician producing the white rabbit from the proverbial hat.

'What? Frances doesn't live in London.'

'She is going to rent a house, but, for the moment, she will stay with some great-aunt, Lady Wilburn...no, Wyburn. Anyway, Frances says she is quite lovely although very old and odd. But she absolutely adores debuts and balls. She will sponsor us both and we will meet wonderful people and you will have no reason to marry Mr Edmunds or worry that Mother might pressure me to marry Lord Harwood.'

'But how will we possibly afford the dresses and such?'

'Well, we are in mourning so we cannot go out a lot, at first. Also Frances still lacks energy, but she said that she could easily get some dresses altered for me and possibly even for you.'

'I am a foot shorter and we cannot possibly descend on some poor elderly woman we do not even know. It is not sensible.'

'Frances wants us to come,' Lil said, with a certain obstinacy of tone. 'And sometimes I think you are too attached to being "sensible".'

Millie gave a wry laugh. 'If you knew… Anyway, Frances is vulnerable.'

'Frances knows that. She says she has to get away from here and that our company would be good for her.'

Millie paused, glancing towards the window and the sliver of sea visible in the distance. It would benefit Frances to leave Cornwall, she thought. It must be a constant reminder of her husband's cruelty and the madness that was Mrs Ludlow. Moreover, Lillian's company could prove helpful. She was young and had a joyful optimism. Providing adequate clothing might prove difficult, but marriage to Mr Edmunds would help.

'It is a good idea,' she said at length.

'See!' Lil clapped her hands with excitement, her cheeks flushing to a brighter hue.

'For you, but not for me,' Millie said hastily, placing a restraining hand on Lil's knee. 'I will marry Mr Edmunds. It will ensure that Mother has a place to live, enable me to help with your wardrobe and be in a better position to thwart Harwood.'

'But I want you to be with me. You do not need to marry Edmunds. Tom…' She paused and Millie saw the sheen of tears in her sister's eyes. 'Tom was wonderful, but he made mistakes. You do not have to make up for them. Or rescue me or Mother. Besides, I told Frances about owing Harwood money and she is quite certain that Mr Garrett or his solicitor can resolve the matter. And we won't see Lord Harwood in London as he is not received in polite society.'

'You seem to have chatted considerably with our guest.'

'Yes, I like her. She did not tell me much about what happened last night though, so you need not worry. Although she said you were brave.'

"She was the brave one." Millie stood and paced to the window.

'Mils, please, will you think about London?'

'What good will London do me? To marry somebody who I know even less than Mr Edmunds? At least this way I can stay in Cornwall.'

'Then do not go to London,' Lil snapped. 'Stay here. But do not marry Edmunds. You have kept this family going through Father's death and Tom's death and while Mother was ill. You have worked with solicitors. You have sold things. You have kept creditors at bay. I cannot believe that it is not possible for you to find another choice.'

Millie looked at her sister, her cheeks now red with emotion. 'I'll talk to Frances about you going. But I will marry Mr Edmunds. I want Mother to have a home.'

Lil pulled a face. 'Well, you cannot talk to Frances now. Marta shooed me away and is quite determined that she rest.'

Mr Edmunds was ushered in by Flora. As usual, he wore knee breeches of an antiquated style. It was also apparent that his girth had increased since the manufacture of his waistcoat as this garment was quite stretched, the buttons pulling over his midriff. Unfortunately, he had not yet abandoned his love for the moustache.

'How lovely to see you, dear Mr Edmunds,' Mrs Lansdowne said.

'Thank you, Mrs Lansdowne. I hope this is convenient. Miss Lansdowne. Miss Lillian.' He bowed in greeting to both young women. 'I am so grateful that you have recovered, Miss Lansdowne. Although I note some injuries. Did you have an accident?'

'I barely escaped with my life.'

'An altercation with a bramble. Nothing more,' her mother said.

'Pesky things, brambles,' Millie agreed.

'I have a particularly robust blackberry bush. Do you like blackberries, Miss Lansdowne? You may well enjoy picking them.'

'I look forward to such agrarian delights.'

That was the thing about Mr Edmunds, he was affable, quite nice really, if one were looking for an uncle or an occasional dinner companion. His children were pleasant and his house nice. He was not overly fond of spending money, but likely this was better than many alternatives.

Flora brought tea and Mrs Lansdowne busied herself pouring and serving. Millie took a cup, adding more sugar than was typical and stirring. She sipped the tea, hoping that the heat and sweetness would create a sense of reality.

Surely after last night, she should be given a day before making any life-altering decisions? Of course, the fact that she'd failed to confide in either her mother or sister rather undermined this argument. She hoped tea and the subsequent proposal would conclude quickly. She wanted to talk to Sally. Was it usual to hope for one's engagement to be expeditious, much as you might wish for the quick conclusion of a dull sermon? She hoped her mother would not become aware of any rumours about last night's events. Or, if this occurred, that Millie was either many miles away or able to block her ears.

Meanwhile, she continued to perform the correct rituals: smiling, talking, nodding, drinking and a myriad of other normal functions, even as her mind circled miles away from this room.

Marriage to Mr Edmunds had initially sounded sensible. But how could she now marry anyone when her mind was so filled with thoughts of Sam? His touch, his smile, lying close to him, talking to him…

'…there are actually several varieties, each of which has a different texture. Which is your favourite, Miss Lansdowne?'

'Pardon?' Good Lord, how could she marry the man when she couldn't even focus on him for two seconds together?

'Type of potato. There are more varieties than people realise.'

'Um…yes… I really hadn't thought.' Would she spend a lifetime learning about potatoes?

The tea dragged. If she had to accept Mr Edmunds's proposal, she wished the deed done. The conversation had moved from the potatoes but, unfortunately, was no more exciting. They were now discussing sheep breeds.

'I quite like the Cornwall Longwool myself. The wool is sturdy. Of course, the Suffolk sheep is excellent and, if I have sufficient funds, I might consider adding some to my flock,' Mr Edmunds explained.

Millie pictured the breakfast table each morning with Mr Edmunds in a too-tight waistcoat discussing potatoes and sheep while straining tea through is strands of his robust moustache.

At last, Mr Edmunds stood, his waistcoat straining with the movement. 'Thank you, Mrs Lansdowne, for a delicious tea,' he said, with another bow.

'We loved having you. So delightful. We live so very quietly, being in mourning for dear Tom and my late husband,' Mrs Lansdowne said.

'Of course, I am glad you let me join you. I wondered if Miss Lansdowne would care for a short stroll with me, seeing as the air is quite pleasant today.'

'Yes, absolutely. I am sure it. A lovely idea, isn't it, dear?' her mother said with palpable eagerness.

'Yes,' Millie replied. She felt like an actor in a bad play.

'Flora, could you get Miss Millicent's wrap?' her mother directed.

The wrap was procured. Millie pulled it about her shoulders, noting abstractedly that Flora had grabbed Lil's wrap by mistake.

Not that it mattered. She was now a bad actor, in a bad play, wearing someone else's costume.

While the weather was much improved in comparison to the heavy rains earlier in the week, it could not be described as warm. With a shiver, Millie pulled the wrap more tightly about her.

'Please do show me around the gardens,' Mr Edmunds said. 'I am so enjoying the air and the many delights of your enviable green thumb.'

Millie raised a brow as she surveyed the straggly grass, cracked sundial and flower beds, bare save for a few intrepid snow drops. 'The many delights are somewhat limited at this time of year. It was kept better when Father was alive.'

'So unfortunate. I myself have experienced loss.'

'Indeed.'

Was it good etiquette to bring up the loss of one's first wife while proposing to one's second?

And now she wanted to giggle, though she felt quite certain giggling during a proposal of marriage was not at all appropriate. And she should have worn boots. Her slippers were getting quite soaked and they could ill afford another pair. She really had not anticipated thinking about her wet feet, which were still sore with blisters, during a marriage proposal.

'Miss…um… Miss Lansdowne, I…um…have heard so many wonderful things about you. You are kind and wonderful with children and have a myriad of other accomplishments. Therefore…' Mr Edmunds paused, inhaling and then exhaling with several whooshes of breath, as though building the required stamina for an arduous task.

He took her hand. Even through the cloth of her glove his palms felt surprisingly warm and moist given the cool temperature. 'I have come to value you very greatly and enjoy our time together and am wondering whether you would do me the very, very great honour of becoming my wife.'

Millie swallowed. Her throat felt dry, her tongue cleaving to the roof of her mouth. She heard the thump of her pulse against her ears and felt her armpits prickle with perspiration despite the chill. She should say 'yes'. It was sensible on so many levels. And while Mr Edmunds lacked personality, intelligence or physique, he was unlikely to break his neck.

Except…

'No,' she said.

Mr Edmunds blinked as though taking a second to properly comprehend the word. Indeed, Millie also felt shocked surprise. Then, the disbelief dissipated, engulfed in a flood of pure elation, a feeling of sudden freedom, like when she rowed on the sea or ran across the moors.

She knew that this was the right decision. It was not even about Sam. It was about something more important. It was about her. It was about choice. One could not choose one's circumstances, but one could choose one's reaction to them.

'But your mother said…'

'You do not want to marry me,' she said bluntly.

'I do not?'

'No,' Millie said, removing her hand from his clasp. 'You want our land because it inconveniently splits your own.'

'Well, yes,' he concurred. 'But—'

'I cannot see that you would want a wife you do not even know. I cannot pretend to care about sheep or potatoes. You cannot pretend to care about me. Surely we can determine an alternate solution which would work better?'

He looked bemused, as though she was speaking a foreign tongue. Sweat beaded on his forehead. 'What did you have in mind?' he asked, his tone apprehensive.

'We sell you the land for a price sufficient to pay off our remaining debt, which is less than the land is worth. You allow my mother and I to remain at the house for the remainder of her lifespan or until she remarries. You would be responsible for the structural maintenance while she would look after its day-to-day operations.'

His jaw dropped slightly. 'Miss Lansdowne, I do not know what to say. You sound—you sound—'

'As though I am presenting you with an alternative and objectively better choice.'

'Just so. Except I am unsure if this agreement is in my

best interest. Purchase of your property would require considerable investment, whereas marriage…'

'One must provide for a wife. Besides, while you are a very nice man, I really do not want to marry you.'

Mr Edmunds frowned, inhaling so deeply that she quite feared for the strain on his buttons. 'I will need to think about this,' he said. 'Is your mother in agreement?'

Millie shrugged. 'I am uncertain, but it does not matter. It is not her story.'

Lil, Mrs Lansdowne and Flora descended on Millie the second she re-entered the house.

'Mr Edmunds has gone. I saw the gig roll away,' her mother said, waving a hand towards the window to emphasise her point.

'I commend your power of observation.'

'But I thought he would come in to share the glad tidings.' Mrs Lansdowne still looked through the window pane as if hoping for the gig's immediate return.

'He is going to see the solicitor,' Millie said.

'Solicitor? It would be better to speak to the rector and read the banns. Have you decided on a date? Of course, it will have to be quiet, given, well, the situation.'

'Mother, I am not getting married.'

Lil clapped her hands. 'I'm so glad.'

Flora produced the smelling salts from her pocket, giving the vial to Mrs Lansdowne.

'I told you to be sensible,' her mother said, inhaling deeply.

'I realised that "sensible" isn't synonymous with marriage. And…' she smiled at Lil '… I determined another choice.'

'But what?'

'I suggested that we sell the land to Mr Edmunds at a

good price, sufficient to pay off our creditors. He will let you live at the house. Lil has apparently already arranged her debut with our guest, Mrs Ludlow, and I will be a companion or governess or perhaps live with you here.'

'But—' Her mother paused, inhaling the smelling salts. 'But what of Lord Harwood?'

Millie glanced at her sister. This was still a worry and certainly she had not included the sum mentioned in the promissory note in her calculations.

'Mrs Ludlow and Mr Garrett will help me determine the best way to ensure that situation is resolved. We will consult a solicitor but I am determined Lillian will not marry him.'

'But you do not want to be a governess or a companion when you could have your own house. A single woman is not respected by society.'

'That much is true,' Millie said. 'Hopefully, society will change some time. Meanwhile, I suppose I must settle for my own respect.'

'I cannot stay at Manton Hall!' Frances spoke the second Sam entered the parlour of the Lansdowne residence.

It was now late afternoon. He had spent the entire day talking to Sir Anthony and writing out a statement and was impatient to see his sister.

However, she was not as well as he had hoped and he felt his apprehension grow as he observed her nervous movements. She stood by the window in the Lansdownes' parlour.

He stepped into the room. 'You do not have to go back to Manton.'

She jumped as though she had not been fully aware of him. She turned briefly to him and then back to the window pane, as if the grey world outside still drew her with a fatal fascination.

'It looks so harmless from here,' she said. 'A silvery streak.'

For a moment he was uncertain of her meaning, but then realised that she referred to the sea which was, indeed, but a streak of shimmering grey from this vantage point.

She took her hand away from the pane, turning abruptly. 'But I cannot stay here either. The sea is still too close. I can hear it, you know.'

He stood still, uncertain. She gripped the window sill so tightly it seemed as though he could feel the tension twisting through her, taut like a piano string wound too tight.

'One doesn't hear the sea from here. It is too far away,' he said.

'No.' She shook her head, the movement almost violent. 'I hear it and them—their voices.'

He felt that horrid feeling of being in quicksand and not knowing what to do or say. It reminded him of the hopeless shock he had experienced last night when she had raised the pistol to her husband's head.

'Frances,' he said gently. 'You do not need to stay here. Or ever go back to Manton Hall. We can go to London as soon as you would like. Your things can be packed and sent later.'

She turned back to the window. 'I had the dream again today. I'd hoped that the dream would stop after last night, but still it came. I saw them. All the men and women and children. Do you think there were children? I hate to think that there might have been children, babies like Noah.'

He had been a fool. He had hoped last night for a miracle cure. He'd hoped that she'd re-emerge as the sister he had once known who had sent letters to school and stopped him from a downward spiral of drinking after Annie broke off the engagement.

But this frail, frightened woman was not that person. He felt lost, uncertain.

'I keep thinking that I should have told someone. I made excuses. I told myself that I did not really know anything. You see, he did not always make sense and talked about it only while in his cups.' She spoke in a monotonous tone, still staring at the silvery streak that was the sea.

'Please, Frances, do not do this to yourself. No one will blame you. Likely they would not have believed you or acted without evidence.'

'But I should have tried! I should have tried.' She turned from the window, stepping towards him, her eyes wide, as though still haunted by her wild imaginings.

'You did. You told Millie and you saved us all. You stopped them. Jason and his mother will not hurt anyone again because of you. You were the hero last night.'

'I do not feel like a hero.'

'That doesn't change the fact that you are one.'

Gently, he stepped to her, placing his hand at her elbow and leading her away from the window to a chair by the hearth.

'Come, sit down.' He stirred it with the poker, more to do something useful than because there was a real need. The fire was already bright. He looked back. Frances sat, perched at the edge of the chair like a bird ready to take flight. He could still see the tension in her shoulders and clasped hands. He sat in the chair opposite. The house was quiet. Flora said that Mrs Lansdowne was resting while Millie and Lil had gone down to see Sally.

'What about London?' he asked. 'You could take Noah. You wouldn't have to go out or socialise if you did not want to do so. Aunt Tilly would love you to stay if you would prefer not to rent a house yourself. You have always said she was quite your favourite relative.'

Her expression eased a little at his words. 'I like Aunt Tilly. I was doing quite well this morning—before the dream. I spoke to Lillian. She would like to come with me to London.'

He felt a flicker of relief. Surely it was positive that she was thinking towards the future. 'That is wonderful,' he said. 'A great idea!' His relief imbued his tone with an over-abundance of enthusiasm.

'I'd hoped Millie would come as well.'

He tensed at the mention of her name and felt again that curious muddle of emotion the woman always invoked: a pulse of unwanted excitement, irritation, but above it all, relief.

His feelings for Millicent Lansdowne were a mush of contradiction, but he trusted her. There was a calm capability about her, a caring which was kind, but without melodrama. He knew without any doubt that Millie's presence in London would be good for his sister.

'I think that is an even better idea. They could both come.'

'She won't.'

'Why?'

'She wants Lil to go, but not her. Lil popped in just before my rest. Marta tried to scare her off, but she was quite impervious to any threat. Anyway, Lil said that she'd just spoken to her sister and Millie is determined to marry Mr Edmunds...'

Sam felt something akin to physical pain. It was as though he had been struck in his stomach. His hands tightened into fists.

'He has made an official offer?'

'He was expected to ask her today. I am uncertain if he did. I slept so much and I only arose now because Marta and Flora said I should. They are rather a powerful force in tandem.' She gave a slight smile.

'Where is Miss Lansdowne now?'

'Down at the village. Flora said that Millie wants to talk to her friends herself before they hear through village gossip. You know, about last night.'

She would, he thought. Millie would not shy from that conversation. She would know it would be better for Sally and the Aimsworths to learn it from her.

Frances turned her head towards the window, the oblique mention of the wrecking pulling her back to the sea and its horrors. Even now, she seemed to teeter on a knife's edge between the sane and the insane.

'I wonder what he looked like?' she said, still turned towards the window while her fingers worked nervously at the cloth of her gown.

'Who?'

'Sally's husband and the other men from the village. And how many there were?'

The memory of Jem's huge, lifeless body flickered before him. He remembered how his face was so oddly unmarked even while his bloodied brains spilled on to the rock. He thought about the old man with his toothless grimace and the rock pools red with blood.

'Frances, why do not you go to London tomorrow?' The need to move her away from this place grew heavy.

She turned back, shrugging. 'I do not know.' Her forehead puckered. Her fingers still twisted at the cloth. 'I feel scared and tired. What will I say to Aunt Tilly?'

'You'll hardly have to say a word; Aunt Tilly will do all the talking. You can take Marta. She can pack up enough for a few days. The journey will be long, but you can sleep. I will write to Aunt Tilly. Lillian can keep you company and I will talk to Millie.'

'You will?'

'Yes,' he said. 'There is no reason why she couldn't go up to London with you, even if she is engaged.'

'And Aunt Tilly would let us stay? She always amuses me.'

'She would love it and her house is large enough.'

'It feels such a huge undertaking.'

'It feels that way because you are still exhausted, but I will arrange everything.' He leaned forward, catching her hand. 'Fran, you will feel stronger away from here. I am sure of it.'

She gave a quick smile, almost reminiscent of the sister he once knew. 'Thank you.'

She rose, stepping to the door. 'I will check on Noah.'

'Fran?'

She turned.

'You saved me once. You helped me to stop drinking and racing Rotten Row. You said that you had lost a father and a mother and that you couldn't lose a brother.'

She nodded. 'I remember.'

'Please know, you aren't alone.'

Sam walked his sister to the stairs and watched as she ascended to the second floor, a thin, almost gaunt, figure. He turned away as she entered one of the doors on the upper landing and found himself face to face with Flora, omnipresent in the Lansdowne household.

'Would you know when Miss Lansdowne and Miss Lillian might return?' he asked. 'I wanted to pay my respects, if possible.'

'Respects? Is that what it's called? Hmmph. You have unsettled her, that's what.'

'The last few days have been somewhat unsettling all around,' he said.

'She should be back soon. You can wait in the parlour, if you must. But do not make noise, I just got Mrs Lansdowne settled. That upset she was.'

'Right,' he said. 'Thank you.'

He went back into the parlour and sat somewhat stiffly on the armchair. He wished there was something to occupy his mind and looked around for any reading material within the room, but found nothing.

Of course, he should not care if Miss Lansdowne was marrying Mr Edmunds or anyone else for that matter. Indeed, he did not care. During his time in society, he had seen any number of convenient marriages and most of them worked out admirably. Love was fickle. If he'd had his way, he'd be married to Annie Whistler. Indeed, he'd been quite certain that he was deeply in love with her. Now he found her vapid in the extreme. In time, he'd realised that he'd merely been attracted to blonde curls, blue eyes and a figure that was bounteous and buxom. Plus everyone was in love with her. She was the incomparable among the *ton*.

He knew now that his feelings for Miss Whistler had never been love. He hadn't even known her. His father had died almost as soon as he'd left school and the grief he'd felt was not just for the austere man he'd wanted to love but also for the relationship that hadn't been.

The social rituals of his class had lacked meaning and he'd found his life empty. Miss Whistler had been a panacea. He'd immersed himself in loving her. It gave meaning to his life. When she'd broken the engagement, he'd been lost, drowning his troubles in too much drink.

But his life had a different meaning now. He belonged to the Philanthropic Society and was working to develop schools and apprenticeships, which sounded boring, but he found it exciting. There was opera and friendships and horse riding. With Millie, it would not be about forgetting. Millie made him more. He felt more and laughed more.

'You wanted to speak with me?'

He jumped as Millicent Lansdowne herself entered the room. Her step was brisk and her cheeks still flushed from the outside air. She'd pulled her hair into a bun, but it was already messy, falling down in tangles about her face.

Just above her collar, he saw the cut from the night previous, a tiny pinprick of a scratch. It was small, a flesh wound, yet it reminded him of what could have been. The memory took the words from him, squeezing at his vitals.

'Is it healing?' he asked.

She touched the cut. 'It is the merest scratch.'

'And you? Not too many aches and pains?' She sat beside the fire, waving a hand to invite him to sit in the chair opposite.

'I am fine,' he said, sitting. 'You were able to see your friend Mrs Strand? That must have been a hard conversation.'

She lifted her gaze to him, huge limpid eyes big with sorrow. 'Yes, but I am glad I was able to tell her myself.'

'I will make sure she gets some money and more books. It must be hard for her with two children. There isn't a school?'

Millie shook her head. 'The vicar tries.'

'I have an interest in schooling.'

'You do?' She looked surprised.

'Yes, I work with a society in London, although their focus is more on helping poor people with apprentice-ships. Not a lot of Greek and Latin.'

'You would like to teach children Greek and Latin?' Millie wrinkled her brow, as though slightly sceptical.

'Diogenes said that the "foundation of every state is the education of its youth" and I am quite certain he did not mean just the youth who go to schools like Harrow. Diogenes was an odd individual. He slept in a jar some-times, but he was right about that.'

Millie gave that warm, wonderful laugh. 'A jar?'

'Yes, it was ceramic, "a pithos".'

'That makes it better?'

He laughed as well and then there was that moment of silence, where the camaraderie became suddenly awk-ward. 'I wanted to let you know that I sent a note to my man of business to talk to Harwood. I will let you know what he learns.'

'Thank you.'

'I…the reason I wanted to talk to you is to ask—will you come to London?' he blurted.

'What?' She startled, her expressive eyebrows rising.

'I need you to come to London. Frances needs you.'

'Lillian will go up with her. And you have a relative, an aunt.'

He stood, pacing in front of the fireplace. 'Your sister

is wonderful and I am happy she will go to London and, yes, Lady Wyburn is lively and eccentric.' He stopped, going to the window and looking out towards the grey of the ocean. 'But Fran needs you. *I* need you.'

Sam threw himself heavily into the chair opposite, leaning towards her. His gaze was intense. The firelight made his eyes darker, highlighting the shadows of fatigue juxtaposed to the lean strength of his jaw. *He needed her.* She felt a pulse of something close to exaltation.

'You cannot marry Edmunds. There must be another option. Indeed, I am certain my great-aunt could figure something out,' he said.

She stiffened. The exaltation turned to lead, anger tightening her belly. 'By "something", I take it you mean that she might introduce me to a more suitable husband?' she said.

He shifted, looking uncomfortable. 'Well, yes, something like that.'

'Then you will be glad to know that this is not necessary. I am not marrying Mr Edmunds.'

'You're not?'

'No,' she said. 'He is buying our land and Mother can stay in the house. I decided that if I could survive this last week, I could find an alternate solution to marriage to Mr Edmunds. Indeed, I aim to find an alternate solution to marriage to anyone. Therefore, I do not need to be introduced to some suitable London gentleman. It is totally unnecessary. Besides, I do not like London.'

'You wouldn't have to live there. You make it sound as though I want you to go into purgatory,' he said.

'Not purgatory, just a location with no great appeal. I do not want or need you to save me from my life.'

'I am not trying to save you from your life,' he said, his voice rising.

'No?'

'I am trying to save Frances from her nightmares.'

She looked at him and again noted the shadows under his eyes and the heaviness in his lids. It was clear he had not slept properly. She thought of her love for Lil and how she had tried to save Tom.

'Lillian said Frances was doing better. I thought last night was a turning point for her?' she asked more gently.

He shook his head. 'She had a dream this afternoon. She thinks too much about the victims. She blames herself. She hears them. I need to get her away from here.'

'Yes,' Millie said. 'I agree and Lillian will be a good companion. She has a natural enthusiasm, an ebullience. She will be as good as, if not better than, me.'

'Fran trusts you. You make her feel safe. Come up for a couple of weeks.'

Millie felt a mix of emotions. She looked towards the sea. It was not the smells or crowds of London that bothered her—although she found neither pleasant—it was that feeling of discomfort. She never knew what to say. London felt like an unknown land filled with people alien to her.

And then there was this man. She glanced at him. It almost hurt to look at his broad shoulders, perfectly outlined in his impeccable jacket, with that dark lock of hair falling forward, the one she always wanted to smooth back.

They lived worlds apart with little in common. To spend more time with him would prolong the inevitable pain she would experience when they parted.

He shifted forward in his chair, pushing back the lock of his hair. 'I have let her down twice already. I should have come sooner. I should have known something was wrong. You heard last night how Mrs Ludlow thought I was a drunk who did not care.'

'She was wrong and mad.'

'I cannot let her down again,' he said.

Millie inhaled. 'Fine. I will go. To London. For Frances. But no soirées and limited chit-chat.'

'All chit-chat will be kept to the bare minimum. And, thank you.'

Chapter Fifteen

Frances, Millie, Lil, Noah, Marta and the nursemaid were conveyed in two travelling coaches and arrived in London just before teatime five days later. Sam remained in Cornwall to supervise issues regarding Manton Hall. Mrs Lansdowne had also remained, with considerable reluctance, as she needed to make final arrangements with Mr Edmunds regarding the house. Flora stayed also, ostensibly to help Mrs Lansdowne, although she saw herself in a supervisory capacity. Millie was thankful for Flora. Her mother was much improved, but Millie still worried she might again take to her bed as she had in the days following Tom's death.

The time prior to their departure had been hectic. Millie had spoken to Sir Anthony and had written several statements. Frances had done so also and found the experience so distressing that Millie again worried for her health.

Jason Ludlow's return to life had created a vast variety of rumours and curiosity which was both irritating and exhausting. Therefore, despite her love of Cornwall, Millie had felt relief when the travelling coaches pulled away and, even more so, when the cumbersome vehicles had neared London.

Lil was the most excited of the company, pressing her face against the pane, much like a child. Indeed, it amused Millie to see the façade of the sophisticated woman slip, if only for a moment. Lil had little recollection of London and had made up for this with all manner of fanciful ideas, gleaned from Mother's descriptions and a variety of women's journals.

Millie was glad for her happy ebullience. It was contagious and she noted Frances smiling several times. For herself, Millie peered at London's congested, cobbled streets with interest, but found it held little appeal. The houses were very close and the sour smell of garbage and sewage was detectable even within the carriage. The streets were so crowded with people, conveyances and stray dogs that she was surprised there were not more accidents and she longed for wide open spaces. On occasions, she would catch quick glimpses of the Thames's slow-moving, muddy waters.

She wrinkled her nose.

'It is better at my aunt's house,' Frances said.

This proved accurate. Eventually, the carriage left the crowded dirtiness and the streets widened, the houses becoming larger and more prestigious. Millie noted several green parks and nannies walking children or pushing huge perambulators.

At last they pulled up in front of an impressive building of several floors with a black-lacquered door. Millie smoothed her serviceable black dress, stretching her stiff limbs as she prepared, somewhat nervously, to exit the carriage. The air smelled fresher here, although still slightly tainted with the city's smell. The weather had changed again and, while not actively raining, rivulets of dirty water wound through the gutters.

She approached the front entrance with little enthusiasm and that familiar feeling of not quite belonging.

The door was opened almost immediately by a stooped and elderly butler. This individual ushered Frances, Millie and Lil into a spacious front hall and, after relieving them of their travelling cloaks, led them into an elegant salon. Meanwhile, the servants set about unloading the carriage while the nursemaid was led upstairs to ensure Noah's comfort.

Lady Wyburn's home was not huge, but everything about it spoke of wealth, comfort and an understated elegance. A fire flickered invitingly from within a marble fireplace, gold trim glittered about the ceiling, long mirrors lined the walls and a red Indian carpet dominated the room's centre.

'Do not worry,' Frances said, catching Millie's expression. 'My aunt isn't anything like her house.'

Millie smiled but was sceptical. While she did not have a vast acquaintance with the aristocracy, she was quite certain they would not appreciate a travel-stained slip of a girl with a dress several years out of fashion and made of a rather cheap cloth in the first place.

Frances was correct in one thing: her aunt was not anything like the house. Indeed, Millie later concluded that Lady Wyburn defied description. She bustled into the salon moments after their arrival wearing a gown of a deep burgundy shade and, despite her obvious age, moved fluidly and with surprising energy. Indeed, she brought with her an eager, almost girlish enthusiasm, her face wreathed in smiles, while a profusion of grey ringlets peaked out from under her bonnet.

'I am so very happy that you have come to visit,' she

said, pressing a kiss to Frances's cheek while greeting both Millie and Lil with genuine enthusiasm. 'We live rather a boring life. Indeed, I am always in search of diversion and poor Merryweather is not a great conversationalist. He is greatly hampered by the fact that he is almost entirely deaf.'

Millie glanced in the direction of the butler, but his face remained impassive.

'Now, first things first,' Lady Wyburn continued. 'Should we have tea now or would you like to freshen up first?'

'I would just like to ensure that Noah is comfortable,' Frances said immediately, her forehead already wrinkled, and Millie noted a nervous jumpiness about her.

'An excellent idea, although I usually find infants travel remarkable well. I think it is because of their size. Lying comfortably in a bassinet seems so much better than bouncing on a seat.' She paused, looking towards the butler and adding in strident tones, 'Merryweather, we will have tea in half an hour.'

'Thank you, that would be lovely,' Millie said as Merryweather departed.

'I am glad we decided to delay tea,' Lady Wyburn confided as she led them through the front hallway. 'It will take Merryweather at least half an hour to even order tea as he suffers from the most dreadful arthritis, but he insists on working and one doesn't want to hurt his feelings. Anyway, it will provide me with ample time to show you to your rooms so that you can get settled.'

Lady Wyburn led them upstairs while still talking, her grey ringlets bobbing every now and again for emphasis.

'Now your bedchamber, Frances dear, is attached to the nursery, which may be unusual but quite convenient. I made up beds for the maid as well. I always feel that the nursery is quite the best place in the whole house and nursery teas are so much nicer than the things one has to eat as an adult.'

They left Frances with Noah and the nursemaid, and Lady Wyburn led Lil and Millie to two adjoining bed-chambers which shared a very comfortable sitting area. 'I hope you will have everything you need but, if not, we will purchase it. I always enjoy shopping and find a spree so uplifting if I am in the least bit despondent. I do hope someone will come with me; the only thing better than shopping alone is to shop with a companion. In fact, I have been experiencing the strong feeling that I am greatly in need of a new bonnet.'

'I would love to come,' Lil said with enthusiasm.

'And we could organise a soirée or tea party. Do you enjoy such events?'

'I do,' Lil said.

Millie nodded somewhat vaguely as Lady Wyburn seemed so kind that she hated to discourage her. Besides, maybe Lady Wyburn's friends might be pleasant. She had to admit that, while somewhat eccentric, Sam and Frances's great-aunt gave one the feeling of belonging and as though one's elbows, knees and feet were, in fact, the correct number.

Lil and Lady Wyburn had kept themselves happily occupied shopping during the first week while Millie diligently did everything she could to avoid shopping. Fortunately, Frances helped with this as they often had tea in the nursery or went for walks with Noah in the park nearby.

Physically, Frances was improving. She did not look so pale and her face had lost that pinched look. She still did not speak much and sometimes had a faraway look, worry and fear visible in her expression. Millie did not pry at these moments, when Frances seemed absorbed and distanced from the world. Sometimes she would distract with an amusing anecdote, but often she remained silent, allowing Frances the time and space for contemplation.

Towards the end of the second week, Sam wrote, announcing that he had finished in Cornwall and would soon be returning to London.

Millie had found that Sam's absence had filled her both with relief and irrational disappointment. This mix of sentiments had irritated her. As well, she noted she had an unfortunate, and equally irritating, habit of dropping things whenever his name was mentioned.

Sam's arrival in London was announced when Merryweather came in with a note laid on a silver platter.

Lady Wyburn took it, scanning the words quickly and smiling in great delight. 'He will see us tomorrow.'

'Who will see us tomorrow?' Lil questioned.

'Dear Sam.'

Millie promptly dropped her butter knife.

'I'll get it,' she hastily said, as Merryweather shuffled in her direction. She was uncertain if, having bent to the floor, he would ever straighten.

'He has to spend the entire day with solicitors, which I'm sure he finds dreadfully dull. Really, solicitors and magistrates should come with some sort of a warning.'

'A warning?' Millie asked.

'Indeed, that prolonged contact is likely to make one dyspeptic. Or perhaps it is the occupation. I have always noted that my solicitor looks decidedly dyspeptic whenever I am talking to him.'

'But Sam *is* going to visit us?' Frances prompted.

'Indeed, although I personally prefer entertainment with less caterwauling,' Lady Wyburn continued.

'Pardon?'

'Sorry, I forgot to mention, the dear boy has invited us to the opera. He loves it, you know, but I find there is too much singing.'

'Singing is rather an integral part of opera,' Millie said.

'Indeed, and I will go, of course, because caterwauling is more entertaining than staying at home. I will invite the dear boy to dine here and then we will proceed to the opera. That way we can have a decent conversation before the caterwauling starts.'

'It will be lovely for us all to spend some more time with him in a less crowded and more intimate environment,' Lil said and Millie promptly dropped her butter knife again.

The following day seemed to involve nothing but preparations for the dinner and the opera. Lil was quite beside herself with enthusiasm because she had never attended any theatrical production in London and Lady Wyburn was also in a high statement of excitement because it was her nature. Meanwhile, Millie's emotions had all the stability of an ill-made weather vane and Frances determined that while she would enjoy the dinner, she did not wish to attend the opera.

'I still do not like leaving Noah during the evening which is foolish, I know. And I also worry that there may be gossip.'

'Lady Wyburn is quite certain that someone will have done something more scandalous and no one will have any interest in us,' Millie said. 'Although a restful evening at home would be pleasant.'

'Stay home? Good gracious, you sound like an antiquity. Do you think the Prince Regent will be there?' Lil asked.

The three women were sitting in Noah's spacious nursery. It was a bright room with a huge, cheerful fire, high ceilings and soft, comfortable chairs. Indeed, Millie felt it was quite the best room the house.

'Antiquity or not, I am quite certain I would also prefer to stay home,' Millie said, leaning back and putting her feet up on a footstool.

'You should go to the opera,' Frances urged. 'Please do not stay home on my account.'

Millie pulled a face. 'It sounds a bit too much like a soirée.'

'Sam has a box, so you won't have to talk to anyone but him, if you do not want.'

Millie felt a sudden flush in her cheeks. The thought of only talking to Sam was not quite the balm on her nerves that Frances intended.

'Well, I'll…um…think about it.'

'But at least let me dress you for dinner?' Frances said, leaning forward with sudden eagerness and enthusiasm which was lovely to see, but also somewhat disconcerting.

'I have been managing fine for the last week. I have not been running around in a state of dishabille,' Millie said.

'But we have a surprise.' Frances looked at Lil. 'Should we tell her?'

'Yes.'

Millie removed her feet from the footstool. 'Now I am truly suspicious. What have you done?'

'Come up to Lil's bedchamber. We have been conspiring,' Frances said.

* * *

Lil's bedchamber appeared to have been struck by an explosion of boxes. They were strewn across every flat surface: floor, bed, chair and night table. Each one appeared open, their contents overflowing in a mess of lace, ribbons and silk.

Millie stepped carefully over the debris, sitting gingerly on the corner of Lil's bed while Frances went to a box. Picking it up, she placed it on the bed beside Millie, carefully removing the lid. With equal care, she lifted up a dress and draped it over her arm in a spill of soft lavender silk.

'It's beautiful,' Millie said.

'It's for you.'

'But—'

'We took one of your gowns and asked the seamstress to make it up. I also got a dress for Lil.'

'You shouldn't. We do not have the money,' Millie said.

Frances laid down the dress, reaching for Millie's hand and holding it tightly in her own. 'Please—it gave me such joy to pick it out and you have helped me so much. I am so glad and grateful you are here. Please, please let me give this to you.'

Millie turned towards the dress and with careful, almost reverent, movements, touched the gossamer silk. Frances's eagerness was so warm and genuine, it seemed unkind to refuse.

'It is beautiful. I have never had anything half as lovely.' A lump formed in her throat and tears prickled in her eyes. It seemed impossible that such a dress could be for her.

'And it's even suitable for mourning. You'll wear it tonight?'

A dress would not magically change her, Millie reminded herself. It would not make her elegant, witty, or in charge of her feet and arms and elbows.

'Yes,' Millie said, with a tiny shiver of excitement.

This, naturally, encouraged both Lil and Frances to suggest that they spend some extra time on Millie's hair. Again, Millie would normally have prevented such fuss and excitement about her appearance, except she could see Frances's eagerness. Indeed, it was Frances who arranged with Lady Wyburn to lend her maid, Heloise, to them.

'I have heard that she is masterful with tongs,' she explained.

Lady Wyburn had been more than happy to lend Heloise and by the middle of the afternoon the diminutive French maid had arrived, complete with scissors, curling tongs, ribbons, combs and all manner of other items.

'I generally do not much suit frippery or ringlets,' Millie told her with some apprehension.

'*Moi*, Heloise, I wouldn't do that to you,' the maid assured her. She was as short as Millie, her speech characterised by a French accent, the strength of which varied considerably. 'However, I do think a fringe would be beneficial.'

Millie eyed the scissors with some apprehension. 'A fringe? You are certain?'

'*Absolument.* One can have too much forehead. I will add some curls.'

'Curls? That is more something that Lillian would have.'

'*Mademoiselle*, you need curls. Beauty is about contrasts. Too many curls with blonde hair and blue eyes is *de trop*. But curls with those severe eyebrows—perfection.'

'I doubt anyone's called my eyebrows perfection before,' Millie muttered.

'That is because the brows with the forehead is too much, *mademoiselle*.'

'They are somewhat hard to separate.'

'Which is why we will have curls, *mademoiselle*,' Heloise said firmly, as though explaining the issue to a wayward child.

Heloise worked diligently. She cut a delicate fringe across Millie's forehead, creating a few loose curls while scooping the remainder of her hair into a low bun. Occasionally, Frances or Lil would come in, providing assistance and encouragement.

'Now we will be putting on the dress and we will be seeing how very, very beautiful you are,' Heloise announced, drawing out the syllables.

Millie questioned this. She doubted very much that she looked even close to beautiful. Indeed, she only hoped she did not look too odd.

'Do not be grimacing until you have the opportunity to look at yourself,' Heloise said, tutting irritably.

'I was only thinking that I have never aspired to beauty. Just to blend in and avoid attention.'

Heloise shook her head. 'The key, *mademoiselle*, is not to blend in. It is about confidence. It is about knowing your value, *oui*? Now we will dress you in your gown. And then you will see a miracle.'

Millie acquiesced, although she somewhat thought it might take something of biblical proportions to provide the transformation the woman seemed to anticipate.

The dress was a shimmering waterfall of a gown. It was in the newest style and had a low neck and no corset, the cloth cascading to the floor in loose folds. Heloise walked around her, adjusting the odd curl or ruffle as she went.

'It is not bad,' she said, at last, with a sniff, stepping back with a satisfied expression.

Frances and Lillie were more exuberant with their praise.

'You're beautiful, Millie.' Frances said with such a happy smile that Millie did not care if she looked like a primped China doll. 'Look.'

Millie stepped in front of the floor-length looking glass. The reflection gazing back at her was quite different from anything she had anticipated. She appeared fashionable and…almost attractive. Soft curls covered her high forehead, making her face less angular. Delicately curled tendrils furthered this effect, framing her cheeks. Her eyes had always been big, but now they sparkled with excitement, their colour enhanced by the lavender gown.

Almost shyly, Millie stared into the glass. The improvement was amazing, indeed almost miraculous.

'Is this quite decent?' Her hand touched her throat. 'The neckline seems quite low.'

'The style is everywhere in London,' Lil assured her. 'Have you been under a mushroom this last week?'

'I go out as infrequently as possible,' Millie said, wryly. 'But I do look nice.'

'What did you expect, you goose?' Frances said, giving her a hug. 'Besides, you always look nice. We have merely made it more noticeable.'

'You will do,' Heloise announced when she saw the women dressed for the evening. 'Almost you are a credit to me. Now, I trust you will not get yourself untidy?'

She directed this question to Millie, pulling her brows together formidably.

'I promise I will do nothing worse than read.'

'Good, at least you are not like Viscountess Wyburn, who invents things.' She gave a sorrowful shake of her head before leaving.

'Invents things?' Millie asked.

'Yes, one of Aunt Tilly's former protégées,' Frances explained. 'She likes to invent things like butter churns. She married Aunt Tilly's stepson. You will like her.'

Millie looked somewhat sceptical.

'You do not believe me?' Frances asked.

'My mother made me come to London when I was younger. I went to these dreadful tea parties with other girls my own age and everyone talked about shopping, fashion or gossip. I find it hard to believe that I would have anything in common with a viscountess.'

'You will like Rilla. Besides, one's early adolescence is never the best time for anyone. Perhaps you should stop judging us all by those tea parties,' Frances said.

'I—' For a moment Millie was going to argue, but then shrugged, laughing. 'Perhaps you are right.'

Sam stood within the entrance hall. Millie jerked to an abrupt stop at the top of the stairs, her hand tightening on the banister and her heart thumping. He looked every inch the Corinthian. He was immaculate, handsome and fashionable, but not in a foppish way. Instead, his clothes merely enhanced his physique, his broad shoulders and long limbs. His dark hair, chiselled nose and jaw gave him the look of a classical statue, making her ache somewhere beneath her breastbone.

Merryweather had taken Sam's outer coat and, for a moment, she had the luxury of observing him without being observed. Then, the moment was gone, as he glanced upwards. Heat surged into her cheeks. For a second, she thought she detected a reaction, a flicker in his gaze as he took in her hair and gown. However, he merely nodded politely in greeting and she discerned no other change in his expression.

She felt a flicker of disappointment, foolish in the extreme. What had she expected—that he would be entranced by a new hairdo and pretty dress? This was his world: a world of debutantes, dances and high fashion. Heloise had made a remarkable improvement, but she could not transform a Cornish waif into a London beauty. Besides, Millie had never aspired to the latter.

Indeed, this entire London trip was to help Frances and pave the way for Lil's successful debut. Millie's own goal was that of independence.

'Miss Lansdowne, you look well,' Sam said as she reached the bottom stair.

'Thank you, you as well.' So much for originality, wit and the avoidance of dull chit-chat.

'Lady Wyburn asked me to show you into the salon,' Merryweather interjected. 'Dinner will be served shortly.'

'Thank you, Merryweather.' Sam offered Millie his arm and she placed her gloved hand on it, conscious of a nervous tremble.

They walked into the salon with its understated elegance. This man in these impeccable clothes seemed quite different from the half-drowned man she had rescued or even the casual gentleman of Cornwall. He belonged here, whereas she was an imposter, dressed in costume and suitably tongue-tied.

'First and most importantly, my man of business spoke to Harwood. Or his solicitor. His health has declined. His

offer of marriage to your sister was real, as he would like
a legitimate heir, however, the promissory note is a forgery and need concern you no longer.'

'Truly?' Millie said, the sudden surge of relief making
her clutch more tightly on his muscled forearm.

'I promised to help.' He glanced down at her and she
felt a rush of embarrassment that she was clutching at
him like an ill-mannered school girl.

'Thank you, indeed, I am grateful for Lillian and myself. It makes my goal of independence the more possible.'

'I am glad I could help.'

There was an awkward pause.

She was glad when he broke it. 'I paid my respects to
your mother before I left and she is well. She sends her
best wishes,' he said.

'I am relieved she is still well. It is strange how one
can worry about someone without even realising one is
worrying. I am glad my mother is still better. Frances is
also much improved. We go for walks frequently.'

'Thank you.' He smiled with that captivating dimple,
which seemed to melt her into a mush of emotion.

This made her again speechless while also causing
her to remember the touch of his lips, the eager movement of his hands pushing down her chemise, touching
her thighs, pulling her close to him.

'Truly, I mean it,' he said, his words jolting her back,
and she felt her cheeks redden, as though he might be
able to read her thoughts.

'It has been nice to see her getting better,' she said,
clinging to this safer topic. 'She hasn't been talking about
her dreams and is taking more of an interest in every-
day events.'

His lips lifted in that familiar half-smile and she found

that the topic no longer felt safe. In fact, as she looked into his dark grey-green eyes, she could no longer remember the topic and was conscious only of the warmth which seemed to emanate from her core.

'Frances wrote that you have helped her so much. I do appreciate it. You have a strength, a sturdiness of character.'

His words made her feel oddly flat and heavy.

'Thank you,' she said stiffly.

Sturdiness? She could not think of a single one of Lil's books which spoke of a 'sturdy' heroine.

'She wrote that she did not want to come tonight, but you will come? To the opera?'

He looked at her with those earnest eyes, as though it was important to him that she come.

And now her inners felt mushy. Gracious, she was a veritable collection of contradictions; hot, flat, mushy. Not to forget sturdy.

She must not, she reminded herself, read too much into his invitation. He was grateful for her help with his sister and wanted to ensure she had a pleasant time in London. It was the sort of thing that Lady Wyburn might do if any country cousins came to town. Kind, but nothing more.

She shook her head. 'No.'

The ludicrous truth was that against all sense, all reason, she liked…cared for…was intrigued by…loved the man. It seemed that, despite her stern lectures, a foolish, unsupervised part of her had been building fanciful castles in the air. Going to the opera, sitting in his box, wearing a fancy dress that she could never afford was a pretence. And the longer she played along with this ludicrous pretence, the more she would be hurt when it inevitably ended.

For a moment she thought he looked disappointed.

'But thank you for inviting me,' she added, realising that she had been ungracious. 'My sister and Lady Wyburn will attend.'

'But not you?'

'It might be too much like soirée.'

He laughed. 'I smile more around you.'

Great—sturdy with comedic abilities.

'And there I thought it was my lack of chit-chat,' she said, perhaps the first spontaneous thing she had said since she'd encountered him at the bottom of Lady Wyburn's stairs.

He grinned back. 'I am grateful that we have thus far avoided an analysis of the weather.'

'And sheep,' she added. 'Very overrated, although the British seem somewhat obsessed with the subject. The weather, not sheep.'

'I recall one young lady attempted to amuse me with a lively discussion of puddles.'

'Puddles? As in rain puddles?'

'Yes, she liked to paint them,' he said, straight-faced but with a twinkle.

'Art can be interesting.'

'Indeed, but not for an entire dinner involving several courses.'

Millie laughed, a rich spontaneous sound. He had missed her. He hadn't realised how much until he'd seen her standing at the stairs. Actually, seeing her there had been revealing, disorienting, confusing. The woman defied categorisation—one moment she was a rebel smuggler, the next a pragmatic competent young woman and now...a beauty. The lavender dress shimmered with her every move. The low neck emphasised the creamy expanse of skin while the loose folds draped down with diaphanous elegance.

She was not pretty, that would be too insipid. Nor was she beautiful. Her face was not cast in classic lines. No, she was striking, inspiring, unique. It was hard to connect this glamorous woman with either the scruffy smuggler or country gentlewoman and yet this enhanced her allure. His every sensation seemed heightened, as though he had been sleepwalking through life and was now awake. This feeling was both discomforting and exciting.

Just then Lady Wyburn swept into the salon, followed by Merryweather, more bowed than ever.

'Dear boy, it is so lovely to see you,' Lady Wyburn said, smiling so that her cheeks bunched up like round, ripe apples. She paused, studying him with apparent concern. 'I do hope that you are eating your vegetables, dear.'

'Pardon?'

'You are looking contemplative and I find thinking leads to irritation. I avoid it when possible which helps me to remain remarkably sanguine. I always tell my solicitor, Mr Begby, that he should eat additional vegetables when he gets a dyspeptic countenance. Likely you have had to spend too much time with your solicitor today. In general, I find spending time with solicitors quite disturbing to my peace of mind.'

'Indeed,' Sam said with some confusion. His great-aunt was his very favourite relative, but following her convoluted thought processes could be challenging.

Merryweather served them drinks and then shuffled away.

'I hope he has some help serving dinner,' Sam said, eyeing the butler's retreating form.

'I have a couple of younger footmen,' Lady Wyburn

said. 'Otherwise, I fear we would never be fed and then Cook would be dreadfully angry. However, I wanted to talk to you about Frances.'

He stiffened. 'I have heard she is doing better.'

'Absolutely, she is much improved. I just wanted to let you know that if there is gossip or anything unpleasant, I could take her away from London. I assured her that she need not worry, someone is always doing something dreadful in London but, well, I wouldn't want her to be hurt by gossip.'

'Thank you, that is appreciated,' he said. 'Jason and Mrs Ludlow are pleading guilty so at least there won't be the publicity of a trial. I was at my club and I did not hear much except an inaccurate rumour that Jason and Mrs Ludlow had been involved in treasonous activity with the French.'

'I do think treason is much better than murder and will likely generate considerably less gossip,' Lady Wyburn said with apparent approval. 'However, we are not at war with the French any more. Is it possible to be treasonous when one is not at war?'

'I am not an expert on such matters, but believe it is possible,' he said, with a wry smile. 'However, there will still be some unpleasantness so London may not be the best place when the rumour mill really gets going.'

'Bath.'

'Pardon?'

'Bath is always good because everyone is ancient, deaf and about twenty years behind the times. I would be happy to take her to Bath. One always needs the waters at my age. Or we could go to Wyburn. Although I would like to stay here at least long enough to launch dear Miss Lansdowne and her sister.'

'I am not being launched,' Millie said, hurriedly.

'Nonsense, you will spoil all my fun. I love organising a debut and I know that you will both be so very successful. Indeed, I am quite positive you will be flooded with offers. There is always something alluring about a female who doesn't recognise her full allure.'

'You do not understand. Truly, I am not interested in marriage.'

'That is very unusual.'

'Did you not know, Aunt Tilly? Miss Lansdowne is somewhat unusual.'

'So, what do you aspire to?'

'I thought I would be an independent spinster in Cornwall.'

'In other words, you would likely live with your mother or be a governess. Sadly, unless a female has wealth, independence is limited and usually results in kowtowing as a governess or companion.'

'What would you have me do?'

'I have no idea.' Lady Wyburn beamed. 'Fortunately, that is your decision. But, talking of independence, I hope we will be able to ensure Frances's freedom from that dreadful Jason Ludlow.'

'I am working on that,' Sam said.

'I suggest a poisoned hatpin.' His great-aunt made this announcement with an enthusiastic nod.

'Pardon?'

'I always fancied poisoning someone with a hatpin,' she added with another bob of her grey ringlets.

'Much as I hate to curtail such heady aspirations I really must put a damper on that idea,' Sam said.

'My great-nephew is absolutely no fun,' Lady Wyburn announced. 'I will just go and make sure Merryweather hasn't collapsed or bent down and got stuck.'

With these words, she stood and with a brisk fluidity which belied her years, moved swiftly from the room, leaving only the sound of the hurried 'tap-tap-tap' of her heels on the hardwood.

The chamber felt quiet without her vibrant energy and Sam was aware of their solitude. He looked across to Millie.

'I wish you would reconsider the opera.'

'Why?' she asked in that blunt way of hers, with her firm brows contracted.

He paused, trying to find the right words. He knew that they had no future. He had found the one woman in England determined not to marry. But they had shared so much. He had learned so much, about himself, the world...

'I'd like to share the beauty of opera with you. I think it is for me like the moors are for you,' he said, surprised by his own words and his own honesty.

The room felt very silent. It seemed for a moment as though it was just the two of them, as it had been at the peat-cutter's hut. 'You shared with me the magic of the moors. Let me share this. It is also magic,' he said softly.

'I'll go to the opera,' she said.

The opera house was full. Lady Wyburn and Lil stopped and chatted with everyone, but Sam steered Millie directly to his box.

'See, hardly any social chit-chat,' he said.

He realised how very much he wanted her to enjoy the activity and to find it magical, yet the very eagerness of this emotion felt odd. He was not used to caring so much about whether someone enjoyed an event. Moreover, he felt as though he was constantly wrong footed. The wild creature from the moors had morphed into a practical young woman and now an elegant beauty.

He watched as Millie leaned forward. Her interest was evident as she took in details of the orchestra pit and mill of people below. As was typical, she made no attempt to hide her interest or pretend a blasé sophistication.

After observing the crowd for several minutes, she turned back to him, her expression curious. 'Tell me what it is that you like most about the opera.'

With anyone else, he would have answered glibly, providing some trite answer, but Millie demanded honesty.

He looked at the musicians tuning their instruments, their sounds still discordant. 'I like the anticipation. I like the way the instruments sound dissonant now and then later they are harmonious.'

But it was more than that. He remembered going to his first opera after his mother's death. He had been alone in his box and for the first time he had felt something. Since her death he had been numb. At school and with his father, he'd learned that emotion was a weakness, a flaw and a vulnerability. The numbness, the ability to function, had been a life skill. Indeed, it had become so ingrained in him, he'd forgotten how to feel.

He leaned towards her. 'You know how you do not like chit-chat?'

She nodded.

'After my mother died, throughout my adolescence, my whole life was chit-chat and pretence, even to myself. But when I am at the opera I am aware of emotion. I feel more alive…' He paused.

She said nothing, as though comfortable with the silence, not needing to fill the quiet with words.

'After my mother died,' he continued, 'I tried to talk to people. I remember talking to Cook, but it made her sad to see me sad. I tried to talk to my father, but it made him angry and made him see me as weak.'

'I do not think it is weak to feel,' Millie said softly. 'I think my father and Tom both went to excess in the attempt not to feel.'

'My mother would have agreed. She said the British aristocracy were emotionally constipated.'

'She what?' Millie gave a wonderful chortle of suppressed laughter.

'We fear bad manners. We fear excess emotion. She loved her Greek and Latin scholars. She loved opera.'

He stopped, staring down at the crowds filling the pit. 'In the end, she proved herself so very British.'

'When she hid her illness.' Her deep blue and intense gaze seemed to understand more than he could put into words.

'Yes.'

'We lie to save our loved ones' pain. But the lie causes more pain. The Cornish peasants are much more honest. Perhaps is their heritage or the hardship of their lives.'

'You have changed me,' he said. 'You have made me think about so many things. Like your friend Sally trying to educate her children. And my mother, so brilliant and yet forced to hide her brilliance. Even our politics are a pretence. More than a decade ago, we made it illegal for Britons to participate in the slave trade and yet it still happens. And we are still making money.'

'I misjudged you when I first met you.'

He shook his head. 'No, I had given money to schools and philanthropic societies. It made me feel virtuous, that I was doing more than just eating, drinking and playing. But I still judged things I did not understand. I thought the law was always right. I thought I was always right.'

'And now?'

He leaned forward, propping his elbows on his knees. 'I still believe in the law, but I think the law can be improved.'

From the first moment the orchestra played, Millie was entranced. It was magic. She forgot about the crowded theatre, the gossip, the smells. She was unaware of Lady Wyburn, Lil and even Sam. The music vibrated through her, giving her soul wings, making her feel as though she understood or had glimpsed some eternal mystery.

It was, she thought, like those moments when the sea and the sky took on a splendour that seemed beyond the beauty of earth.

For the first time, she could understand London's appeal. To hear something like this was remarkable. To have such a multitude of instruments—cellos, violins, flutes—playing together. Moreover, it was not only music. It was movement, dance and song. It was like entering a separate world of golden light, music and magic—Oberon's palace, peopled with faeries.

Chapter Sixteen

Sam sat in front of his pianoforte. He should go to bed. He had told Banks to retire, but the man was likely waiting up with a sad expression. Banks did not trust him with the proper maintenance of his jackets or cravats.

Sam felt tired, but he couldn't go to bed quite yet. Usually, the opera both thrilled and calmed him, leaving his soul feeling freshly laundered. He'd enjoyed every second, but he also felt a heady excitement, which precluded sleep. He remembered the way Millie had held her breath during certain arias, releasing it with that breathy gasp. He remembered how she'd leant forward, propping her elbows against the edge of the box and cupping her chin.

Much of the time, he had not looked at the stage. It was more fascinating to watch her in the glow of the candlelight. Her skin had flushed with excitement and, as she concentrated on the music, she bit her lip. He would like to take her to the opera again. Or the symphony. There were so many things to show her in London.

His fingers ran over the keys. The tune was pretty, but lacking in power. His mother would sometimes arrange for an orchestra to play at their home. He'd liked that. He would sit at the back of the room, forgotten by the musicians, and listen.

A solo is but one song. It is when instruments play together that there is magic.

That thought, those words, struck him anew. Almost, it seemed as though he heard them from a source external to him. It felt as it did when he looked up at the stars and imagined Socrates, Themistocles or Epictetus viewing a similar skyscape. He felt both overwhelmed and enlightened.

He had feared love. He had lost himself in his love for Miss Whistler. And with his father he had felt a need to be different, to pretend. Indeed, it had appeared to him that pretence was a prerequisite for love.

Except perhaps that was not true.

Plato said that every heart sings a song, incomplete until another heart whispers back.

Sam had never expected to hear that whisper. Indeed, much as he respected many aspects of Plato's work, he had thought him misguided in this.

Very gently, he tapped on a key, listening to its pure note and realised that maybe, perhaps, if he was lucky, life need not be a solo enterprise.

Millie woke up the next day with the music still pulsing through her. For one evening, she'd allowed herself to people her world with happy fantasies. Everything—her gown, the opera, the man, the huge chandeliers heavy with candles—had added to that feeling. Even now she could picture his dark hair, mesmeric eyes, strong jaw and chiselled cheeks. It had been wonderful. The memory would warm her during Cornwall's winter nights.

But she could no longer let herself indulge in foolish thoughts. She was Cinderella and the midnight hour had struck. Sam had given them a wonderful night. They had a bond. People who survived peril formed a connection. But the danger had passed. They would write occasional notes and send Christmas cards. A bond did not equal a future.

Millie spent the day either roaming restlessly about the house or sitting staring somewhat blankly at the wall. Lady Wyburn and Lil had gone shopping while Frances, Marta and the nursemaid went for a walk. Both groups had asked her to come, but she found that she did not have the energy. Instead, she sat listlessly in the sitting room that she shared with Lil. She started a letter to her mother but soon found herself staring into space, the letter incomplete. After numerous false starts, she tossed the crumpled balls into the basket. She'd tried to read, but found herself rereading the same line over and over with no memory of its content. She attempted her needlepoint, but tossed it aside in a tangle of silk.

So instead, she stared into the flickering flames. At some point she must have fallen asleep, as a tap at the door jolted her awake.

'Mr Garrett is here, miss,' Merryweather said.

'His sister and aunt are out, I'm afraid.' Her voice sounding rather squeaky, which made her flush.

'I mentioned that Lady Wyburn, Mrs Ludlow and Miss Lillian were out, miss, but he stated rather emphatically that he wished to see you.' Merryweather spoke lugubriously. His doleful tone was likely not personal. The man could make the cheeriest greeting melancholy.

'Well…um…send him up.'

'Yes, miss. Do you wish any refreshment?'

'No, I do not think so.' She could not spend any more time with Sam than was necessary. Nor could she indulge in any more intimate chats or shared confidences. It was

confusing. It muddled her emotions. It was playing with
fire and was not sensible.

Indeed, likely he merely wished to talk to her about
Frances or perhaps he had some further information
about Lord Harwood. She straightened, composing herself and trying to assume a businesslike expression.

Just then, Sam strode into her small sitting room as
Merryweather bowed his way out. The room felt instantly
smaller. And Sam seemed taller. And broader. His eyes
were more piercing and his jaw and cheekbones more
angular.

There was a brisk energy about him and a determination.

'Sam? What is it?'

'Millie, I— We need to talk,' he said.

She startled at the urgency in his tone. 'About Frances? Or the investigation? Has something happened?
They are not releasing Mrs Ludlow or Jason, surely?'

'No, not about Frances or the Ludlows.' He threw
himself into the chair opposite her, as if angry at her
suggestion. 'I need to talk about us. I know you want to
be independent. I respect that. I will talk to a solicitor to
determine how best to do so, if necessary. But Plato had
it right. We have a connection. We are like an orchestra.'

'What? An orchestra? Is this about Harwood?' she
asked, fearing that some shock must have caused such
disjointed confusion.

'What, no, what has Harwood to do with it?'

'Nothing. You were talking about your solicitor.'

'Right. Yes. Sorry, I am not doing this well.' He
paused, inhaling as though forcibly collecting his
thoughts and ideas. 'Sorry. I have gone about this all
wrong. What I wanted to say is, Millicent Lansdowne,
will you marry me?'

She gasped. She felt her mouth hang open as she stared at his dark eyes, the perfect contours of his face, the firm lips and the tiny crease of his dimple which lined his cheek. 'Are you mocking me or asking out of pity or gratitude?'

'Of course not. I do not go around offering to marry women out of pity or gratitude.'

'But...'

He hurried on. 'And I know you do not want to marry anyone. I know you want to be independent and, in our society, it is hard for a married woman to be independent. I am certain I can determine something. That is why I mentioned a solicitor. The two of us, together, are greater than the individual.'

'Sam, it is not just about independence. You live in London. I am not the type of woman that someone like you should marry. You need someone witty and beautiful.' She stood, needing to distance herself from him, hoping the physical space would provide clarity.

He stood also. 'But that is what I love about you. You are not a "type". You are a person. You are a strong, caring, obstinate, brave, funny person. And you are also witty and beautiful. That's why I love you.'

'You...love...me?' she whispered.

'Yes, I have been afraid of loving. I have been afraid of being vulnerable. But with you, I do not feel alone, I do not feel as though I am in this world alone and I love that feeling.' He stepped towards her. 'I love you.'

Joy and hope tangled with doubt and fear in a confused mush. She reached up to him, cupping his face with both hands, and staring into the dark grey-green of his eyes. 'I love you, too, but we cannot pretend that our differences do not matter. I do not want to be in London society. That isn't me.'

'It isn't me either.'

'It isn't?'

He shook his head. 'I am still discovering who I am and I want to keep discovering that with you.'

'You do?'

'Yes.' He kissed her, tentatively at first and then with a growing passion as one hand reached up into her hair and the other caressed her back, pressing her tight to him.

'But,' she said, breaking free of his drugging kiss, 'I have to write my own story.'

'You can write anything you want,' he muttered, feathering kisses across her nose and her cheeks, his hands stroking her backbone in a way that made her arch into him. 'Did anyone ever tell you that you talk too much?'

'Frequently. But I cannot live in London all the time.'

'Fine. What about Cornwall?' he asked.

'You'd live in Cornwall? I did not think you liked it.'

'It is growing on me. Besides, I want to open a school.'

'A what?' She stepped back from him. 'What are you talking about?'

'Likely it is a foolish notion,' he said, looking chagrined, colour flushing into his cheeks, making him appear younger and less certain.

'Tell me,' she said, eager to reassure.

'I wanted to explain my idea in an organised way.'

'Do not worry about organised.'

'You have changed me. You have made me think about so many things. Sometimes the world feels too huge to change. And it is absolutely too huge to change all at once. But maybe we can take small steps, like opening a school in Fowey.'

She went to him. She wound her arms around him, pressing herself tight to him.

He claimed her mouth. Her hands slipped from his

shoulders, as she caressed the muscles in his chest, moving under the cloth of his shirt. She heard the wild drumming of her own pulse. She felt him respond to her touch. She thrilled to his soft, needful groan.

'The answer is yes,' she whispered.

She felt an exaltation, an awareness of her body and a cessation of thought and reason with a singularity of focus on this one moment. It seemed that her body became molten, no longer bone and muscle, but sensuous and fluid. She knew a wild freedom, moving without thought, instinctively responding to the driving heat which started at her core, pulsing and expanding throughout her body.

'Where is everyone?' he muttered.

'Out. Or deaf,' she said.

They shifted backwards in an intimate dance, moving into her adjoining bedchamber until she felt the mattress at the back of her legs. Half-stumbling, they fell to the bed. The mattress sank under their weight.

Cupping her face, he caressed her slowly, gently, tenderly.

'You're sure?' he whispered.

'Yes. Yes,' she said. 'Occasional risk-taking may be necessary.'

He kissed her; long drugging kisses. He stroked her neck, pressing his lips to her collarbone and the skin at the neckline of her dress.

She heard him remove his shirt. Through half-closed eyes, she watched the way his muscles moved, highlighted by the low amber glow of the fire. He pulled back the blankets and he lay beside her. He felt warm and strong. He kissed her slowly, gently, moving against her. Darts of feeling pulsed through her. She clung to him, her body demanding something which was foreign to her, but in a heady, wonderful way.

Sam groaned as he undid her buttons, pulling away her gown and chemise. He kissed her chin, her neck, her collarbone, cupping each breast. He pulled off her skirts, her chemise and pantaloons, peeling them off her body. She felt the whisper of air against her nakedness, but knew no hesitation or embarrassment.

Instead, she felt only a needful joy as he lowered himself so that his body covered her own.

The glow of the firelight flickered against the white walls. He leaned against a pillow with Millie curled against his chest, her dark hair soft and silky. They should get up. It was shifting into late afternoon and someone would be home soon. Yet he felt a heady content as he looked at her. Her long lashes lay like fans against her cheeks, her soft pink lips twisted into a half-smile while her cheeks were flushed and rosy. With one finger, she lazily drew circles across his chest.

'You smell good, much better than in the cabin,' she said drowsily.

'You, too.'

'I will have to teach you to love the moors. And the sea.'

'I'll learn,' he muttered into her hair. 'I will teach you some things, too.'

'And fishing.'

'I was not thinking of fishing. And not in a storm.'

'No,' she said. 'And if you're going to live on the coast, I'll have to teach you to swim.'

'Sounds cold.'

'I'll keep you warm.' She raised herself on her elbow,

looking at him with her serious, dark gaze. 'Tell me about this school?'

He smiled a little shyly. 'Right now, it is just an idea. I realised that you and Sally are right. People deserve choice. Education is one way to give people options so that it is not a choice between the mines or smuggling.'

She kissed him. 'I love that idea. We can get a building, hire a teacher or I could teach.'

'Maybe we will open schools in other towns or run for political office and change the world.'

'One coastal town at a time. Sam, I never thought—I have never felt like this before.' She spoke with an appealing wonder, curiosity threading the soft huskiness of her tone. 'Like the world has options and choices and excitement.'

'I have not either.' He looked at her and the soft movement of her finger against his chest. 'I feel, for the first time in for ever, that I am not a solitary creature.'

'And I feel for the first time ever, that I am the sort of woman to find romance. I never thought I was.'

'And what sort of woman finds romance?'

'The debutante type. I am more...dull.'

He laughed. 'Dull? You saved me from drowning and chased down criminals. You're anything but dull.'

'Very well, I have adventurous moments, but not exactly in a "happily ever after" way.'

He ran his fingers down her cheeks so that he cupped her chin. 'That's because this is not about happy endings. This is the happy beginnings. This is our happy beginning.'

Epilogue

Millie sat at the desk in the small cottage which had been converted into a schoolroom. Gerald added some fuel to the fire and a flurry of sparks chased up the chimney. There had been frost this morning and the air felt chilly with the nip of the coming winter.

'Go now,' she said to her young helper. 'I see your mother and sister are here.'

He left and she waved to Sally through the window and watched them leave, heading towards the harbour. From this vantage point, she could see the ocean. It was a nice day, but the sun was already low in the sky so that the sky was a pink gold and the waves were bright with diamond sparkles.

Sam rounded the corner and she smiled, waving. Standing, she started to collect her things, ready to go home. She paused for a moment, watching his fluid movement as he strode forward. Silhouetted against the diamond sparkles, he looked strong, broad and purposeful. He carried several books, which had most likely arrived in the afternoon post.

There had been some initial hesitation among the villagers about the school. Some children feared it might limit their freedom and a few determinedly remained down by the sea. Sam had been smart and had merely walked down with the other children and they'd scrambled among the rock pools, learning about the fish, the tides and the crustaceans. He'd made it all so lively that attendance had grown. Flora's fresh baked bread or, on occasion, tea treat buns, served mid-morning had proved an added enticement.

Sam entered. 'Two new volumes of Virgil.'

'And the primers for English?' she asked.

'They should arrive soon. I have also translated *Row, Row, Row Your Boat* into Latin if you would care to teach it to the younger children.'

'One cannot start a classical education too soon,' she said.

'I also have some new ideas for mathematics and thought that next year we should go to London. I believe I could convince the Philanthropic Society to support us.'

'Sounds wonderful, but let us get home now. I am so excited that Frances and Noah have decided to visit. Mother is so much better now that she gets such constant news from the city.'

She stood, packing a few items before pausing, frowning briefly.

'You do not think that a visit to Cornwall will negatively impact Frances's health, do you?'

He pressed a kiss to her head. 'She is much better,' he said. 'She will be fine.'

They started to walk across the floor to the outer door, before Millie stopped, hurrying back to her desk. 'I mustn't forget my knitting.'

She pulled open a drawer. She had experienced limited success with tatting or netting and hoped to manage better with knitting.

'I'm making something for Noah,' she explained, pulling out a bundle that included a ball of wool and two needles, one of which was attached to a five-inch square of knitting.

'A woolly handkerchief?' Sam asked dubiously.

'It was supposed to be an article of clothing.'

'Clothing? He does have arms.'

'A scarf,' Millie said. 'And I have every hope that I will achieve this by Christmas.' After all, it was only October.

With the knitting collected, they gave a final look about the small school and then exited, closing the door behind them and walking into the village. They were going to meet Lillian, who wanted to do a little shopping, and then take the carriage home together. Flora was organising preparations for Frances's visit and had been giving the cook all manner of directions. Indeed, she was in her element now she had a staff once more.

Millie sighed, tucking her hand into Sam's elbow.

'Happy?' he asked.

'So very, very happy.'

* * * * *

*If you enjoyed this book, why not check out
these other great reads by Eleanor Webster*

No Conventional Miss
Married for His Convenience
Her Convenient Husband's Return
A Debutante in Disguise